A Wicked Hunger

Published by Kiersten Fay
Edited by Rainy Kaye

This book is a work of fiction. All of the characters, names, and events portrayed in this novel are products of the author's imagination.

ISBN- 0-9835733-9-5
ISBN-13: 978-0-9835733-9-5

A Coraline Conwell Novel

Kiersten Fay

To Arlene and Jimmy: Your encouragement and support is incredible, and appreciated more than you know.

To Heather: If you were here, we'd be laughing our asses off and sipping on Corona's with juicy limes.

And to my editor Rainy: You are wonderful at what you do. Don't stop being as awesome as you are.

Chapter 1

There was much in the world that Coraline Gordon feared: a revival of the revolution, being claimed by one of the countless vampire clans, dinner parties...but nothing compared to what she was about to put herself through now. Who would have imagined the most frightening event in her life would turn out to be seducing her husband?

Cora glanced out her car window at the luxurious high-rise hotel as she mentally rallied her courage. It shouldn't be such a difficult task to entice one's own husband—probably wouldn't be for any other wife—but Winston was a cold man, hard to read, fearsome at times. She knew if she didn't find a way to please him, she'd eventually be tossed back out on the streets where he'd found her. By his recent treatment, she wondered why he had married her in the first place. Was it because she'd been so destitute as to be indebted to him for her new station? Had he merely desired a picturesque wife, one that he'd molded perfectly to his taste? She'd been so pliable, wanting to please him. She hated to think she'd somehow fallen short. That he'd given her up as a failed experiment.

There had been a time when she'd cared for him more than anything, maybe almost loved him...in the beginning, anyway. Goddess of light and dark, had it only been seven months ago? She still did care for him. Craved his attention. But it wasn't the same. Soon after their week-long honeymoon, he had grown distant, burying himself in his company: Gordon Exports.

She disengaged the motor and tugged the key from its slot.

Her hand froze just inches from the ignition as indecision warred in her mind, tempting her to start the car back up and peel away before there was no turning back.

She sighed. She had attempted to be the dutiful wife, did everything in her power to make herself presentable to his wealthy friends and acquaintances. Yet somehow she had been found lacking. No longer was she invited to the gatherings, shindigs, and charity events that Winston often attended, even though she always donated the max that he would allow.

Had his friends discovered her paltry origins and unanimously shunned her for it? Subsequently, had that caused Winston to see her as the street urchin she once was? Or was there another reason for her being cast out of his society?

If only he'd inform her of what she'd done wrong, she would strive to fix it. It wasn't as if she hadn't changed so much of herself already. Her once ragged sandy-blonde hair now gleamed from the regular high-end salon treatments. Her skin was kissed by the medically induced tan that was guaranteed never to fade. All the hair but that on her head and brows had been permanently removed, leaving every inch of her like silk.

She was finding there wasn't anything she wouldn't do to regain the acceptance she'd only known for a short while. Which was why she now sat in the vintage Aston Martin that Winston had given her as a wedding present, clad in thousand-dollar lingerie that was hidden only by a long elegant trench coat. Cliché? Maybe. But she wasn't adept at being sexy, so she had to go with what she'd seen in movies.

After pocketing the key, she checked her makeup in the rearview mirror and straightened the sleek, dark wig she'd purchased this morning. Around her, folks bustled in and out of stores that lined the street. The outdoor seating area of a nearby café was packed for lunch.

She opened the car door and swung her legs out, making sure the tall heels of her knee-high boots found solid purchase before she pushed to a stand. Her heart thumped against her ribcage, but she ignored the meager protest as she crossed the parking lot.

The lobby of the five-star hotel was typical in its splendor. Gargantuan crystal chandeliers hung from the vaulted ceiling, gold-plated embellishments rested over banisters and other surfaces, beautiful artwork decorated the walls—no doubt originals, refurbished. The first few uprisings had devastated much of the world's art. What wasn't destroyed had been purchased, stolen, and horded up by wealthy collectors.

She couldn't help but note the stark contrast of her well-to-do surroundings to the one-room shack she'd shared with several other street urchins not so long ago. The gap between the rich and poor was likened to an ocean of quicksand, nearly impossible to cross without a helping hand. And if one did manage to claw their way out of the muck, any new-found status depended on the good favor of a wealthy patron.

For her, that patron was her husband, Winston.

She hadn't openly sought his favor, though she had always thought him handsome. She would spy him here and there, strolling the streets of her neighborhood with a barrage of bodyguards while he prospected the land for new properties, or some such. No, he had come to her, wooed her, seduced her with promises of a better life and possibly a family. She had been so easily enamored. Then again, like most of the women from her district, a snap and crook of a finger would have swept her off her feet.

But it was her, not them, that Winston had set his sights on. To her that he had promised the world. Yet now those promises felt like trying to grip a puff of smoke in her palm.

Her heels clicked over the marble floor as she crossed to the elevator. Inside, she tugged her tie-belt snugly around her waist and then pressed the button for the ninth floor. Winston was in room nine-eighteen. She knew because she'd ordered the room for him before he'd left on this trip.

When the doors slid closed, she took a succession of rapid breaths. Anxiety siphoned the moisture from her throat. She swallowed, feeling her pulse rise. It was being boxed in that did it to her. She still wasn't used to the fast-paced world of the upper class. The majority of the lower classes kept to the outskirts and dilapidated districts that had been most affected by the recent wars—the areas that remained neglected, some buildings still half falling down. Surprisingly enough, it was safer for them there, where they could watch each other's backs, where gangs ruled both by brute force and strength of number. Those who braved the city limits were either outcasts, junkies, loners, or criminals looking for a score. Either way they risked much.

She'd been a loner, for the most part.

Gangs might be safer when dealing with outsiders, but they did no good when the threat came from within. Which it often did for the weakest of the bunch.

The glassy doors opened, and a bit of her anxiety waned. As she stepped out of the elevator, a wave of dizziness assailed her. Though the floor was as sturdy as could be, her body instinctively knew how far it was from the true ground. The sensation was odd, but fleeting. Still, nausea rolled through her. Her nerves pushed adrenaline through her veins like a battering ram as she made her way down the empty hallway.

She told herself that most the buildings of today were made to withstand a nine-point-zero earthquake as well as bomb impacts. There was little chance she'd relive the terrifying disaster that took her parents and baby brother all those years ago.

Since that terrible day, she'd always hated tall buildings. She hadn't set foot in one till Winston came along—it just so happened most his business was conducted in tall buildings.

Just outside room nine-eighteen, she swallowed hard, closed her eyes, and took a deep breath. The walls weren't closing in. The ceiling wasn't about to crash down on her.

Winston always scoffed at her phobia. He called it ridiculous and embarrassing. She agreed her fear was irrational, but not unfounded. All the same, he'd instructed her to "get over it."

Right now, it didn't look like that was going to happen. Her heart had already started its familiar staccato beat, her breaths shortening. She felt hot, and a light sheen of sweat formed across her forehead. She leaned one hand on the doorjamb.

She mentally cursed. The very last thing she portrayed at this moment was sexy. Perhaps she should attempt this seduction thing when Winston returned home. As it was, he would take one glance at her and burst into laughter.

She was about to turn back down the hall when the soft murmur of voices from within the room gave her pause.

Oh, goddess, she hadn't considered he might have visitors. He *was* on a business trip, after all.

Another sound filtered through the door...a giggle of sorts, followed by a string of words Cora couldn't quite make out, yet her instincts sprang to life. The voice—the *female* voice—had sounded overtly sensual. Winston, for that was surely his deep tone, responded with a rough chuckle.

Her mind delved into a dark place, a place where every issue that had cropped up between her and Winston suddenly made sense.

But it couldn't be. Infidelity was one thing in high-society that was still frowned upon. Fear was making her jump to conclusions. Surely he was just in a business meeting or schmoozing clients.

Phobia forgotten, she raised her fist to pound on the door just as the door at her back whooshed open. Strong fingers clamped around her wrist. She started to turn to see who had stopped her and why, but the large hand left her wrist to cover her mouth. At the same time, a thickly muscled arm wrapped around her midsection and yanked her backwards. She managed a single muffled cry before she crossed the threshold and the heavy door closed her in. Her limbs flew into a panic before her brain could make sense of what was happening. She thrashed wildly, bucking to get free. But for all her struggling, her abductor might as well be made of stone.

While the man kept her still, another man dressed in dark

clothing moved into her line of sight. The gun he held in her face inspired immediate capitulation. She stilled, eyes wide, heart pounding. Her own terrified gasps echoed in her ears.

In his other hand, he held up a badge. Her mind was too panicked to read the words on it, but the unique oblong shape was all too familiar. Vampire Enforcement Agency.

Another whimper crawled through her throat.

"Yeah, you know what this is, don't you?" The dark-haired man at her front said.

She managed a weak nod. Her abductors hand was still tight against her mouth.

"So you're going to cooperate, right?"

Another nod.

"No sounds, no sudden movements. Got it?"

One more nod.

"Put your hands up. My partner Mason here is going to remove your coat and search you for weapons."

Her hands shook as she obeyed. Undoubtedly, both her captors could hear the sudden rushing of her pulse. The man at her back, Mason, released her, circled around, and then pulled her tie-belt lose. She flushed and lowered her gaze to the floor as her coat fell open.

The men stared at her partially see-through bustier with a strip of black coverage over her breasts and matching sheer micro mini that revealed black string-bikini underwear. Leather boots that reached above her knees completed the ensemble.

"What did he do," Mason asked his partner, "order another hooker?"

Mason's hair was a slightly lighter brown than his companions, but cut just as short. Both men were taller than her by a half foot at least, and it was easy to imagine the compacted muscles that lie beneath their dark suits.

"When did he manage that?" his partner countered.

To her, Mason ordered, "Drop the coat and kick it toward Trent." He gestured to the other man with his head.

She let the coat slip over her shoulders and then shoved it away with her foot. Trent lowered his gun to retrieve it and began digging through the pockets.

"Hands on the wall." Not giving her much time to obey, Mason turned her around by the shoulders.

Her palms met the wall. A second later, a set of firm hands traveled along her sides and down each of her legs before retracing their steps and moving toward the undersides of her chest. Her jaw clenched. Clearly there were no weapons hidden on her person. How would she even manage such a thing?

Next, Mason pulled her arms behind her back, and metal cuffs bit into her wrists. Her stomached dropped three floors down. She wanted to ask why she was being arrested, but she was too terrified to form the question. If these men truly were vampires, simply looking them in the eye could be seen as a direct challenge.

He maneuvered her to sit on the edge of the bed.

Trent tossed her coat to the floor and held up her ID.

A set of brightly lit monitors in the corner of the room caught her eye. One displayed a split screen of the hallway from either end. The second showed different angles of a room similar to the one she was currently in. On the bed, two figures lounged. A man and a woman. The woman was dressed in a sexy outfit, not unlike her own. The man was...Winston! Shirtless, arms behind his head, smiling like she'd never seen him smile. A familiar giggle erupted from a set of tiny speakers as the woman on the screen ran her hand along his chest and then toward the clasp of his trousers.

Cora's jaw dropped. The sting of betrayal tightened the muscles in her throat.

Mason glanced at the screens, then back at her. He gripped her chin between his thumb and forefinger and tilted her head up, capturing her hurt gaze. Something like recognition fired behind his eyes. "Oh, shit. It's his wife."

Confusion mounted and she took in his features, wondering from where he might know her. He had a sharply angled jaw, a bit wide, but it fit his face perfectly. His nose was nearly straight with only the slightest bump that added a dangerous cast to his already glowering expression. His eyes were an odd bluish-grey color with the appearance of being backlit.

His brow furrowed.

She tore her gaze away, realizing she was staring directly into his eyes.

"Coraline Gordon," Trent announced, handing him her ID.

Mason didn't even look at it. Instead, he reached out and tugged the dark wig off her head. Golden locks tumbled over her shoulders.

A ripe, guttural curse made her jump. She glanced up for only a moment, wishing she hadn't. Mason's jaw was locked tight, his eyes bright with fury. A hint of his fangs verified his species.

She cringed and studied the floor as if it held the key to her survival.

A whistle rang out from Trent's direction. "Nothing against Marissa, but with a wife like that...?" He shook his head. "And the man's only been married for what? A few months?"

"Enough," Mason barked and turned toward the surveillance screens. "We have movement again."

The split screen of the hall showed three males in dark clothing, each carrying a black duffel bag, walking toward the camera.

"Dammit," Mason sighed. "This floor is supposed to be off limits to occupants." He looked to Trent. "Did we confirm that with the front desk?"

Trent's gaze widened on the screens. He pulled out his gun. "They're not here for a stay."

As the men glided swiftly down the hall, they opened their duffels and retrieved from within an automatic weapon. They stopped at room nine-eighteen. The one in front slammed his foot into the door, busting it open. Gunfire erupted. One half of Winston's head explode while blood splattered onto the bed and walls behind him.

Cora felt dizzy from the sudden raging of her heart. A scream rang out. Had that come from her? A second scream filtered through the monitor's speakers.

"Shit!" Mason yelled. "Get down!" He pushed Cora off the mattress to the floor. With her hands still cuffed, she landed on her shoulder between the bed and the wall farthest from the door. Her body curled into a ball automatically.

The maelstrom of gunfire that came next seemed to last forever, though in hindsight, it was probably only a few seconds. The other woman's scream went silent, but echoed faintly in Cora's head. Was she dead? She was having a hard time processing that.

The only thing Cora was able to comprehend was the fact

that she couldn't get enough air. What she did manage to suck into her lungs was tainted by the dusty scent of the carpet near her face. Her body shuddered violently and the cuffs dug into her skin, but she didn't dare move. Didn't dare draw attention to herself.

The gunfire ceased.

Who were the victors? She couldn't tell. Moreover, she didn't know what would benefit her more: if the strangers had survived, or the vampires.

One thing was undeniable. Winston was dead. She closed her eyes and tried to shake the gruesome image of his death away, but it seemed stained into her mind.

She began to hyperventilate.

A voice came back into the room, possibly Trent's, sounding sullen. "Human officer down, dead on scene. Suspect has been taken out by three unknown assailants." He paused. "It looked professional. One is still alive, just barely. Mace is questioning him now."

There was another pause.

"Yes, sir. Mm-hm. There was another complication. The suspect's wife showed up just before the assailants. We don't know if it's connected...Oh really?" He paused. "Oh, shit. Are you serious?"

"Serious about what?" Mason's voice sounded from the hall. Footsteps announced his reentry.

Trent's voice went low. "It's possible this wasn't an isolated incident." Then he went back to his normal tone. "Yes, sir. Be there within the hour."

"He's dead," Mason said matter-of-factly. "I didn't get anything out of him. What do you mean this wasn't an isolated incident?"

"That's all he said. Said he'd brief us when we bring in the wife."

The room went silent. She could practically feel their gazes slip to her. Her heart stopped dead before jack-rabbiting out of control. Oh, goddess! They were going to take her in. Humans who crossed the VEA didn't just go to jail—they disappeared. Panic iced her veins.

"Okay," Mason said. "You go inventory the crime scene. I'll take her down to the car."

At some point, Cora had managed to mold herself into a tight corner of the small space, but that didn't keep Mason's strong hands from lifting her up off the floor. With both palms on her shoulders, he steadied her and didn't let go till he seemed sure she wouldn't fall back over.

"Turn around," he ordered. When she did, he added, "Don't move." Then he uncuffed one of her hands.

The urge to wring her fingers around her free wrist was strong, but she kept as still as possible.

The familiar fabric of her coat came over her shoulders. Mason guided her arms through the sleeves and then turned her back around to face him. He snatched the belt string and tied the trench closed. "If it so happens you're here by coincidence, you picked a hell of a day."

If her voice box had been working she'd have told him that was the understatement of the year.

Once more, he cuffed her wrists behind her back and then guided her by the elbow out into the hall. Red splotches decorated the previously spotless walls. A body slumped lifelessly on the floor. A frightened noise escaped her lungs, and she stumbled.

Mason held her steady and rushed her forward.

In the elevator, after the doors slid closed, he studied her for a long while. She tipped her head down and became like a statue, except her breaths heaved erratically. The weight of his gaze was nearly physical. She was acutely aware of who in this small space was the predator and who the prey.

Vampires functioned on a different level than humans. They were twice as strong and thrice as primitive.

After another moment, his hand stretched toward the panel, and he pressed the button marked G for garage. This time, the ride down was not fast enough, but finally, the doors parted, revealing a badly lit space stuffed with vehicles. As he tugged her forward by the arm, her heels clicked loudly against the concrete. The sound bounced off the solid concrete walls.

He led her to an unmarked black car and then situated her in the back. She was surprised by his gentle treatment of her thus far, but then, there could be witnesses anywhere, cameras. Vampires liked to keep vampire business behind closed doors.

He slid into the driver's seat and started the engine, but kept the car in park. In the rearview mirror, their gazes locked before she turned her eyes down. The silence stretched on, and she took the time to assess the unfortunate turn of events. More likely than not, her old life was forfeit, her future precarious. Winston, for whatever reason, had caught the eye of the VEA. Never a good thing. And now he was dead.

She felt as though she should be experiencing more sorrow over that fact. In truth, she only felt numb. Maybe she was in shock. Maybe her survival instinct was overruling her emotions. Unwanted thoughts from the past bubbled up from the back of her mind.

After the disaster that had made her an orphan, she'd been rendered a street-beggar at the age of ten. While scrounging for scraps in a back-alley dumpster, she'd caught the attention of a low-level vampire soldier.

She had tried to run, had managed a laughable attempt, but he'd caught her throat in a death grip. Not a breath later, his fangs had pierced her shoulder. When he was done nearly draining her, he'd introduced himself as one would a new acquaintance. "I'm Edgar. What's your name?"

Through her sobs, she'd whimpered out a shaky, "Coraline."

Then he'd tried to hypnotize her into following him, only to find her immune to vampire compulsion. A surprise to them both. His crazed blood-drunk eyes had grown excited. To this day, she couldn't say why that had enamored him so. Or why it made him want to torture her. Her only explanation was that vampires were sadistic by nature.

She mentally skipped over the worst of her captivity. That was where she'd learned how to go unnoticed by vampire kind, how to be still and quiet and the importance of averting one's gaze. That was where she'd learned they were more like animals than humans.

She thanked the goddess that he hadn't abused her in a sexual manner, though he did make threats of the kind. At the time, he seemed more interested in making her his personal snack pack.

Edgar had been a kind of foot soldier for a militia clan meant to squash the human uprising. When his leader discovered her chained in Edgar's quarters, he ordered a tribunal. Apparently no one in that particular clan could claim a human without express permission from the higher-ups. Edgar had made his case with her cowering by his side in front of his entire clan. He'd revealed her affinity to resist compulsion and claimed to want to keep her for further study.

Whether it had been extreme luck, or merely that Edgar was genuinely disliked by his superiors, the commander refused his request and ordered her immediate release. He'd called her a liability before bringing up that she was a minor. Cora was surprised to learn they did have some laws against such things. However, she might never understand why they hadn't just killed her then and there.

Edgar had protested and openly challenged the leader's decision. The result was Edgar's blood coating the walls. Her child's mind must have blocked out his execution, but the horror often slipped back to her in dreams.

After disemboweling Edgar, the leader had turned to her, and simply said, "Go."

Her thoughts were disrupted by the passenger side door opening. Trent folded himself into the seat. "Forensics has arrived. Clean up team's not far behind. Let's go."

Chapter 2

Mace watched the little human in the rearview mirror with too much interest. He always watched her with too much interest, which was why he often considered transferring to another case. Yet in all the months he'd been tailing Coraline and her rat-bastard husband, something had stopped him from doing just that, even when his unexpected infatuation had nearly blown his cover a few weeks back.

What the hell was she doing here?

Dressed like every guy's wet dream, for shit sake!

He slammed the car into reverse and then peeled out toward the exit. Trent didn't comment on his aggravated maneuver. His partner was too busy contacting Rolo, the newbie assigned to watch the Gordon house while Mace, Trent, and Marissa set up this little sting.

Marissa, though only human, had been a tough cookie, willing to snuggle up to that slime in hopes of garnering information on his dealings. Her chief was going to be pissed about losing one of his best over a vampire blood smuggling case.

The humans rarely cooperated with the VEA as it was. Now

they'd be less likely to do so than ever, especially after this particular clusterfuck.

Trent's tone was clipped when Rolo answered, clearly not wanting to give too much away with Cora in the back. "You seemed to have lost something, Rolo," Trent hissed into the phone. "What the hell?"

With his superior hearing, Mace caught Rolo's answer through the tiny speaker. "What are you talking about?"

Trent sighed. "Where are you?"

"I'm where you told me to be, but I'm a little busy right now."

A faint round of gunshots vibrated the phone's speakers from the other end of the call.

"What's going on?" Trent asked.

"Just a little Mexican standoff. A group disguised as a painting crew broke into the Gordon house. They're packing some serious heat." A few more gunshots rang out. "I don't know where wifey-poo is. She never showed up after I took my shift."

"We, uh, have *the package* with us," Trent said obscurely.

"No shit? She's with you now?"

"Yes. We're heading to the police station."

Cora perked up at Trent's words. For another frustrating second, she met Mace's gaze in the mirror before lowering her head. He knew she was from the ghetto, but something in her behavior told him she had a little more experience with vampires than the average human. The suspicion only made her more intriguing.

"Do your best to capture at least one of them for questioning, then meet us at the precinct." Trent hung up. "Fuck all," he muttered. "Something serious has just gone down under our noses."

They remained silent for the rest of the ride. Mace pulled into the police garage and parked as close to the entrance as possible. Before he killed the engine, Trent was already out of the car, opening Cora's door and helping her out.

Cora had almost cried from joy when she saw the police station. The only reason for them to bring her here would be to hand her over to the human authorities instead of condemning her to vampire justice. She might yet survive this calamity.

Inside, Trent guided her to a room with dreary stone grey walls and a single table with several chairs. Then he undid her cuffs and exited, leaving her alone.

She examined her appearance in the wide, one-way mirror—standard issue, she thought. Her blonde hair was ruffled from the wig that remained back on the hotel room floor. Her light-brown eyes were stark, shell-shocked. And her coat was a little disheveled.

She was insurmountably grateful that the vampire called Mace had been kind enough to allow her to cover the outfit that now seemed like an ode to stupidity.

How had she ever thought it was a good idea to follow Winston in an attempt to surprise him? She should have just stayed home and fretted over his return, per usual. But then, he wouldn't have returned, would he? Perhaps even now she would have been called to the door by Frederick, the butler, and greeted the police officer assigned to give her the terrible news. She would have cried and mourned and despaired.

Instead, she had to discover just how little Winston valued

their marriage. The stinging realization was only muted by the horror of having witnessed his murder. It seemed silly now that she had thought seducing him would be the most terrifying thing she'd endure today.

The reflection in the mirror smacked of so much desperation, hopelessness, and misery, she had to look away. Almost without her willing it, she slipped into one of the plastic chairs, folded her arms on the table, and lowered her head into the dark crevice created by her body.

It could have been minutes or hours later when the sound of the door opening jerked her awake. She hadn't even realized how exhausted she was until slumber was stolen from her.

"Hello, Ms. Gordon." A balding man took the seat across the table.

Mason and Trent entered as well. Trent crossed to lean against the wall. Mason stood beside the officer, arms folded behind his back. Why were they still here? A sense of foreboding chased away the last of her drowsiness.

The balding man handed her a cup of water. With shaky fingers, she took it from him and downed a large gulp.

"Has someone come in to take your statement yet?" the man asked.

"No," she replied.

He glanced at the mirror and then back at her. "Well, I have a few questions for you, but I'd like to get your statement on record first. Why don't you tell me what happened?"

She blinked twice, suddenly nervous. She was going to have to explain why she'd been there. "I wanted to...surprise Winston." She wrapped her arms around her torso before continuing. "He's been working a lot lately, and we hadn't had much time for...romance—"

"Working on what?" the officer interrupted.

She hesitated. "Well, his import-export company. Anyway, I went to his room at the hotel and..." She assumed he knew exactly what happened at that point, but she went through it anyway, all the while avoiding glancing at Mason or Trent. "The next thing I knew, gunshots were going off, and I saw...I saw my husband's head...um..." Her voice quivered, making it impossible to speak for a moment.

"Can you tell me about your husband's company?"

She cleared her throat. "Not much. It's an old company. He inherited it from his parents. They transport goods in and out of the country."

"What kind of goods?"

"Anything you can think of."

"Anything illegal?"

She paused. "I...I wouldn't know. It wasn't something Winston ever talked to me about. Is that why he was being watched? Was he doing something wrong?"

Mason snorted. For a split second, she forgot herself and shot him a glare. One of his sleek eyebrows rose, and she fixed her gaze back on the human officer.

The officer continued. "If there's anything you know regarding what your husband and his associates were into, now is the time to tell us, Coraline. Even if you were involved in any way, we could—"

"Involved in what?" she asked.

The officer shared a look with Mason, and Mason took over. "We believe your husband was involved in the abduction of vampires and harvesting their blood for sale on the black market."

Cora's mouth fell open. She didn't even attempt to wipe away her dumfounded expression. Could Winston have been so stupid as to tempt the wrath of the vampire nation?

"Why would he do anything like that? Gordon Exports is a multimillion-dollar company. He had no need to—"

"Clearly, your husband got bored easily," Mason said coldly.

Her mouth clamped shut. Was that a dig at Winston's infidelity?

"It tends to happen when you want for nothing, when you're handed everything from the time of birth and never have to work for it. There's no doubt Winston was smuggling vampire blood, but we weren't sure if he was the mastermind or just a middle-man. Marissa, the woman you saw with Winston, had been seeing him regularly."

Cora flinched. The corners of her mouth tugged into a frown and a set of salty, burgeoning tears burned her eyes.

Mason's tone softened. "Her objective was to find out where the blood was coming from and who else was involved."

"How long had they been...?" She trailed off, staring at Mason's upside-down reflection in the metallic gleam of the table.

"Since before you," he replied simply.

Devastation crushed her chest.

"In fact, Marissa had been hinting about marriage just before he met you. You came as something of a surprise, actually..." Mason paused for a moment. "We weren't sure if you were involved somehow, so we assigned someone to follow you as well."

Cora's head jerked up. She'd been followed? For how long? The thought sent a shiver down her spine. "And what did you find?"

"For the most part, it seemed you were ignorant of everything. But several months ago, something was discovered. If a human had been tailing you, it would have gone unnoticed, but…the scent of vampire blood was in your veins."

Finally, she met Mason's gaze head-on. Surely he was joking. His deadpan stare bore into hers.

"That's impossible," she said.

"It's a fact. I smell it on you even now."

She shook her head. "I've never even tasted vampire blood, not even when…"

Both males canted their heads, and she knew she would be forced to finish her sentence.

"Not even when I was offered it in my youth."

After Edgar would brutalize her, he'd tear open his own wrist and present it to her, claiming his blood would heal her if she choose. She had always refused, hoping her wounds would kill her instead.

"You've ingested it within the last week," Mason insisted. "But you don't have to take my word on it. We're preparing a warrant to have your blood tested. That will not only confirm what I say, but it could identify which missing vampire it came from."

Cora's heart slammed to a halt. What would happen to her if they found something in her system? When could she have possibly ingested vampire blood? And if she had, how could she not have realized it? Didn't that stuff affect humans in noticeable ways?

She gasped as a memory knocked the wind from her lungs like a blow to the stomach. It was something she wouldn't have thought twice about had she not been forced to reconsider everything she'd known over the last seven months. She glanced at her right forefinger, at a spot that probably should brandish at the very least a scab, but the skin was smooth and even, flawless.

"What is it?" The vampire asked.

"Last Monday Winston and I were making dinner. He was cutting some carrots, and I reached over to grab the pile next to him. The knife slipped, and my finger got cut. I thought it would need stitched, but Winston wrapped it in gauze and convinced me not to worry about it. Then he finished dinner and poured me a glass of red wine." She paused at the memory of thinking how kind it had been of Winston to take such care of her. "The next morning, I checked the cut and it was already closing up. I figured it just hadn't been as bad as I'd originally thought."

Had Winston been feeding her vampire blood behind her back?

"Blood-laced wine is a popular method of consumption," Mason replied. "It masks the color and taste."

"Something happened before that," she continued as another suspicious memory assailed her. "There was a dinner party at the Montgomery home three months ago. Not a huge event, just a few people I had never met before. Ms. Montgomery had taken me upstairs to show off a new painting of her posing by the pool with her miniature chow. On our way back down, she lost her footing and fell into me. I took a hard tumble and landed wrong on my arm. I remember thinking I must have broken it. It swelled up pretty bad. But same as last week, Winston convinced me to wait before we sought medical attention. We all sat down to dinner and had wine. Before the night was over, most of the pain had dulled and the swelling had gone down. The next morning it was only a little tender."

Mason and the officer shared another look.

"I recall that gathering," Mason said. "The Montgomery's home is like a fortified castle. We couldn't get a man inside. Do you remember the names of everyone who had attended?"

"I was introduced to them all at once earlier that night, but I hadn't been able to memorize all their names. I might be able to identify some of their faces, but you could just ask the Montgomerys."

Once more the two men locked eyes.

"What?" She glanced between them.

Mason sighed. "The Montgomery home was infiltrated at the same time those assassins came for your husband."

"Oh my goddess. Are they...?"

"Dead." He said it as though he were discussing the weather.

"Hold on, now," the officer bit out. "I'm not ready for that information to be made public."

Mason ignored him. He seemed to be gauging her reaction, and she thought she knew why. "Am I a suspect?"

"You would be, if your home hadn't been targeted as well."

Her head jerked up, and she again met his intense gaze. "Targeted?"

"The operation was carried out with military precision. Synchronized to perfection. Every suspected conspirator, and several we didn't even think to add to the list, was executed."

"Mace," the officer hissed. "Would you shut your mouth?"

"She's not involved in any of it," Mason replied.

"And what makes you so sure? Her home was attacked, but she was conveniently away at the time."

"About the time Winston married her, tainted blood was circulating through the black market. People were dying from it. I believe he needed someone to test his product on before distributing it to his rich friends." He gestured toward her.

Her frown grew more pronounced.

Was that all she was? A guinea pig?

She had always wondered why Winston had chosen to marry her when he was constantly surrounded by beautiful, sometimes too obviously willing, women of his own class. Gullible guinea pig made too much sense.

The officer shook his head. "That's just your opinion until all the evidence is examined."

Mace shrugged. "Right now, there is no evidence. No leads. Only her."

The officer sighed. "Ms. Gordon, is there anything else you can tell us? Did your husband ever mention anything about his little side business?"

"No. Never."

He stood as if to leave. "If you think of anything, I won't be far. Someone will be by to take a sample of your blood and then you'll be free to go."

"Actually, she'll be coming with me."

Cora gaped at Mason.

The officer paused and swiveled his head in the same direction. His jaw tightened, and she thought he might protest.

Please protest.

Mace became stern, as did Trent, their expressions hardening. The three seemed to be having a silent conversation. Or a battle for dominance. If the VEA wanted her, she couldn't imagine there was anything the officer could do.

Apparently, he'd come to the same conclusion. "She'll be released into your custody once we get the sample."

"What does that mean, released into his custody?" She

gripped the edge of the table as if she could bolt herself in place.

"This is a VEA investigation," the officer informed her. A bit of pity seeped out with his words. "We're only providing assistance."

She leaned forward. "You can't let them take me."

"Sorry, little lady." He hiked his thumb at Mason, pity quickly evaporating. "These guys are in charge. You know that."

She did. Since they'd revealed themselves to the world one hundred years ago, the vampires had *graciously* allowed the human institutions to proceed with almost no interruption, but there was no illusion that vampire law didn't overrule human law, which was the underlining cause of most of the uprisings.

"But he'll kill me," she muttered. Anyone caught with illegally obtained vampire blood was dealt a swift death. No trial necessary.

"I've no intention of killing you," Mason proclaimed.

Terror dropped her heart into her stomach. Then what did they plan for her? She knew first hand that surviving in the custody of a vampire could be even worse than death.

"Can't I stay here...in a human jail until all this is sorted out?"

Mason narrowed his gaze. "No, you can't." Then he addressed the officer in a demanding tone. "Fetch the person to administer the blood test. I want to be on our way."

The officer's features pinched slightly, almost like a sneer, but not quite. He left without a word.

Cora kept her eyes lowered to the table. Her tone came out no more than a whisper. "Please. I don't want to go with you."

The vampires made no response, which was answer enough.

Chapter 3

"Can't I at least get my suitcase from out of my trunk?" Cora pleaded, wanting more than anything to change into normal clothing.

She stood, hopelessly, in the police station garage, next to the same black car that had brought her here.

Mace opened the passenger side door for her. "Your car and everything inside it is considered evidence at the moment. I'm afraid it will take some time to clear it."

She glanced longingly to her left, down the sidewalk that fronted the police station. A brief, ridiculous fantasy of making a run for it trickled through her mind.

She wouldn't even make it a step.

Mace waited, seemingly patient, for her to get into the car. Something in his expression told her he knew the way of her thoughts and was somewhat amused.

As she settled in the car, she wrung her fingers nervously while Mace walked around the front and took the driver's seat.

The engine roared to life with the turn of the key. The sound was like an ominous prelude to an execution.

She wondered briefly where Trent was. He'd allowed Mace alone to escort her out of the police station while remaining behind with the human authorities.

In the small space of the car, sitting so close to Mace, Cora automatically reverted back to the mindset that kept her alive during her time with Edgar. She forced her lungs to work slow and even. She tilted her head down, and went as still as a possum. From the corner of her eye she saw Mace shoot her a sidelong glance before putting the car into drive.

"Put your seatbelt on," he ordered.

She yanked the strap across her body and snapped it into place, then returned her hands to her lap just as he pulled onto the street. A moment of silence followed. She kept her eyes on her hands.

She felt the car speed up, slow down, stop, then speed up again, but never looked up, never glanced out the window.

After a long while of quiet driving, Mace said casually, "Are you trying to make me forget you're there?"

Her chin jerked slightly, but she made no response.

"Believe me. Nothing could accomplish that."

She swallowed, keeping her eyes downcast.

"Where did you learn to do that, anyway?"

Her heart stuttered, and silence crushed the space around them.

"Well, anyway, you don't have to do that. I'm not a threat to you."

He took the highway on-ramp, heading out of town. She prayed he would stop trying to engage her in conversation, but she wasn't so lucky.

After another stretch of silence, he said, "Don't you have questions about where we're going? Why you're with me? How long we've been watching you? You can ask me whatever you like."

She was sick with curiosity, but she shook her head.

"It's going to be a dull ride then, and we have a ways to go."

He paused as if that should have been enough to entice her into asking. He obviously wanted to tell her, so why didn't he just get on with it?

He sighed. "I have loads of questions for you, but I don't want this to feel like an interrogation. You're a witness, not a suspect. You're no one's captive."

"Then let me go," she heard herself reply, instantly regretting her desperate tone.

"She speaks," he said on a chuckle. "And where would you go?"

She thought about that for a moment. There was only one place she could go, the large home she had shared with Winston. Thinking of him now sent a flurry of mixed emotions through her heart.

"You can't go home," Mason said, as if reading her mind. "Aside from the fact that assassins broke in with too much ease... specifically to murder you, I might add—"

"Why me? Weren't they just looking for Winston?"

"They knew exactly where Winston would be. No, they were looking for you. Still might be. These people, whoever they are....well, it's like they're cleaning up their entire operation, or perhaps eliminating the competition. We're not quite sure yet. Whatever the reason, they left no loose ends. None but you." He shot her a look. "It was more than Winston and the Montgomerys. All our suspects were targeted, and then some. Entire families were executed, children included. You can't go back there."

He allowed her a moment to take that in.

"But aside from all that," he continued, "Winston wrote you out of his will the moment you said 'I do.'

Her head snapped up. He met her bemused expression with one of complete seriousness.

"That prenup you signed waved away any claim you might have had to Winston's wealth. He had already prepared his will before the honeymoon was over. In case of his death, the money, the cars, the three homes? It all gets split between his blood relatives. You get nothing."

A deep chasm of despair crashed in her chest. "You could be making that up."

"You know I'm not. Not after all you've learned today about your rat-bastard husband."

The venom with which Mason ended his sentence was shocking. Almost as shocking as the realization that she was now back where she'd started. Street urchin. Worse, actually—a street urchin who'd drawn the attention of the largest vampire organization known to man.

Tears billowed, quickly drenching her cheeks. Even if the vampires didn't kill her, going back to the streets might. She was too different now. Not only did she look like a *whale*—street slang for a female of means—but now she knew, really knew, what it was like to live without fear, in a soft, safe bed, not having to sleep with one eye open. Not worrying every minute of every day where her next meal would come from or having to beg for coins while trying not to resort to more desperate acts like the ladies who lined up on corners at night.

Mason said nothing as she quietly sobbed.

"You must think I'm despicable," she stammered.

"Why would I?"

"Because I'm crying more for losing the money than losing Winston."

Mason laughed. "I think you're a survivor. You married that bastard because you had no other prospects. You did it to get out of a terrible situation. Anyone would've done the same."

She sniffed, a little taken aback. "I did care for him in the beginning."

"Of course you did."

His tone grated. "I did. He was sweet and generous at first. He didn't make me feel inferior. I truly thought he loved me." She buried her face in her hands. "I feel so stupid."

Mason cursed. "Don't cry. That shithead isn't worth it."

She worked to get control before Mason grew irritated with her. And though it was bound to happen eventually, she wanted to delay seeing Mason when he'd lost his patience. Vampires were unpredictable in the best of moods.

"Did you know him or something?" she asked. "The way you talk about him, it's almost as if you hold a grudge."

Mason pursed his lips, and his eyes narrowed on the road.

"Forget it. I don't want to know. In fact, I want to know as little as possible about all of this."

"I'm afraid that's a fantasy, sweetheart. You already know more than enough."

Anxiety crawled along her skin, raising the hairs on the back of her neck. "What does that mean?"

"It means you're under our protection until we say otherwise. I'm taking you to a safe house."

A hard ball of dread pushed down on her stomach, making her nauseous. A safe house? A prison was more like it. He was going to drive her somewhere isolated and keep her there until...well, as long as he wanted.

He must have noticed her distress because he said, "You don't need to fear me. I've been assigned to keep you safe. No harm will come to you as long as you're in my charge."

She just kept from rolling her eyes. A vampire's idea of harm varied greatly from that of a human's. Before his death, Edgar had sworn to his commanding officer he'd done nothing to *harm* her. The commander hadn't even looked twice at the marks on her wrists and neck.

The scars were healed now. That was the miraculous thing about vampire bites. The evidence of them never lasted.

Mason transferred to the left lane to pass a slow-moving vehicle.

Cora turned her head to watch a graveyard of tree husks rush past. They were almost out of the upper class zone, St. Stamsworth, founded just after a devastating fire had toppled the original city. She'd heard this area used to be a national forest, boasting an array of wildlife and lush greenery. Whatever weaponry had been used during the first of the uprisings now kept any new growth from springing up out of the black-charred soil, even though Lake Tahoe still sat full as ever.

"Why were you offered vampire blood?" Mason drew her attention away from the scenery.

"Excuse me?"

"Back at the precinct, you said you'd never tasted vamp blood even when it was offered to you."

"I, uh..." She didn't want to talk about this with him. She often feared she'd somehow be blamed for Edgar's death. "It was a long time ago. I don't even remember the circumstances."

Mason frowned. "We vampires have what you humans might call a fable. Long ago, two vampires befriended a human female, and took her under their protection. She grew to care for them both, but over time, the human fell in love with one of the vampires. However, she discovered that both the vampires felt the same for her. Wishing not to hurt the one she considered only a friend, she claimed no love for either. Late one night, in secret, she went to her beloved, and the other vampire caught the lovers together. He became so enraged he ripped both their throats out."

Cora gasped. Why would he offer such a gruesome story? Was he threatening her? "Are you suggesting humans are deceitful or just confirming that vampires are ruthless?"

"I'm saying lies could get us both killed."

She watched his profile for a moment, and then slumped back in the chair. Vampires were always too perceptive. Most of them were walking lie detectors. "It's inconsequential, and I don't want to talk about it."

"It sounds very consequential."

She cringed away from him.

"Oh, now don't start that disappearing act again—"

A hard jolt brought Cora's head up just as her equilibrium shattered. The car listed to the side. The world tilted. Her hair fell over her face, hovering there oddly, as if defying gravity. The seatbelt pulled tightly against her chest, nearly cutting off her air. And the world outside the car folded over on itself, the ground kaleidoscopeing in all directions. Her body jerked painfully, and agony speared her skull.

The car slid on its roof to a stop, but her body still felt like it was rolling. Muffled curses echoed through her brain. Warm liquid leaked into her eyes and blurred her vision. Where was Mace? Had he jumped out of the car, hoping the crash would kill her?

"Cora?" Mason's voice sounded from outside. The passenger side door creaked open and then was nearly ripped from its hinges.

She closed her eyes, expecting the final blow of death.

"Cora, are you alright? Can you move?"

"Mace, I don't want to die."

"I know, sweetheart. Tell me, can you move your arms and legs?"

"I think so."

"I'm going to cut the seatbelt and pull you out. I'm sorry if I hurt you." He didn't wait for a response, and she tried not to cry out when he extracted her from the vehicle and laid her on the gravel. "Someone rammed us off the road," he explained, looking around. "They kept driving, but they could be back any minute. Are you okay to walk?"

"I think gas leaked all over me," she said instead of answering. She lifted her arm and wiped along her forehead. When she pulled her arm away, red coated her sleeve. She couldn't make sense of it. Red gasoline? "Oh, goddess."

"Shh. It's not as bad as you think," he said, but his eyes went tight with worry.

Something like a giggle escaped her. "Lies could get us both killed," she mocked, then laughed harder. She stopped when pain and dizziness cut into her brain. The harsh bite of exhaust and burning rubber tortured her lungs, and she coughed violently.

Her vision wavered.

"Damn, you're out of it." Mace helped her sit up.

He cinched one arm under her legs, the other around her back, then carried her from the crash site, laying her back down a few yards away.

Kneeling next to her, he retrieved his phone from his pocket and tapped Trent's name under his contacts. The line rang once, and then Trent answered, "You miss me already?"

"We have a problem."

Trent went silent and waited for him to continue.

"Someone just side-swiped us off the road, a black SUV, tinted windows."

"License plate?"

"I didn't get a chance to write it down while I was death-rolling," Mace snapped.

"Alright, untwist your panties. Is the girl okay?"

He glanced down at Cora. Her face was locked in a grimace, and blood gushed from her head wound. The sweet scent of it had his fangs descending; a purely unintentional, primal response.

"She's alive, for now."

Cora's eyes shot wide, and he cursed her inherent fear of his kind. The way her voice had sounded when she'd told him she didn't want to die made him realize she'd assumed that was why he had returned to the car. Not to help her, but to end her.

"I need to get her somewhere safe," he said, loud enough for her benefit. "Our attackers could be doubling back to check their work."

"I can have someone there in twenty minutes?"

"Not soon enough."

The roar of a motorcycle drew his gaze. The biker slowed and eased off the road toward them, looking concerned. Blessed good Samaritans.

"Besides, my ride just showed up. I'll be in touch." He hung up.

"You guys need help?" The biker zeroed in on Cora's wound. "I have some EMT training." He dropped the kickstand with his foot and lumbered off the bike.

"Thanks, man." Mace locked eyes with him. "But I'll be taking the bike."

The compulsion went to work instantly. The biker's pupils expanded, eating away the brown of his irises. "Okay."

"You'll walk to the nearest town and call a cab to get you where you're going. After four days, you'll report the bike stolen, not before."

"Okay," the biker repeated. As soon as Mason released his stare, he strolled away.

Mace turned back to Cora and lifted her off the ground.

She made a sound of complaint, pressing the heel of her palm against her head.

He settled her on the bike's seat, making certain she wasn't about to fall over. She glanced at the vehicle nervously.

He slipped in front of her. The engine still rumbled softly. He knew by its make that it was a fast piece of machinery, but he would take it a bit slower with Cora on the back.

"Put your arms around me and hold on tight."

She hesitated.

He pulled her arms around his torso. The act caused her chest to press up against his back. He called back, "If I feel your grip loosen, I'll cuff 'em together, understand?"

"I-I don't know how long I can hold on. Also, I've never ridden on a motorcycle."

"Don't worry, I'll be doing all the work. Hold on for as long as you can. Keep talking if you have to."

He heeled up the kickstand and eased the bike forward. Cora tensed, as he figured she would. Her grip around his torso became vice-like, and her legs squeezed his hips. Any other time, he would have enjoyed the way she clung to him. Who was he kidding? He still enjoyed it.

Instead of heading north, he crossed the median and went south. As he picked up speed, Cora buried her head in his back. Then he kicked it into high-gear, and she let out a squeal.

Soon enough, St. Stamsworth was several miles behind them. The setting sun sent shadows stretching across the road. Mace exited the highway, deciding it might be safer to maneuver through the back roads from now on. Now that he'd had a moment to think, he had to assume that the driver of the black SUV had somehow known he and Cora would be traveling the highway at that time. The bastard had appeared from nowhere—most definitely hadn't been following them the whole way—which meant there was an informant.

Mace turned onto a gravely road and eased off the gas a little. Here, a bit of green was fighting strong, creeping up from the black rocky ground along the roadside. A few sporadic trees sported buds along lucky branches.

Cora's grip loosened a bit. "How are you doing back there?" He yelled over the din of the wind.

She made no response.

He turned the wheel and coasted into a wooded area, not stopping till he was far enough from the road that no one would see what he was about to do.

He toed down the kickstand and twisted around to look at Cora. Her eyes drooped, and blood coated her head all the way down her right side. He feared the damage she'd sustained was more significant than he'd originally concluded. Head wounds were tricky like that. He hoped he hadn't waited too long to heal her with his blood, but he'd had to find a safe spot first.

He looped her arm around his neck and pulled her from the bike. Her body was limp, and she wasn't staring at anything in particular. A black cloud of dread moved to the forefront of his mind.

"Cora?"

She mumbled something he couldn't decipher.

He set her down, letting her lie back against the dried ground. A soft moan left her lips. Her features scrunched painfully. Then her eyelids cracked open; her pupils were pinpricks, unseeing. She was already deep in shock.

He lifted his wrist to his mouth and sank his fangs into the flesh. Then he moved his now bleeding wrist to her lips, allowing his blood to drizzle into her mouth. She flinched. With a languid touch, she tried to push his arm away.

After a moment, her vision seemed to clear and she met his gaze. Realization flashed over her. Fear replaced her previously zombified expression. She began to struggle, pushing harder against his arm and shoving her feet on the ground to move her body back.

Quelling the attempt to get away was akin to holding a

bunny rabbit in place. The weight of his body pressed her into the soft turf. He reached up with his free hand and gripped the hair at her nape in his fist, tilting her head back to open her mouth wider. Instead, she clamped her mouth shut, clenching her teeth.

"You have to drink it," he said. "It will heal you. I can't risk taking you to a hospital."

She made a noise of complaint, her eyes angry and boring into his. That look chased away his dread. Better angry than dead. But when she turned pleading, his heart squeezed.

"This will heal you, not turn you," he explained. "Drink it. I won't let you up until I'm satisfied you've had enough." When she still didn't open her mouth, he threatened, "I can stay here all night." He tightened his grip on her nape.

She let out a whimper as her lips parted. He shoved his wrist between her teeth and felt the sting of her bite. And though she'd done it out of spite, the effect was a substantial amount of his blood gushing into her mouth. By reflex, she swallowed and then began to cough, trying to hack it back up.

"Don't you dare spit that out!" he growled.

She stilled. Then after a moment of trembling hesitation, she swallowed more of his blood, only gagging a couple more times.

"There's a girl." He removed his wrist from her mouth, stifling a grin at the red marks on his skin that matched the pattern of her teeth.

Cora glared up at Mason, but exhaustion stole the memory of why she was so angry with him. Her head lolled, and she was confused by the sharp scent of dirt.

"I'm so tired," she heard herself say.

"I know, sweetheart. Give me a little time to set us up with a room for the night. There's a motel about a mile back."

Her vision dimmed. Mason said something else, but she didn't hear it. When she opened her eyes again, the sky had morphed into a white, splotchy ceiling. A tiny lamp in the corner of the room gave off a soft glow. Mace hovered over her, fumbling with the belt of her coat. Automatically, her hands flew out to slap him away.

He paused, but didn't move from his position at the edge of the bed. "I drew you a bath. You look like you're straight from a massacre."

Using her elbows, she pushed to sit up. It took more effort than it should have.

The motel room was small, with only one bed. She'd consider that little nugget later. Her hand went to her forehead, which still throbbed.

"It's healing, but it needs to be cleaned," he informed her.

Healing? Her mind zeroed in on the word. "You forced me to drink your blood!"

"I did. And you don't have to sound so disgusted. It's considered a privilege among my kind."

"How dare you—"

"I already told you, if there had been any other way, I wouldn't have done it."

"When did you tell me that?"

"When you were cussing me out all the way here."

She tilted her head. She didn't remember doing that. She wouldn't have the nerve to do that.

He knelt before her and began undoing her coat belt again.

"Stop it!"

"The water is getting cold." Foregoing the belt, he reached for her left foot and started undoing the ties that ran the length of the boot. His actions were clipped, and he seemed irritated with her.

Oh, goddess! What had she said to him in her stupor? It suddenly registered that she had a very strong, very unpredictable vampire on her hands...and he was undressing her.

In a demure tone, she said, "I can do that myself."

"I'm sure you can," he replied, slipping her boot off and setting it aside. Then he started in on the second one. Soon it joined the other on the floor. When he reached for her belt once more, she cringed away from him. He stilled, but only long enough to send her a look that said she wouldn't win this battle.

She forced herself to calm.

He noted her capitulation and then resumed undoing the strap.

Her coat fell open, and a fiery blush entered her cheeks. *Damn this outfit!*

Without a word, he stood and held his hand out to her. She debated the probability of talking her way out of this. It wasn't good. Hesitantly, she slipped her hand in his, and he helped her to her feet. In the next instant, her coat plopped on the ground.

Standing now in her expensive lingerie, she kept as still as possible, focusing on the floor. Mace paused for only a second before he went to work on the rest of her garments. The micro mini fluttered to join her coat. Desperately, she wrapped her arms around herself, protecting the partly see through bustier that barely covered her breasts.

Mace let out a deep sound. She couldn't decide if it was a growl or a groan. Neither would bode well for her.

"Alright. I suppose you can keep the rest on, if you're so inclined." Again, he held his hand out for her, then led her into the bathroom. The tub was filled nearly to the top. Steam skimmed the surface.

"I don't need your help for this," she insisted.

"That cut is in an awkward place," he said. "You can't clean it properly by yourself. Besides, I owe this to you."

She dared a quizzical glance at him.

"I promised you would come to no harm, and that promise was broken not fifteen minutes later." His features contorted into an angry mask, but swiftly melted back toward repentance. "Please let me care for you."

Figuring he would only persist in carrying out whatever he planned no matter her protests, she dipped one foot into the warm water, then the other, and sank down. The material of her outfit clung to her skin, but she was grateful for the small amount of modesty it offered.

A tingling sensation permeated over her skin. On the counter sat an opened container of bath salts and other products, one of which was probably responsible for the bouquet of floral-mint in the air.

Had Mace hat time to stop by a store? How long had she been unconscious?

Sitting on the wide, flat edge of the tub was an array of items: soap, shampoo, tweezers, a plastic cup, and a sponge.

Was she really about to get a sponge bath from a vampire?

The concept was irreconcilable in her mind.

He dipped the cup into the water. "Tilt your head back," he

commanded gently.

When she did, he drizzled the water over her forehead. There was a tiny sting, probably from where the liquid met her wound. He dampened the sponge next, running it over her face with an almost feather touch. Then he reached for the tweezers. She went tense.

"It's for the glass," he said. "My blood in your system has already sped the healing process. I need to remove any glass or your skin will heal over it."

She relaxed a bit—well, as much as one could relax while being half-naked and bleeding in front of a vamp. She was the picture of a tasty meal to one such as he.

"Forgive me if this hurts." His expression became serious, his brows furrowing as he methodically worked. With the tweezers, he pulled a glistening shard and dropped it into the now empty cup. It made a dull thud.

Cora counted twelve more dull thuds before Mace set the tweezers aside, dumped the glass in the trash, and then returned to rinsing the excess blood.

Next, he drizzled shampoo into his palm, lathered, then folded his fingers through her hair. She couldn't help but close her eyes as he massaged her scalp, all the while thinking how surreal this was.

His hands moved to her shoulders, and he applied a slow gentle pressure with his thumbs. She had to suppress a groan. The warmth of his skin matched the temperature of the water, and for a second, she imagined him touching her lower.

She stiffened at the thought, and he paused.

"You alright?"

"Mm-hm," she said, not trusting her voice. Her body remained tense, however, even as he continued rolling his thumbs between her shoulder blades.

What was wrong with her, conjuring up such a scene? Had rational thought been crippled by that accident?

And yet, she couldn't stop sensual pictures from invading her brain.

An internal thrumming started a low beat inside her, steadily growing stronger. She cursed her body's wayward response and fought to get it under control, clenching her muscles.

He must have assumed his actions were bothering her, because he stopped the massage and grabbed for the sponge again.

"Look at me," he commanded in a light tone.

She did so without really meaning to meet his gaze, but his grey irises captured hers. A lump formed in her throat. Was it her imagination, or did he appear turned on?

To escape from his stare, she dropped her eyes to his mouth. Not a much better idea, but at least she didn't feel like he had full access to her increasingly disturbing thoughts.

He curled his finger under her chin and moved her head to the side, then ran the soft sponge along the line of her jaw and down her neck. She closed her eyes and shuddered. Why did that feel so hedonic?

"Mason?" She sounded breathy and a little rough.

He froze.

"Please stop...I..." She didn't know what kind of explanation she could give him. Her skin seemed hypersensitive to every nuance of his touch. Even the air, disturbed by the slightest of movements, seemed to brush her flesh like a caress. She shivered again. The thrumming that had started in her lower half was now a banging pulse that raced through her veins in a fiery rush.

She needed to get her body under control.

"Right," he said, his voice more guttural than before. "You should be able to finish up." He handed her the sponge and stood. "There's a night shirt for you to change into in a bag out there. I need to run out for a little bit. Don't leave this room, and don't open the door for anyone. I'll leave my number by the phone if you need me for anything, but I shouldn't be long."

"Um, alright."

He left, closing the bathroom door behind him. She didn't fully relax till she heard the motel room door open and close.

A pent-up breath left her in a rush.

Chapter 4

Cora peeled off what was left of her outfit to finish bathing properly. By the time she was done, the water was stained pink by her blood. After stepping out, she pulled the drain, wrapped herself in a towel, and then glanced at herself in the mirror for the first time tonight.

Just above her temple, a rough hook-shaped scar ran into her hairline. To her surprise, it already looked as though it was few months old. There were other, smaller marks, almost like splatters, that marred her skin just around her eye, undoubtedly where the glass had embedded into her flesh.

She couldn't remember most of the accident. She hadn't even seen the guy who hit them. But there was no way it was a coincidence. No doubt, whoever it was had hoped the crash would kill her. They couldn't have hoped to kill Mace. Taking a vamp's life was much more difficult than that. Witnessing Edgar's death had been a frightening experience to say the least.

So, all in all, one thing was certain: Her life was in danger, and as crazy as it sounded to her, a vampire—the thing she always thought she feared more than death—might be the only thing keeping her from it.

Outside the bathroom, she found the cheap, plain white gift-shop shirt in a bag on the chair and put it on. It was an XL, which hung to her knees. She searched the bottom of the bag, saddened to find no clean panties, or any other garments for that matter. The only pair of underwear she had were drenched from the bathwater. She decided to let them dry on the towel bar in the bathroom, then slipped under the covers of the king-sized bed.

That thrumming that had started with Mason's touch had not yet dissipated. In fact, it seemed to be growing worse. The soft synthetic-cotton shirt whispered over her breasts, kissing the taut skin of her nipples, making them bud into tender nubs. The sheet glided over her legs like silk rubbing against silk.

Against her will, unwanted, impossibly urgent, and undeniably carnal desire pooled between her legs.

A panicky whimper rushed past her lungs. She reached under the hem of her shirt to alleviate the pressure, but it soon became clear there would be no end to this torture.

She'd felt physical need before, but nothing like this. It was as if release was detrimental to her sanity. As though if she didn't orgasm soon, she'd explode.

* * *

Mace sank his fangs into the dazed waitress he'd lured into the dark alley behind the late-night diner. She let out a little moan from the erotic effect of his bite, making the trade of blood beneficial to both parties. It wasn't sexual on his part, not this time.

It was necessity.

Breathing in Cora's essence had brought forth his true nature, his hunger...as well as his inexplicable animalistic desire for her. Yet the woman who fed him now did nothing for him. She looked wrong, she sounded wrong, she even smelled wrong. Nonetheless, he needed to slake his hunger before returning to the motel room.

Not that he doubted himself around Cora. He could control baser instincts better than most. But still, Cora did something to him that he couldn't describe, made him crave more than just her vein and a quick fuck.

Giving her his blood hadn't helped matters. A connection was always formed with the blood-gift, which was why it was so rarely done, and always with a mutual understanding of what to expect.

Taking from humans was a different matter. There was little to no risk of solidifying a bond. Ultimately, their essence wasn't strong enough to leave a lasting mark. Taking from other vampires, however? That was a whole other bag of problems. Mace, himself, had never shared blood with one of his own kind. Bonds like that went both ways and, depending on the strength of the vampires and the frequency of the act, took longer to fade.

Whatever nexus Cora gleaned from his blood would resemble the spirit with which it was given and wouldn't last more than a few weeks. If anything it should help her to trust him, at least for the time being.

He hoped she hadn't ingested too much, though. Her wound had appeared worse, slathered in her own blood, than his examination had revealed. The good news was that it should heal fairly quickly and leave no scar behind. However, too much vampire blood, without proper faculty, would overload the system and bring on...specific urges.

He sucked the woman's vein more deeply.

He'd suspected as much when he'd been cleaning Cora's wound. The massage, he had to admit, had been a misstep. He wasn't the only one to become aroused.

He needed to be strong, mentally prepared, to deal with the situation in a detached, chivalrous manner. There was no doubt in his mind she would never trust him again if he couldn't manage that. Not to mention, if he took advantage of her now, it would enforce her already forged hatred of his kind.

Not nearly satisfied, but no longer thirsty, he compelled the waitress to forget him and sent her on her way. He retrieved the to-go bag that he'd ordered beforehand and walked the twenty yards back to the eclectic single level motel with cracked faded paint and burned-out parking lamps. The lot was empty but for the stolen motorcycle in front of room one-oh-three and what looked like the husk of a pre-uprising hick-mobile. Rust eaten and dilapidated, the truck perched at the end of the lot like a sad memorial to bygone days.

When he entered the room, Mace was relieved to find Cora already in bed. Her head was sandwiched between two pillows with her arm slung over the top. Maybe he hadn't given her too much of his blood after all.

He crossed to the table and set the food down.

"Mace?"

The tremors in Cora's voice made him go tense. She peeked at him from under the pillow. From what he could see of her expression under her fluffy shield, she appeared to be in pain.

"Are you alright?" he asked.

She shook her head. "Something's wrong. I feel...I'm...I can't..."

Mace squeezed his eyes shut. "Shit." Definitely too much blood. The scent of her desire invaded his nostrils. He clutched the back of a nearby chair. The aroma was like an electroshock wake-up call to the section of his brain that was purely primordial. He went instantly hard. His fangs lengthened, more from anticipation than hunger.

Cora continued sputtering, her cheeks flaming. "I-I...need to..." She let out a frustrated sound and buried her face back in the pillow.

"You don't have to explain," he said. "It's my blood that's affecting you now. It should pass in a few hours."

She smashed the pillow into her face with her palm and exhaled a protesting scream. Then she flung the pillow away. "A few hours? I can't stand this a second longer. I ne...uh...need your help. Need you to make it stop."

He shook his head, pity burrowing into his gut.

"Please." She squirmed uncomfortably under the covers.

"I won't do that. You wouldn't be happy about it in the morning."

Her lip quivered. "Please, Mason. I'm going to go insane."

Generally, Mace thought of himself as a vigilant, uncompromising individual, but he had never wanted to fold so quickly.

"Cora," he warned. "Think on this. You know you don't want me touching you."

She started to respond, but he tuned her out. He had to put some distance between him and the sweet scent of her arousal. The bathroom wasn't far enough, but he wouldn't risk leaving her alone in this state.

He ran the tap and splashed cool water on his face. When he reached for a towel, he found, instead, a soft bit of cloth. He fingered the material and let out a guttural sound. Christ, she was out there in bed, no panties, and begging for his cock. Even if he didn't have a special attraction to her, any man would be hard-pressed to resist.

Her moaning pleas assaulted him mercilessly from the other room. She sounded both tormented and salacious—the sweetest sound that had ever graced his ears. He braced his palms on the counter and lowered his head, cursing. Who was he kidding? He wouldn't be able to deny her for another minute, let alone a few hours.

He reentered the room a defeated man, but Cora's pleas continued uninterrupted. Unshed tears sparkled in her eyes. It broke his heart.

"Mason, please," she implored, looking miserable.

"Coraline." He paused at the edge of the bed. "I don't want you to hate me for this in the morning."

"I won't hate you. I won't even be mad. I promise. Please... I've never felt like this before. It's too much." She shoved the blankest away and ripped the shirt over her head, tossing it to the ground.

Normally she was a little shy and reserved. He always liked that about her. Now she was completely lost to lust, and fuck if he didn't like that too.

Selfishly, he feasted on the vision of her lush curves, while at the same time feeling like a deviant. She crawled toward him, stopping with her knees on the edge of the bed, her hands urgently roaming his chest and shoulders.

This wasn't her. This wasn't the kind, bashful female he had come to know over the last few months. He realized in this moment, he would take her in any form.

But only with her full, rational consent.

She reached for his fly and had his zipper down before his body caught up with his resolve. He stayed her hand. She responded with a tiny sound that bordered on a sob, her beautiful eyes pained.

"I won't be having sex with you tonight, Coraline. But," he added swiftly, before she completely lost her shit, "there are other options. Ones that you might approve of later, when you're in your right mind."

"Like?" she urged.

His gaze dropped to her mouth. He brought his hand up to rest his palm on her cheek while his thumb caressed her bottom lip. Unabashedly, she sucked his thumb into her mouth.

The little witch nearly broke him then and there.

With his free hand, he clutched the hair at her nape, and slowly extracted his thumb. Cora froze. Somewhere deep beneath the predominant lust, there was fear behind her eyes. His extended fangs probably didn't help that.

However, he didn't loosen his hold. "I want it noted that I could have had you any way I wanted, and you would've begged me for more, but I restrained myself. For now, stay still while I make you come."

Before she could manage a response, he gripped the backs of her knees and yanked her body out from under her. Her back met the mattress, leaving her legs spread wide for him, her ass hanging over the edge of the mattress. Foreplay was obsolete at the moment. He knelt to the floor and placed his mouth directly on her heated core. They both groaned in unison. The exquisite fragrance of her arousal penetrated his mind, making him drunk with the need to hear her scream from pleasure.

Deliriously, he laved her tender folds, sucking her clitoris between his teeth, mindful of his throbbing fangs. The urgent sounds she made had his cock straining painfully against his partly undone jeans. He shoved the material down and ran his palm over the length of his shaft as his tongue rode her undulating hips. She was utterly lost now, writhing, taking from his willing mouth what she needed.

He pumped his fist in rhythm with her movements. Her body shuddered violently, mindlessly, from their cresting passion. In the next instant, a harsh cry erupted from her. She barricaded a hand over her mouth. Mace was on the verge of following her climax and continued his sensual assault.

Too late, he realized this was ready to cross a line he hadn't intended.

As Cora cried out from a second orgasm, the beast in him took over. He turned his face toward her inner thigh and sank his fangs deep. Cora's moan deepened, her body arching as if an electric jolt had seized it.

His mouth filled with her succulent blood. Euphoria scrambled his brain. All his thoughts reduced to mush. All but one: she tasted better than he could have ever imagined.

His ecstasy slowly abated, leaving behind an almost mind-crippling pleasure. His orgasm came so fiercely, his vision faltered. It took him a moment to realize he'd removed his fangs from her thigh and was hunched over, his hands on the floor, trying to cope with the intensity of what had just happened.

Absently, he muttered, "Every bit of you is like heaven on

my tongue. You have me addicted already."

He could hear short gasps coming from her as she hurriedly slipped her shirt back over her head. If he hadn't just experienced essentially what amounted to a swift kick to his mind's balls, he probably would have seen what was coming.

Propelling off the bed, she threw the door open wide and rushed outside before the knob ricocheted off the wall and the door slammed shut behind her.

"Shit." He buttoned his fly and raced after her.

She hadn't gotten far, just to the middle of the lot. When he closed his arms around her torso from behind, she screamed and began kicking her legs wildly.

"Calm yourself," he ordered, finding no trouble holding onto her.

"Let me go!"

"I can't do that," he replied in a reasonable tone, his body still thrumming with pleasure.

She sniffed and let out a terrible sob, all the while thrashing in his grip. He wasn't worried about the noise. This was a deeply rural area where people kept to themselves.

He dragged her back inside the room and caged her with his body against the closed door, locking gazes with her. "Relax and calm down." He pushed only the slightest bit of compulsion into the command, hating to have to resort to that much. When she didn't respond, he tried again with a bit more zeal.

Still nothing.

Her face was red, panic stricken, and streaked with tears. Her thrashing continued.

Pushing the full force of his compulsion into his voice, he growled, "Stop crying."

A sob filtered through her lungs, and her tears came harder.

He cocked his head. "What the fuck?"

That's when she went utterly still, as though she'd come to a terrifying realization. She peeked up at him through tear soaked eyes.

"*Rheol Eithriad*?" he gasped. The exception to the rule. Otherwise known as, *Lurela*: a person that cannot be compelled. He'd never come across one before. Of course his first would have to be Cora! "Dammit all to hell."

Although she seemed to be calming, weighing his reaction—which told him she knew about her natural resistance—the look in her eye said she would run from him at the first opportunity.

How could she be so upset after the blissful, mind-rocking experience they'd just shared? Religions were built around such things. His masculine pride took a pile-drive to the gut.

He glanced at the clock. It was nearly midnight.

"We'll talk about this in the morning." Maybe then he could muster up an authentic apology. Right now it would seem insincere to her ears, especially because it would be. "We have a ways to go tomorrow, and we both need to get some sleep."

He released her and pointed to the bed.

She looked at it and mumbled, "I'll sleep on the floor."

His mood darkened even more. "I don't think so. You'll just try to run when I fall asleep."

"No, I won't." She lied so easily.

"I'm not taking the chance." He guided her by the elbow to the bed.

Thankfully, she appeared to be out of defiance for the moment. She crawled onto the mattress and pulled the covers around her like a cocoon, then placed a pillow in the middle of the bed as a barrier between them.

After shutting off the light and claiming the opposite side of the bed, he snatched her faux wall and disgruntledly shoved it under his head. Then he reached under her refuge of blankets, hooked his arm around her waist to pull her flush against him.

"What are you doing?" She brazenly swatted at his arm and bowed away from him.

"It's either this, or I tie you up for the night. Your choice."

"I prefer to be tied up, then."

"I lied. It's my choice. Go to sleep."

Cora cosigned herself to Mace's arms and settled in. She didn't have much of a choice. She was just glad this was the only retaliation for her attempted escape, which had been spurred by his powerfully erotic snuffing of her lust. She had been too surprised to think straight.

Humans had once thought of vampires as cold, undead creatures, who required blood to survive. Mason was anything but cold at the moment. The warmth of his body seeped into her back, as did his pulse, which was noticeably slower than hers—adrenaline still spiked wildly in her veins.

No, vampires were flesh and blood, same as humans. Whether evolved or otherworldly was debatable, but definitely top of the food chain.

Currently, she was on the bottom, right underneath krill.

As for needing blood to survive? That part was all too true.

As Cora lay there, immersed in one of her greatest nightmares, she evaluated the end of her life as she knew it. Mace now knew she could not be compelled by him or, as far as she could tell, any other vampire. She could not be made to forget the salacious act they'd just shared, the location of wherever it was he intended to take her, or this whole illegal vampire blood business.

She'd been inclined to hope for a swift and immediate death when this fiasco was over...but now? Now he would claim her, take her to his clan and demand to keep her, just as Edgar had.

For the sole purpose of being cruel, Edgar had explained in gory detail what happened to lone humans amongst vampires. And it all started with a bite.

Well, Mace had bitten her.

And once her brain had pushed past the unexpected and consuming pleasure of it, the realization had made her rash. She couldn't believe she tried to run from him—the stupidest thing one could do in the presence of a vampire. They were animalistic by nature. Running only invoked their urge to chase, to hunt.

Edgar had explained that as well, which was why she'd been too scared to attempt an escape, and she'd been too scared to run the instant his commander had told her to go, directly after having killed Edgar.

That fear may have actually saved her life that day. More than one vamp had studied her with glossy-eyed interest as she'd turned and forced her feet into slow but sure action, counting the steps till she was outside the old abandoned building.

The heat of the sun in mid-day on her skin had lifted her spirits like nothing else ever had, even though vampires were not hindered by it—another false rumor that had spread through humanity. They could have still gone after her if they'd wanted.

But they hadn't.

Still, it had been several months till she felt out of danger. Even then, she treaded with more caution than a field mouse in an aviary if she even imagined a vampire might be near.

She should have been just as cautious of humans, she supposed. Among others, Winston had found her easy enough to take advantage of. She'd been so enamored with him and his elaborate life-style, she'd turned a blind eye to the warning signs. It was too easy now to look back and recognize the reality of the situation. Especially that time she had tried to refuse that glass of wine he'd offered her after she'd injured her ankle. He had been livid and practically forced the wine down her throat.

How many times had he fed her blood and waited to see if it would make her ill, or worse, kill her? How many times had she brushed off the fact that she healed far too rapidly than should've been expected?

She didn't know how long she ran through every scenario, berating herself for each one, but eventually her mind eased till she nodded off completely.

Chapter 5

The musky scent of dampened soap, along with the sound of rushing water, lulled Cora awake. The edge of morning seeped through the drawn curtains. She sat up, surprised to find herself alone in the bed, and the shower running with the bathroom door left open.

The water cut off, and her heart jumped. She wouldn't be surprised if Mace could hear it hammering from within the other room. He emerged a moment later, a white towel around his slim waist.

Because she hadn't fully shrugged off the haze of slumber, her eyes unabashedly took in the impeccably sculpted muscles of his chest and arms, seeming to get stuck on his six-pack abs. He scrutinized her for a moment, and the corner of his lips quirked upward.

She frowned. The last thing she needed was for him to think she appreciated what she saw.

Her gaze shifted to the door, longingly.

"Woman, I will chase you butt-ass naked if I have to," Mace

said in a tone that brokered no doubt.

That brought her attention back, specifically toward his crotch. Heat flooded her cheeks as well as other parts of her anatomy.

What was wrong with her? Had the lust carried over from the previous night, or had she just woken up insane?

He arched a brow. "I think I used up most of the hot water," he announced, and then smirked. "But maybe that will work to your advantage this morning."

Her flush deepened. Even though she hadn't meant to, she had become aroused, and, to her extreme embarrassment, he could tell.

"Wasn't expecting a compliment like this after the kick to my ego you delivered last night."

Her brow furrowed. What did he mean by that?

She didn't bother rationalizing his words. Instead, she slipped off the bed and crossed to the bathroom, not meeting his gaze as she passed. Still, she could feel him watching her go with an intensity that was almost tangible.

Inside, she closed the door. Her jaw dropped as she took in her reflection. Aside from her wild mane of hair, she looked... great. There were no marks on her face to indicate she'd been in a horrific accident less than twenty-four hours ago. Her eyes sparkled the color of warm mocha dipped in gold. Her skin was smooth and even, almost radiant, like porcelain. Even her lips, which she'd always considered too plump, now seemed to complement her features.

If this was the work of Mason's blood, she could see why Winston's rich friends would covet the stuff. What she couldn't understand was the risk they courted by procuring it illegally, especially for people who had practically everything they could ever want. Why play with fire when the pit created under the flames could so easily swallow you up?

As Mace predicted, the water grew cold by the end of her shower. No matter. This far from the city, having warm water at all was an unexpected luxury. In the ghetto, most resorted to heating water in pots and transferring it to a tub for what was, at best, not a freezing cold bath.

A soft curse graced her lips as she stepped out of the stall. She'd forgotten to grab her clothing before entering the bathroom. Now she would have to waltz out there in front of Mace in just a towel.

She gnashed her teeth and held her chin up as she stepped outside, but her posturing was unnecessary. The room was empty.

She had no illusions that Mace had gone far, however. Trying to run now would only piss him off.

With no other option, she dressed in her obnoxiously tight outfit. Once again, she wished she had chosen something that wasn't so overtly sexy. She'd just finished tying the belt of her trench coat when Mace returned. He too had dressed in his clothing from the day before: dark slacks and a black buttoned up shirt.

He paused in the doorway when he saw her, and his gaze traveled her length as if he were imagining what resided under her coat. Her first instinct was to shoot him an indignant glare. Then she remembered herself and turned her eyes down.

There was a small paper bag in his hand. His fist tightened on the folded top before he thrust it at her. "Here. I got you some breakfast. Eat quickly. We have to get a move on."

For some reason, she got the impression she'd done something to displease him, but couldn't fathom what it could be.

Accepting the bag, she peeked inside and gasped. "Where did you get this?"

She pulled out the large slice of coffee cake. Of all the treats in the world, coffee cake was by far her greatest weakness. When she was younger, she would sometimes stand outside the bakeries every morning just to smell it. Up until it became more of a punishment than a pleasure. Few people threw away such delicacies for the vagrants to fight over.

After marrying Winston, she'd eaten a slice nearly every morning. A couple of times, she had even purchased an entire cake and left it near her old stomping ground where the old-timers who had always been kind to her hung around. However, that stopped the day Winston caught her. She still couldn't understand why it had made him so angry.

"One of our mountain neighbors was in a baking mood," Mace replied. "Been smelling it all morning."

She frowned as realization struck her. "You compelled someone out of it?"

Mace rolled his eyes. "Do you want it or not?"

Conflicted, she bit into the cake and groaned out loud. Mace actually smiled, looking satisfied. But why would he be? For that matter, why would he care if she went hungry? Perhaps he was afraid she'd start complaining during their travels and didn't want to deal with it.

Or maybe keeping her fed worked to his advantage, like a farmer with his livestock. She shuddered.

Cora ate every last crumb and even contemplated licking the bag—who knew when she'd get a treat like this again?—but Mace was in a hurry.

Outside, Cora climbed onto the back of the bike and waited for Mace to take his place at her front, but he just stared at her.

"What is it?" She checked to see if she had dropped crumbs down her front, finding none. When she looked back up, Mace had his phone out and snapped a picture.

"Now that's a sight to remember," he said.

She was stunned into silence, trying to see herself from his perspective. Her boot-clad leg, the one closest to him, was stretched to the ground, holding her steady on the bike, still tilted on its kickstand. About four inches of her thigh showed between her tall boot and the hem of her coat. Her other leg was bent, her foot resting on the peg. One of her hands gripped the back rest, angling her torso toward Mason. All in all, it made for a pose that reminded her of those biker babe magazines, but Cora was anything but sexy. She probably looked more like a drowned rat with her hair still wet from the shower.

And Mace was laughing at her.

She scowled at him. He snapped another picture, then slipped his phone back in his pocket and mounted the bike.

"Hold on," he ordered.

Grudgingly, she obeyed, and he fired up the engine. The motorcycle sprang forward with unexpected speed. Cora flexed her arms tighter around Mace, fixing her torso flat against his back. Over the roar of the engine she couldn't hear it, but she could swear he chuckled at her.

Several hours later they were still winding through tight, nearly abandoned mountain roads. She would have been bored out of her mind if it wasn't for the brilliant scenery. The dead burned landscape had given way to lush green forest, blanketing endless hills and valleys that were only broken up by steep stony mountains.

Winston had never entertained the idea of visiting the countryside. This part of the world was inhabited by what he would call "crazies." Whether that was true or not, they preferred to live alone, or in small groups, surviving off the land. She'd heard that those types of people, the kind that lived in camouflaged huts and flossed with bark, were reclusive, often paranoid, and could be violently territorial. Anyone who ventured this far without proper protection risked, well, everything.

Most of the time, the rest of the world left them alone.

Maybe that wasn't such a terrible way to live, she thought, considering the struggles of her own life.

Then again, who knew what kind of existence that would mean, especially for someone like her. In life—whether in the slums, or a high-rise, apparently—the strong preyed on the weak, and she was about as weak as they came...

Before Winston, she'd only just been capable of protecting herself, mostly by keeping her head down and making herself as unassuming as humanly possible.

That tactic had worked for her on occasion, though, not always. She eyed the back of Mason's head—case in point.

Suffice it to say, unstable mountain folk would eat her for breakfast if they had the chance. It was dangerous just to be out here on the road in plain view where anyone could be tracking their movement from a high summit.

Yet, miraculously, she wasn't worried.

A frightening thought popped into her head: she wasn't afraid of the crazies because nothing matched the savagery of a territorial vampire. Nothing would get her while she was in his custody.

Nothing but him.

She shivered, and he eased off the gas, giving her his profile. "Do you need a break?"

"I'm fine," she replied.

He slowed and halted the bike on a narrow pull-off by the side of the road that was cut short by a small cliff. Below was a wide bank hugging a slow, winding river. The surrounding overgrowth was thick with trees, man-sized bushes, and other unkempt shrubbery.

"I'm old enough to know that when a woman says she's fine, it usually means the opposite." He toed down the kickstand, making it final.

The instant she dismounted the bike, her legs nearly gave out from the strange jelly sensation.

Mace reached out to steady her, and she flinched away. "I'm fine, really."

He frowned. "I hoped you'd be less skittish toward me today."

She wasn't sure how to respond to that, so she said nothing as she walked around to stretch her legs. A light breeze carried the scent of fresh soil in the air. It wasn't a smell often found in the city, where pungent exhaust and trash perfumed the streets.

Out here the air felt new, fresh, and unsullied, almost giving the illusion of freedom.

Almost.

Mace watched Cora come to a halt several feet from the edge of the short cliff and wrap her arms around herself as she gazed out. Her expression was one that he'd seen all too often, but only from afar, across a restaurant or through military-grade binoculars. What that expression meant, he didn't know. He could only describe it as forlorn.

He hadn't liked it then, and he abhorred it now.

Mace approached her. "Look, I'm sorry you're so unhappy with what happened, but it was necessary."

Her head turned his way, though she studied the ground at his feet. "It was anything but necessary. Do what you will with me, but there's no need to lie."

Mace paused, surprised by her response. "You needed my help. And if you recall, we didn't even have sex." Though the temptation had almost destroyed him.

"No, you only made me beg for it." Her expression hardened, but then she turned away as though ashamed. She nearly choked on her next words. "And you *bit* me."

He went still. Was that what bothered her the most? A dark thought settled in the pit of his stomach? "Did it hurt…? When I bit you?" He'd never come across anyone who didn't find pleasure in the act. But then, he'd never met a *Lurela*.

Her brow furrowed as her cheeks flushed. Even though she didn't answer, he could tell she had liked it…at least a little. And yet, she shouldn't be surprised by that. He recalled her suggesting she had been bit before. So then what was the problem?

"My bite helped to alleviate most of your need," he explained. "I assumed it would be better than the alternative."

Truthfully, he'd been so overcome with desire for her he'd taken her vein without thinking.

She went silent for a long while, scanning the landscape.

"I hadn't intended for any of that to happen, you know," he said. "I just gave you too much of my blood, that's all."

"For future reference, if it's a choice between me dying and you giving me your blood, I'd rather die."

Red coated his vision as he spoke through clenched teeth. "The offering of my blood was a gift not to be taken lightly. Think twice before you scoff at my benevolence."

"Benevolence?" She dared a sardonic sneer and actually met his gaze head-on, which managed to deflate his anger. "Oh, you're so magnanimous, aren't you?" Then she crossed the space between them and slapped him on his chest. He took a step back, and his jaw went slack. "So gracious to let me live...?" She slapped him again. "To keep me alive...!" Her hands turned to fists, and she brought them against his torso again. "That it should be an honor for me to give you my blood?" Her fists slammed his chest several more times as she spoke, rocking him backward, but he held his ground. Tears started streaming down her cheeks. "I should be happy to let you take whatever you want?"

Her words sounded out of place, as though she were talking about something other than what had happened between them last night. He clamped his hands around her wrists when his chest began to sting from her attack, but the verbal assault continued.

"Are you to be my *master* now? Will you talk of benevolence when you take me to you clan and loan me out?"

"Whoa, what?"

She tried to rip out of his grasp, but he held firm.

"Let me go!"

He didn't. Instead, he allowed her to exert herself till she finally stopped and surrendered to his authority, although her tears never ceased. Once more, her eyes went downward.

He wished he was one of those vampires who could read

minds.

"What happened to you?" he finally asked.

She flinched, but didn't respond.

"No one had ever acted so negatively toward a vampire's bite, and it's not because you're a *Lurela*. You've been bit before, correct? So you should've known what to expect, but for some reason, I don't think you did."

She'd gone completely still, like an animal in the grips of a predator sensing death was imminent.

He released one of her wrists and hooked his forefinger under her chin to tilt her head up. When she reluctantly looked into his eyes, he said, "I have no intention of taking you anywhere besides a safe house, or sharing you with anyone. And as for master, I'm not one to claim lordship over unwilling women. But I won't lie, I enjoyed giving you pleasure last night, and that's all my bite was meant to do, nothing more." He paused. "Now tell me what happened to you that has you reacting this strongly?"

Her shoulders hunched, and she looked away. She remained silent so long that if it weren't for the open debate raging behind her eyes, he would think she had no intention of answering him at all.

She inhaled a sharp breath and raised her chin. "I was held captive by a vampire named Edgar when I was ten."

With that simple revelation, white-hot anger flashed through every cell in his body with his imagination acting as fuel. What had she endured? In an instant, he'd shuffled through the memories of every vampire he ever met, trying to recall any named Edgar, a death warrant already issued in his mind.

"Mason?" Cora came back into view. Her eyes were wide, her body shaking. He realized she was terrified...by him.

And for good reason. His fangs had emerged with his rage. His body had tensed. His expression? He could just imagine how ruthless he appeared now.

He released her and stepped away, focusing on schooling his features.

Still wary, she fell back a couple paces.

"Where is he now?" he hissed through his clenched fangs.

"He's dead," she replied, taking another step back.

"Don't move," he warned her.

She froze.

"Just give me a moment." He'd never been driven to fury so quickly. If she ran from him now, it would only exacerbate his rage. "Tell me how he died." Humans often assumed vampires were dead when they really weren't.

"He was torn apart by his commanding officer right in front of me."

"Commanding officer?"

"It was near the end of the last uprising when there were pockets of militant groups all over. I think Edgar was a low-level soldier. His commander found me in his quarters and ordered him to release me. Edgar had refused."

"The fucker must have been really young, then." Disobeying an order from a superior—which generally meant an older and much stronger vampire—was an amateur move.

"I wouldn't know. He never revealed his age, just liked to divulge his future plans for me."

"And what were these plans?"

She shrugged. "Things he would do to me, or things he wanted to watch others do. He would ravage my neck and then try to make me beg for his blood. Stuff like that?"

Her flippant tone didn't quite hide her obvious pain or the terror she'd endured.

He glanced at the delicate column of her neck. There were no scars, but that meant little. Winston had been giving her vamp blood for months. It had cleared her of any scars, making her skin flawless.

"Did Edgar ever manage to give you any of his blood? When you were too weak to protest, maybe?" Jealousy turned Mason's hands into tight, white-knuckled fists.

"No. I'm sure of it."

He wasn't sure if he should be elated or more furious about that. Her wounds would have had to heal naturally. "What else did he do?"

"He just drank from me and told me horrid things."

"He didn't...touch you?"

"Not in a sexual way, if that's what you mean. I think he got his rocks off by hurting me."

Mace scrubbed a hand down his face, relief softening him further. "I'm sorry that happened to you. We aren't all like that. Just like your human race, we have our share of criminals, too."

She stared blankly at him, giving him the impression she didn't quite believe him. He couldn't blame her for that. It was no wonder she found it difficult to trust him, and how she had learned her near-perfect submission act.

It was born of necessity.

"If this Edgar were alive today, I would hunt him down and make him suffer horribly before I killed him."

She canted her head. "Why would you bother?"

"Because you deserve that much and more."

His reply didn't seem to alleviate her confusion. She looked at him now as if to figure out what manner of treachery he engaged in. He reached out for her shoulder, intending to reassure her.

Something slammed into his chest, knocking the air from his lungs and tossing him back.

Pain stole his sight. He lost his footing over the cliff.

For a moment, Cora couldn't understand what had just happened. Mason's chest had...exploded!

He stumbled back, falling over the bluff.

Adrenaline spiked. She screamed. He had to have been shot, but by who?

She darted her gaze around, searching.

A mud-covered jeep sped over the dirt road toward her, screeching to a halt just behind the motorbike.

Three scruffy men in grungy clothes jumped out, all of them eyeing her with cruel grins.

She rushed to the cliff face and leaned over. Mace lay face down at the bottom, about twenty feet below, unmoving. "Mason!"

Boots crunched against rock, closing in on her from behind. She couldn't take her eyes from Mace.

Callous fingers threaded through her hair, dragging her back toward the jeep. One of the men stepped to the edge where she had been, aimed a gun down, and fired twice, presumably at Mason's corpse.

"No!" she screeched.

"Shut that banshee up!" one of the men yelled.

In the next instant, pain laced her cheek from the backhanded slap. As she tried to clear her jarred brain, her coat was ripped from her body. A disgusting string of appreciative noises came from her assailants, and she was slammed up against the burning hot side of the still running jeep.

"Is she the one?" the man near the cliff asked. His voice was odd, harsh and scratchy, like he'd been smoking since birth.

"Looks like it," the man next to her replied. He was the youngest of the three. "We should bring her in, just in case."

"We only need to bring in her head," the third man laughed.

Cora gagged on a sob. Her eyes blurred from both horror and the pain that still stung her cheek.

"Shame to kill such a sweet ass," Scratchy Voice said apathetically.

"Well, we don't have to kill her right away. Is the vamp dead?"

"I shot him three times. What do you think?"

A pair of rough hands pulled her forward and pushed her toward Scratchy Voice. "You hold her. I call first crack."

"No way. I'm the one who brought you in on this. I go first." He shoved her aside.

"Screw that. I don't do sloppy seconds," the young man said.

"Fuck you."

Fists swung between the two, while the third held a gun to her head and waited indifferently for the outcome.

Cora stood, shaking, heart thundering, as she contemplated what was sure to be the end of her life. What a sad, pathetic, useless end. How utterly unimportant her life turned out to be. Nothing but an ode to endurance with less than a few short months dedicated to happiness. Or as close to happiness as she would ever experience.

What was the point of life, anyway, if there was nothing but sorrow, heartache, and pain? If everyone was nothing more than cruelty wrapped up in the facade of civility. Morality was a joke created by cynics and con artists. Evil reigned at every turn. Anything good decayed like fruit and turned sour, hateful, greedy, and selfish.

She wasn't fit for this world.

A snarling roar made the men freeze mid-fight.

Cora looked up.

A mountain lion stood atop a pile of rocks, some fifty feet away, its fangs bared at them.

The men swore and scrambled back.

The young one yelled, "Shoot it!" and the man with the gun to her head turned it on the animal.

Three loud shots echoed off the mountain ridges, but the sound hadn't come from the directions she'd expected.

The three men fell lifeless, blood oozing from each of their skulls, staining the gravel.

Heart slamming, Cora crumbled to the ground, gasping and sobbing uncontrollably.

She gathered herself enough to glance around and take stock. The humans were dead. The lion was gone, most likely scared by the gunfire. She spied Mason's upper body slumped over the edge of the cliff, a pistol in his limp hand. It seemed he had managed to pull himself up, but looked to be unconscious again.

"Mason?" she called, her voice shaking.

He didn't respond, didn't move.

The space around her now seemed eerily quiet, except for the jeep's engine, which had been left idling.

Her mind jumped into overdrive, still riding on the heels of adrenaline. The wisest course of action would be to take the jeep and put as much space between her, Mason, St. Stamsworth, and vampires in general. Drive till either the car died, or she did.

At the thought, numbness coated her. Run till she died? It sounded no better than going back to the streets. Besides, Mason had saved her life. What was it? Three times now? She owed him for that at least.

Beating back her trepidation, she rummaged through the pockets of the dead men, claiming whatever cash she found. It wasn't much. For good measure, she kicked one of them twice in the stomach. As pointless as it was, it made her feel better.

"Mace?" She knelt beside him and rocked his body. "Mace? Can you hear me?"

His eyes fluttered. "Cora..." He finished with an incoherent mutter.

"If you can make it into the jeep, I can drive us out of here and find help."

Mace seemed to understand. His head tilted up to gauge the distance between them and the jeep. His arm moved to push against the gravel, slowly elevating his torso. She helped as much as she could, which was almost not at all. When he inched forward, she caught the sight of his back. One of the shots had probably penetrated his spine. She spotted another gory wound at his shoulder. That didn't include the first that had gouged his chest. All three wounds oozed a foul-smelling green substance. She couldn't imagine the kind of pain he was in.

As he lumbered forward, dragging himself along the ground

on his hands and knees, she yanked him by the arm, urging more than helping him along. He paused, breathing heavily, then slumped down. His lungs heaved for air.

Her gaze darted over her surroundings. They were in trouble if those men had back up. Then she remembered that mountain lion. Any moment, it could return, enticed by the fresh scent of death.

"Get up, get up," she chanted.

Mace pulled his arm forward and began to drag himself once more toward the jeep. Cora pulled up on his forearm when he tried to stand, offering leverage. He got to his feet, but went back down to his knees directly after. Again she helped him up, panting and sweating as she used all her strength to aid him in conquering another few feet.

With a sound of pain, he went down once more, catching himself by one strong arm. With the other, he clutched his chest wound. His face twisted in a grotesque mask of unimaginable agony.

"Not far now," she encouraged.

Inch by inch, she helped him crawl across the gravel toward the jeep. The whole process must have taken twenty minutes or more, but eventually they succeeded in getting to the jeep.

His muscles bulged angrily as he pulled himself into the passenger seat while she tried to lift his lower half. When he was fully inside, he let out a harsh breath. His body folded forward over the dashboard.

Cora closed the door behind him, took the driver's seat, and drew in a deep breath.

What in the hell am I going to do now?

Chapter 6

"Mason? Mason, wake up. Please wake up."

The soft, feminine voice lulled him out of a deep slumber and then dunked him into the fiery pits of hell. His blood burned as though laced with sulfuric acid.

He cracked his eyes open, confused at first to see a dark, shadowy world rushing past him. Cora rigidly leaned over the steering wheel as she drove much too fast through the darkness. How long had he been out?

The nauseating smell of his own cooked flesh pierced his nostrils. The ammunition those men had used was designed for vampires. Too bad for them it wasn't potent enough to kill, only meant to incapacitate. Mace wondered if they had known that.

Probably not. Otherwise they would have been sure to finish him off.

"Mace?" Cora glanced at him with wide, bloodshot eyes.

"Watch the road," he chastised. "How long have I been out?"

"Two hours. Do you need...do you need to drink?" There

was an unsteady note in her tone.

He blinked at her.

Was she offering? Even after all she had revealed? Without turning her head from the road, her eyes darted nervously his way. Tenderness for her warmed his chest. However, there was no way he would take from her again. Not when it drudged up such terrible memories for her.

When he didn't answer right away, she let off the gas, and the jeep began to slow.

"Keep driving," he ordered, then he reached for his phone, ignoring the agonizing pain that shot through his spine as he moved. The time was just after eight in the evening. He scrolled to Trent's name, but paused. Just like that black SUV, those hicks had targeted him and Cora. Any number of police officers had known which road they were to take out of the city, but only Trent had known where to find them today.

Mace wasn't about to entertain the idea that his longtime friend and sire might betray him. More likely, Trent was keeping both the VEA and human enforcement agency informed of their situation. Which meant anyone of them could be responsible for issuing the hit.

Still, Mace refrained from calling for now. He needed to find a safe place where he could heal first.

His phone's GPS map put them approximately twenty minutes from the closest town. Lucky break that Cora had continued along this road.

He typed the name of their destination and mapped out a route, then handed the phone to Cora. "Go here. I have an acquaintance there who owes me one."

Cora read the name of their destination: Ever Nights. The place was located in Cloverdale, one of the many cities that had been burned to the ground—mostly due to hysteria—after the vamps had first been exposed, and rebuilt. Before that, the vampire population in Cloverdale had probably been countable on one hand. After? Out of the ashes, a new city arose, its vampire demographic in the hundreds, if not thousands.

Of course that was where Mason would want to go—a place where sane, intelligent humans endeavored to avoid.

"Mason? Is it necessary...?"

Mace grimaced painfully and clutched his chest. His breathing sounded labored, like air rushing through a clogged exhaust.

"You need blood. I'm going to pull over."

"No...keep going. Cortez...will..." He groaned. "The shrapnel's..." His words dwindled to a babble of incoherency. His eyes fluttered. Then he passed out completely.

"Shit, Mason. You're essentially sending me into vampire territory with no protection. You better not've been bullshitting me earlier." She recalled how angry he had become over her story, furiously so. And then he'd sounded so earnest, so sympathetic to her plight that she'd found herself actually softening toward him. And for the moment, it seemed impossible that Mace could be as cruel as Edgar.

She hoped she could hold him to that. Because if she couldn't, she was so screwed.

Twenty minutes later, Cora pulled into the parking lot of Ever Nights. The neon lights were indicative of—

"A strip joint?" Cora groaned and then doubled checked

Mason's directions. She had followed them to the T.

She turned to him. He was still unconscious in the passenger seat, head tipped back, arms limp by his side. A light sheen of sweat coated his forehead. On the way here, his big body had fallen over onto her, pushing her into the driver's side door. It had taken all her strength and a surge of adrenaline that was surely her last to prop him back up and keep the car from veering off the road.

He bled heavily from the lesion in his chest, and an abnormal discharge bubbled around the edges. Any mortal would be long dead, judging by the severity of the wound.

"Mason. We're here. Wake up." She jostled him lightly by the shoulder.

He hissed out a pained sound, showing his fangs, though his eyes remained closed. She yanked her hand away just as he snapped at her.

He must need blood badly. How much had he already lost? She owed him a debt. The only thing she could offer was her vein. However, after his aggressive display just now, she wasn't sure she could trust him not to drain her dry in his stupor.

With him incapacitated, it wouldn't do to risk her own life. Besides, according to Mace, there was someone named Cortez who might be able to help.

She hopped out of the jeep and rushed inside, coming face-to-face with a very large, very frightening, undoubtedly vampiric, bouncer. His all-black ensemble, thick chain necklace, leather arm cuff, silver-tipped steel-toe boots, and all those tattoos weren't necessary to add to the aura of menace that clung to the broad-shouldered vampire. Neither was the deep scowl aimed directly at her. Wasn't necessary, but it worked all the same.

Cora lost her voice for a moment.

The vampire's lips curled ever so slightly as he took her in. Her mouth was hanging open as if she fully expected eloquent, well-thought-out words to emerge.

All that came was a scratchy, high-pitched, "Cortez?"

The part of her brain that recognized she was but a wee fluffy mammal in the presence of a powerful, meat-eating predator infected the section dedicated to bravery. It was almost physically painful to plant her feet and keep her body in place when all she wanted to do was run in the opposite direction.

One thing kept her staring flatly into the eyes of that vampire: The solid, bone deep, and undeniable knowledge that if she ran now, she was as good as dead. Even if this monster of a vamp let her go, she wouldn't survive much longer if Mace didn't pull through. Mace, and his promise to keep her safe, was all she had in the world.

She mustered up all her bravado and straightened her spine. "I need to see Cortez."

"The man owe you money or something, honey?"

She wasn't sure if it was wise to inform this brute that a nearly dead fellow vampire lay mere yards away. She didn't know who to trust, if anyone. And since Mace only mentioned one name...

"Or are you looking for a gig?" He leered down at her body.

She had completely spaced her manner of dress. Her tan trench coat remained back with the three dead would-be murderers.

The vampire smiled, revealing long white canines. "Perhaps you're looking for something else? You don't need Cortez for that."

She swallowed a painfully thick lump in her throat. "Cortez

will want to see me right away, and if you don't go get him and bring him here, you will regret it." Every bit the lie it was, she had somehow managed to sound assiduous and grave.

The vamp's dark, almost black eyes narrowed. "You expect me to *fetch* Cortez for you?"

She got the impression that Cortez wasn't one to be fetched *for anything*. That maybe he ordered the fetching.

"Take me to him, then." She tensed her arms at her side, resisting the urge to fidget. Bringing Mace to a vampire den was one thing. Asking for entry was entirely another.

Suspicion bloomed on the bouncer's face. "Cortez has many enemies, and your heart's pounding like a little critter. Would you say that's from fear, or insidious intentions?"

She offered a half-truth. "It's from urgency." Of course it was mostly from fear.

"I smell blood on you, little critter. And not your own."

"So? You're a vamp. I'm sure you smell blood all day long."

"True. But not many use it as perfume. What business do you have with Cortez?"

"That's between he and I."

The bouncer took a menacing step toward her, glowering. "It'll be between you and six feet of dirt before I let you in here, honey. If Cortez wants to see you, he'll seek you out."

She felt hope dwindle. "Please. This is life and death."

The bouncer remained unmoved.

Mace was teetering on the brink of death. It might already be too late. She couldn't wait another second. "Cortez!" she screamed, then sucked in a breath and used the full force of her lungs to scream for Cortez again.

The bouncer slammed his palms against his ears. One of

those men on the mountain had called her a banshee. Right now, she didn't mind the distinction.

"Woman! Do you have a death wish?" The bouncer growled, but didn't budge from his post.

A part of her was surprised he hadn't snapped her neck just out of irritation. She yelled out once more.

"Dane, what's the fuss out here?" A voice came from a darkened corridor that she hadn't noticed before.

"This broad is wack," the bouncer replied, gesturing toward her.

Cora strained to see past the darkness. A shadowed entity, outlined by thick muscle, loomed just inside.

"Cortez?" she asked.

"She clearly doesn't know Cortez," the shadow told Dane. "Get rid of her. She's disrupting Kenzi's act."

"No, I don't know Cortez," Cora rushed out. "But I need to see him, please. I need his help. Someone he knows is dying. I don't have time to explain." Through her speech, her eyes had adjusted slightly to the darkness, though she could only make out the chiseled jaw and full mouth of the other man. Yet she could tell the two shared a look.

"Who?" They both asked in unison, dubiously.

She didn't see any way around it. She couldn't barrel past them on a mad dash. And even if she could, which would be a miracle in and of itself, she'd still end up bumbling around an unfamiliar place looking for a man she didn't know from Adam.

"His name is Mace...uh, Mason. I don't know his last name. He's with the VEA, and he's hurt."

Both males turned their heads to the left as if looking at something, or someone, out of sight.

From that same direction, a third vampire appeared, stepping fully into the light. He was decked out in a jet-black, tailored button-down and charcoal slacks. His short, dark, tussled hair was styled in a way meant to appear effortless. Winston spent hundreds on a look similar to that, yet always managed to fall short. But this vampire owned it. He oozed sexuality. Even if he were dressed in a ripped stained T-shirt, he would ooze sexuality.

He stepped past the other two and approached her at a quick pace. Instinct overrode her courage and she stumbled through the entrance, back outside. As her feet touched the pavement of the parking lot, he gripped her by the arm and caught her in a hard-as-ice gaze.

"Where is he?"

"Er...are you Cortez?"

One of his brows lifted.

She probably should have answered him right away. It hadn't occurred to her that this vampire would try to compel her. She realized her mistake too late, but she couldn't bring herself to care just now. She would deal with that later.

"I am," he replied. "Now where is Mason?"

She pointed with her free arm to the jeep. "He's in there."

Cortez spared a glance at the jeep, then looked back at the other two, gesturing to it with this head. With that, they crossed the lot to the vehicle and checked through the window. As she followed them with her gaze, Cortez watched her closely. His words, however, were not for her. "Is he conscious?"

"Not entirely," Dane replied. "Looks like he's been shot with acid rounds."

"Take him in through the back," Cortez ordered, still staring at her as though she were a puzzle lacking a couple pieces.

Dane yanked the passenger side door open and the two vamps hauled Mace out, carrying him like a sack toward the alley behind the building.

She tried to follow them, but Cortez was still holding her arm. "Let me go," she demanded.

"They'll take care of him. I have questions for you," Cortez replied.

"I can answer them later. Let me go with him."

"I don't think—"

"I'm going with him!" She yanked her arm out of his grasp.

The two vamps toting Mace paused to fix shocked stares at her.

Her gut dropped. She had never acted so carelessly around vampires. She pictured a lonely grain of sand bouncing wildly around the funneled top of an hourglass, circling the chasm where its counterparts had already plummeted to a heaping pile of shit-out-of-luck.

After a moment of tense silence, Cortez waved his cohorts on. Then he strolled after them, allowing her the option to follow or not.

Cora managed to suck in a breath she didn't realize she was holding as the flash-freeze in her veins thawed. She eyed the Jeep, debating once more if she should take her chances and hightail it out of here.

"Are you coming then?" Cortez called without looking at her, almost sounding amused.

As she fell in step behind him, she wondered when the sand in her hourglass of luck was finally going to run out.

Chapter 7

The phrase "polar opposites" came to mind as she took in the interior of the strip club's back rooms. If the outside was one of those warehouse stores reserved for the lower class, the inside was Saks Fifth Avenue. The exterior had been almost run-down, flat and rust colored.

Yet the long hall she traveled now was anything but.

Vibrant hues of gold, brown, and every other warm color known to man, merged effortlessly with fine looking art in museum-quality frames. Full, potted palms and other exotic plants were placed every few feet. The line of chandeliers would have appeared gaudy if they were as large as the ones Winston preferred, but these were the perfect size for the space and offered just the right amount of light.

It was as if the storefront was deliberately dull while the inside was a hidden gem.

Cora followed the train of vampires into a large bedchamber. Across the room, Dane and the other vamp laid Mace down on an elaborately carved four-poster bed.

Cora took up an unassuming stance by the chaise, hoping to avoid drawing attention.

No such luck.

After ordering Dane to fetch someone named Rita, Cortez turned a blazing gaze on her. "What happened to him?"

Forcing a steady voice, she described all she could. While she spoke, the unnamed vampire retrieved a first-aid kit from an adjoining room Cora assumed was the bathroom. He opened it to retrieve a large bottle of rubbing alcohol and proceeded to bath Mason's chest with it. Mace woke instantly, crying out in pain. He blinked, dazedly searching the room till his gaze landed on her. He seemed to relax then.

"I smell him all over you." Cortez claimed her attention with the accusation in his tone. "I assume you are his consort. Why have you not fed him? He desperately needs blood."

"I—"

Mace hissed out a straggled, "No. Not from her. Find someone else."

Cortez appeared perplexed by that, but didn't argue. "Balthazar, go help Dane find Rita."

Balthazar nodded and left the room.

"Mace, I don't mind—" Cora started.

"No. Anyone but you."

For some reason, Cora felt slighted by that. But why? She was off the hook, right? Someone else would be expected to open a vein. So then why the sting in her chest?

When she noticed Cortez still watching her, she relaxed her clenched hands and forced a blank expression. He scrutinized her a moment longer, making her self-conscious. Then he turned to Mace. "Since when are you with the VEA?"

Mason's breath was clipped and his expression was pained as he replied, "Joined them soon after Brayden went missing."

Cortez went dangerously still. "I thought his case had been closed, presumed dead."

"It was, until a steady supply of his blood started showing up on the black market."

Expression darkening, Cortez said, "Why didn't you tell me?"

"I had nothing concrete, and it would have just pissed you off."

"He's my brother!"

"Exactly!" Mason's outburst cost him. He clutched his chest and heaved for breath.

Cora didn't realize she had moved to his side till she was already there, swiping a tendril of sweat-dampened hair from his face.

He seemed both surprised and eased by the action. "Are you alright, Coraline?"

"Of course. You're the one with the problem." She forced a smile.

"I'll say," a feminine voice shot from behind.

Cora turned to see a scantily dressed female, her dark hair done up in high pig-tails. Compared to the black one-piece outfit that showed more skin than it covered, Cora was dressed damn-near modestly. The woman was probably no older than Cora, but her eyes held the mien of experience beyond her years.

"Rita," Cortez greeted and gestured to Mason. "I'll need you to feed my friend here."

As if it were nothing, Rita crawled onto the mattress and situated herself next to Mace. Cora had the strangest instinct to pull the woman away from him by the hair.

"Coraline," Cortez called, waving for her to join him by the door. "We have a well-stocked kitchen. Come. You look as though you could use a glass of wine."

She felt the color drain from her face.

"Or if you don't like wine, perhaps a bit of ale. Whatever you like."

She glanced at Mace, unsure if she should leave him, but something told her she wouldn't be able to stand watching him feed from Rita.

"Go with him, Cora," Mace urged. She imagined he didn't want her witness to his feeding either. Goddess, she hoped that was all they were going to do.

The stray thought alarmed her as she followed Cortez into the hallway. Why should she care? A moment later, she determined she didn't.

The kitchen was stocked with a wide variety of food, which told her Cortez often entertained humans...or had them over for dinner. She snorted out a small laugh. When Cortez gave her a what's-so-funny expression, she shook her head. Her overtired brain must be making her dippy.

An object in her hand buzzed, causing her to jump. She realized only now that she hadn't once put Mason's phone down. It had been in her anxiously tight grip this entire time. The name on the caller ID read Trent.

She thumbed the phone on. "Hello?"

"Who's this?" Trent demanded.

"Uh, it's Coraline Gordon."

"Coraline? Where's Mace."

"He's okay. He's recovering. We were attacked on the mountain and…"

"Attacked? By who?"

"I'm not sure, but I think they were sent to kill me and Mace. They shot him with acid rounds, but he managed to kill them."

Trent let out a low curse. "Where are you now?"

"We're, um…" Something made her pause. A sense that she shouldn't reveal their location without speaking to Mason first. "I don't know. When Mace gets better, I'll have him call you."

"How badly is Mason hurt?" he replied slowly. Perhaps he'd registered the uneasiness in her tone. "If you're in danger, I can have someone pick you up."

"I…I think Mace will recover quickly. When I see him next, I'll—"

"You're not with him now?" Trent interrupted, alarmed. "Coraline, if you're in trouble, tell me now. Is there someone there with you?"

She glanced at Cortez, unsure if she was safer here than she would be anywhere else. Cortez raised a brow at her.

"I believe we're safe for now," she told Trent. Not a full lie; not the wholehearted truth either. "I need to go, though. I'll have Mace call you later."

She hung up before he could object.

"Trent sounded more harried than normal," Cortez said with a smirk.

She blinked up at him. Vampires were known to have superb hearing, but she never expected they could listen to the other end of a phone conversation.

She tried to act aloof. "Do you know him?"

"He and I are…acquainted." A snide smile played along his lips. "Tell me what you know of my brother."

She shook her head, disarmed by the sudden subject change. "I don't know anything. I'm sort of unintentionally involved in all this."

"How do you mean?"

The last thing she wanted to do was confess to this intimidating vampire that she had apparently ingested his brother's blood. Once again, she pictured that solitary grain of sand, circling.

"Didn't you say something about ale? I could really use a drink."

Cortez studied her for a moment. "We brew our own here." He crossed to the fridge and retrieved a dark bottle, popped the top, and handed it to her, waiting expectantly.

She took a swig and then offered her compliments, hardly having tasted it. Cortez smiled and waited patiently, his question still hanging between them.

"Seriously, I don't know anything. I've never met your brother. I never even knew there was an underground market for vampire blood until a couple days ago. I was married to someone who might have been involved. A man named Winston. He was murdered, and now I'm under Mason's protection."

He narrowed his eyes. "There'd be no need for protection unless you know something more than that."

She shrugged. "People keep trying to kill me. That's the extent of my knowledge."

"Even still. Unless there's more you're not telling me, there'd be no reason for the VEA to protect you. That's not really their forte."

She considered that for a moment. He was right. Why would the VEA bother keeping her safe...from *anything*? Especially when one of their own was in the crossfire? Mace had said she was a witness, but witness to what? She'd been completely ignorant of Winston's testing his *product* on her. She hadn't known he was involved in nefarious activities. She didn't know who killed him, or exactly why. True, she'd witnessed his murder, as well as the woman he was with, but Mace and Trent had seen it for themselves. Plus they had surveillance of it. They didn't require her testimony.

So then what did they want from her?

Cortez seemed to be reading the progression of her thoughts just by her features, while his own betrayed nothing. Something in her expression made him back off. "Feel free to eat whatever you like. Someone will be by shortly to show you to a room."

"Aren't I staying with Mason?" she blurted before she could think better of it.

"If you prefer."

After a thoughtful hesitation, she nodded. She was feeling dangerously exposed being away from him after only this short period.

"That is, unless Mace wants to have the room to himself." She recalled the beautiful woman brought in to feed him. A faint—almost unnoticeable, really—twinge of chagrin pinched the forefront of her brain.

"Very well. I'll check with him." He moved to the door. "I hope I don't need to warn you not to wander the club on your own."

"I think you just did."

The corners of his lips quirked. "Indeed. Have a pleasant evening, then." He inclined his head and then left her alone.

She waited in nervous silence for a moment before she decided it was safe to raid the refrigerator, which, surprisingly, was filled with the most normal, as well as boring, food one could imagine. Bagged, precut lettuce, an array of unusual vegetables she couldn't even begin to name. Gourds, maybe? Some kind of melon? There was tofu...ugh...kale, a pink liquid that looked like fresh squeezed juice, and a package of uncooked chicken.

Although vampires could eat some food—their main form of sustenance came from blood—it was clear by the contents in the fridge they had no taste buds at all.

On the counter beside the fridge was a stack of green and red apples, among other fruits. She grabbed a green apple, washed it in the sink, and then sank her teeth in. It was perfectly ripe and juicy. She took another bite.

Then, out of curiosity, she checked the freezer.

Jackpot. Ice cream! Or, rather, sorbet. Chocolate Caramel, Strawberries and Cream, and an interesting one called French Mango Sunset.

She hunted through the dark stained cabinets for a bowl and spoon, intending to snag a hefty scoop of each.

Chapter 8

Just about the time Rita crawled off the bed and sauntered from the room, sans a couple of pints, Cortez entered. How long had he been waiting out there for Mace to finish up? Not that Rita would have minded her boss watching, Mace thought. Cortez had undoubtedly seen her engage in more sultry acts than a simple feeding.

"How are you feeling?" Cortez asked, though it was clear there were more pressing questions burning in the back of his mind.

"Been better." His chest ached as his healing flesh battled against the encroaching acid and shrapnel. Luckily, the alcohol Balthazar had poured over him earlier help to nullify most of the destructive chemical. "Should be on my feet by morning," he added. "There are a couple things I need you to do for me."

Cortez cocked his head. "Now you ask for favors?"

"Yes," Mace replied simply. "The jeep outside in your parking lot will need to disappear, preferably tonight. Same with the three bodies I left on the mountain pass. There's a motorcycle up there as well. It'll be reported stolen soon. Take it, sell it, strip it for all I care, but it shouldn't be traced back here."

"Is that all?"

"No. I'll need a replacement vehicle. Cora and I will leave here in the morning."

"I'm going to need some answers, Mason. What the fuck is going on?"

Mace let out a breath. There was no getting around it. "The night Brayden disappeared, arsonists burned down his apartment building."

"Yes, several other vampires had resided there. They labeled it a hate crime."

"Right. And with all the bodies virtually incinerated, and Brayden missing, the local investigators easily declared him deceased. It was Trent who came to me last year with the news that his blood was discovered on the black market."

"Why didn't he come to me?" The fire behind Cortez's eyes betrayed his cool tone.

"You know why."

"I could have helped in the search. There are witches I could call upon to scry—"

"Don't you think we tried that?" Mason paused, waiting for Cortez's rebuttal, but none came. "Anyway, I joined the VEA the next day. With Trent's connections, he was able to streamline the process and we've been partners ever since, with our main goal finding Brayden. I was going to tell you when we had...something, but it was like we were always chasing shadows." He let out a haggard breath. "Then came Cora."

"Yes, the female. If you're so intent on finding my brother, why are you taking time to guard this girl?"

"It's...complicated. I...well, she's the only clue we have at the moment. Part of the theory is her late husband was testing product on her before approving it for sale. She had no idea. We have samples of her blood being analyzed now, but that's just schematics. Trent and I both smelled Brayden on her."

Yet, now it was his own scent all over her.

The thought was too satisfying.

"Toward the end," Mace continued, "her husband was giving it to her more and more. Often for no reason at all. We figured he'd received an influx of blood that needed testing, so we beefed up surveillance on him and his associates, hoping to catch a drop off. That was probably our biggest mistake. Two days ago, our suspects were eliminated as if by well-trained assassins, creating a virtual dead end for us."

"Still, why bother with the girl?"

"Should we just leave her life in the hands of fate then?" Mace hissed.

"If she has no further use in the investigation, I see no point—"

"Whoever killed her husband and the others wants her dead in a bad way. Think about it. Why bother hunting down one ignorant female? Why spend time and resources searching for her when the first attempt on her life failed? Why risk being caught over someone seemingly insignificant?"

Cortez went silent.

"I've wondered about the excess blood her husband was pushing on her. I have a theory about it. Trent has his own opinion..." Mace drew in a breath and let it out slowly before going on. "I think Winston and his cohorts were trying to figure out how to turn a human."

The sound of something shattering in the hall drew their

attention. Cortez yanked the door open.

Coraline stood pale and motionless but for a quiver in her hands. At her feet lay a multicolored mess surrounded by bits of glass.

Mason cursed.

Her voice came so faintly that normal human ears would not have heard. "That won't happen, will it?"

"No," Mace assured. "And it's only a theory of mine. Winston and his cohorts were arrogant enough to believe they could live forever."

Cortez regarded his stained rug with an air of indifference. "But it *is* possible—"

Mace shot him a scathing look as Cora went stark white.

"You care too much for this female's feelings, Mason," Cortez chastised. "It *is* possible to turn a human. That much is common knowledge. Yet not even most vampires possess the wisdom of how it's done. It's a secret guarded closely by the eldest of our kind. If you're right, that means a group of humans are trying to discover what very few of us know. It could provoke a new chapter in their war."

"I said it was only a theory," Mace growled, trying not to let Cora's horrified expression bother him. "We have no concrete evidence, except..." He darted his eyes to Cora and averted them too quickly.

Her shoulders slumped. "I'm evidence." It wasn't a question, but a bleak understanding. And in that single phrase there seemed to be a farewell of sorts; a goodbye, perhaps, to her old, safe life. Maybe even to her previous, not so safe life, both having been free of vampires and blood. Mason felt a twinge of sympathy over that, but it was overshadowed by something far more powerful, something that gave him too much satisfaction than he was willing to admit at the moment.

Cora met his gaze as if she were sensing from him what he was trying so hard to bury. And for the first time, it was he who looked away.

* * *

"Really, I don't mind letting you have the whole bed to yourself." Cora repeated yet again.

Cortez had provided her with a slip of a nightgown, black and lacy, giving Mace a conspiratorial wink before taking his leave. Mace didn't know whether to thank or curse the man.

Mason rolled his eyes. "I already feel unmanned as it is, I'll not have a female in my charge sleeping on the floor while I'm babied on a comfortable mattress."

After their host had left, Cora had spent an hour in the adjoining bathroom crying. If he thought she would have accepted him, he would have ignored the agony of moving and gone in there to comfort her. Yet he had no idea what he could have done or said to cease her tears. He was just as much responsible for her sorrow as Winston's callous use of her, or the discovery that her entire life with him had been a lie. Worse, Mace was the one who had stripped away her rose-colored glasses and shoved her into a world she wasn't ready for, a world that terrified her. And he was the one keeping her there.

Her puffy eyes tentatively glanced his way as she finally slipped under the covers next to him.

"There, see?" He offered a reassuring smile. "Plenty of room for the both of us."

She returned his grin with an inadequate, thin-lipped facsimile.

She didn't bother with the pillow barricade tonight. Was she becoming more relaxed around him, or did she believe he was too injured to try anything lascivious? A broken spine wouldn't stop him if she offered him a fair chance.

She snapped off the bedside lamp and then settled back, pulling the covers to her chin. Mace closed his eyes and focused on her breathing, trying to determine the moment she fell asleep. Only then could he fully relax. Although she'd been fairly silent since exiting the bathroom, he was getting the impression a cyclone of questions circled around in her head. She had kept pausing and staring off into space as if in deep thought, shaking herself free of it moments later. He wasn't looking forward to the inevitable interrogation.

Unfortunately for him, she wasn't anywhere near sleeping, and it wasn't long before the cyclone broke free. "Mason?"

"Mm?"

"What would have happened to me if I'd been turned, if that was truly Winston's purpose?"

She'd gone straight to the one question he didn't want to answer. "What do *you* think?"

"He might have continued using me, I suppose. Started selling my blood on his black market."

"Or used your blood to turn himself and his friends." Mace added bluntly.

"And then what?"

"I guess they'd've had no more use for you."

She shuddered. "You said Trent had a difference of opinion. What was his theory?"

"He was more inclined to think Winston was receiving blood through several other sources, but I never smelled anyone except Brayden on you."

"What do you mean *never*? When were you ever around me besides that day in the hotel?"

Mason's pensive silence guided Cora to the truth.

"You were the one watching us," she gasped. She didn't know how she hadn't put it together till now—with all his cryptic comments about Winston, his knowledge of their life. She automatically began listing the obvious clues that had previously eluded her. "You instantly recognized me in the hotel, even with the wig, while Trent had not. You knew I liked coffee cake because you saw me eating it. You never answered when I asked if you had known Winston."

Mace let out a sigh. "Ten months ago, a tip about Winston's involvement in the black-market blood came in and I was assigned to tail him."

"So then, were you there when I first met Winston?"

It took a few moments for Mace to answer. "I was."

How surreal to look back with the knowledge that someone had been watching her that day...and then on. And not just anyone—a vampire. This vampire.

She waited for the jilt of indignation, the ire that should be forming deep in the pit of her stomach. The only reaction she could muster was a jaded *meh*. After all that had happened to her—orphaned at a young age, Edgar's torture, life in the slums, her rags to riches fairytale love story, and her fall from grace via Winston's betrayal, subsequently being targeted for death—a vamp-stalker who seemed bent on protecting her was all of a sudden low on her outrage meter.

Or maybe she was just too tired to fully assimilate the information.

"If Winston had been feeding me more and more blood, how could I not have noticed? I didn't drink *that* much wine."

"He had you see a doctor once a week, right?"

She nodded absently. "Doctor Albright. I was malnourished. She was giving me weekly vitamin shots to boost my immune system."

"I don't think that's what she was giving you. I couldn't follow you inside without soliciting suspicion, but when you left there, you always smelled strongly of Brayden. After your first visit six months ago we started watching Albright and her staff."

"Oh goddess, how many people are in on this? Wait...you said I *smelled*? How close would you get to me?"

"Once I was assigned solely to you, I was never very far."

"Meaning?"

"Close enough to guess which perfume you used that morning."

She swallowed the tiny lump nesting in her throat. "Am I that unobservant? How had I not noticed you?"

"It's my job not to be noticed."

"But seriously. It's not like you're inconspicuous by any form of the word. Yet never once did I think, 'hey, there's an inhumanly handsome man following me around'? And you'd been following me for how long? A month? Two?

"Since two weeks after your wedding."

She drew an astonished breath. A vampire had been watching her for seven months and not a note of alarm had tickled her intuition? She had always assumed her experience with Edgar had made her more adept at spotting—as well as evading—his kind. She'd gone years without a single encounter. Or so she'd thought.

"So, you think I'm handsome?" Mace inquired in a teasing tone.

"Inhumanly," she qualified sharply.

"An even better compliment."

"Hardly," Cora replied, beating back a traitorous grin. Who'd have thought she would ever banter with a vampire? After a short stretch of silence, she asked, "How can the blood sample determine if your theory is correct?"

"Humans have three main types of blood cells: red, white, and platelets. Vampires have an extra cell type not found in human blood, referred to as dark cells. These are what speed healing and muscle growth, among other things. If your blood sample reveals the presence of even a single dark cell, it would give weight to the theory."

"If it doesn't?"

"Wouldn't change my mind on the matter, but we wouldn't have any evidence."

"What if I have some dark cells? What does that mean for me?"

"You won't turn, if that's what you're asking. There are other steps necessary for the transformation than just the introduction of dark cells." Mace hesitated. "Or so I'm told."

Cora contemplated that for a moment. "Are you sure? What if the dark cells multiply?" She wasn't even sure if that was possible, but it was a distressing thought nonetheless.

"When dark cells enter a human's bloodstream, the white

cells rightly see foreign matter and target them for destruction."

"So then, they should be gone pretty quickly."

"Right. Which is why we had your blood drawn as quickly as we could. Trent should be getting the results back any day now."

"Oh, that reminds me. He called earlier." She felt Mace tense next to her.

"You answered?"

"'Course."

"Did you tell him where we are?"

"I...no. Why?" She didn't like the change in his tone.

He relaxed a bit. "I just don't want anyone knowing our location for the time being."

She could read between the lines. Someone had sent those roughnecks on the mountain, someone who had to have known exactly where she and Mace would be. "You think your partner—"

"No," Mace interrupted. "More likely the human police have a mole. Where's my phone?"

"In the bathroom." She'd still been clutching it during her emotional breakdown. "You want me to get it for you?"

"No. I'll contact Trent in the morning."

They both became quiet and the darkness suddenly felt heavy on her chest. Her eyes drooped, and she yawned. "So, what happens now?"

"We'll leave here in the morning and head to a safe house as planned. Just not the one Trent and the human police intended for us to go. From there, I'll decide the best course of action."

"And what might that be?"

She sensed him smile. "I don't know yet. Sleep now. We have a long trip ahead of us."

Chapter 9

Cora yawned and stretched in the passenger seat of the black sedan.

"Do you need to stop?" Mace grumbled, not taking his eyes from the road. They hadn't said much to each other after their awkward morning. She wasn't sure when, but at some point during the night Mace had settled her in the cradle of his body. She recalled the heat permeating from his skin, cocooning her as light from the rising sun coaxed her awake. The feel of his powerful build. The heavy appendage pressed against her ass...

Apparently human males weren't the only ones plagued by morning wood.

In her dreary, half-sleepy state, she had turned her head to verify it was actually Mace's arm folded so tightly around her torso.

And as she did so, she'd come face to face with a pair of razor-sharp fangs.

In retrospect, the spike of adrenalin and instant alarm was fueled purely by surprise, not an actual threat. Mace had still been sleeping. But it wasn't often she found herself up close and personal with a vamp's chompers and her reaction was instinctual.

She'd cried out and scrambled wildly under the covers, jarring Mace awake in the process.

Unaware what caused her hysteria, he bolted up and surveyed the room.

Freed from his grasp, Cora's body, along with the covers tangled in her limbs, gracelessly poured over the side of the bed.

She'd landed with a grunt.

When she'd peeked over the edge of the mattress, Mace had regarded her stiffly, his frown prominent.

Her cheeks had burned even after he'd gone into the bathroom for a shower. After a few minutes, he'd emerged with dampened hair and a towel around his waist, forcing her to flush once more. He was all hard planes and packed muscle.

Then her eyes had dipped to his chest wound.

Although it was probably normal for him, it astounded her that it was almost fully healed with only the remnants of angry redness that could be mistaken as a rash. She would have commented on it, but his phone was pressed to his ear and he was responding to someone on the other end in short, curt grunts. To her, he'd jerked his head in the direction of the bathroom as if to say, "You'd better get a move on it."

She hadn't dawdled, knowing she might not get the chance to bathe in a while.

While she'd showered, Cortez, or maybe Rita, had dropped off an outfit for her, though she hadn't seen either of them before the club was in their rearview mirror. She wasn't sure if she should be grateful for the clothing that was equally as tawdry as her outfit from yesterday. Her top was a grey knit wrap blouse with a plunging neckline. Her black heels were too high for her comfort. Throughout the drive, she nervously tugged at the hem of the dark skirt that barely covered her upper thighs. More than once, Mace had growled for her to stop, as if her fidgeting irritated him.

He seemed to be extra grumpy today.

"There's a town ahead," he continued. "Are you getting hungry yet?"

"Surprisingly no," she replied. All that had occurred in the last few days had affected her appetite negatively. The thought of food made her stomach flip over on itself. She'd only managed to eat half the apple from last night and her dessert had ended up on Cortez's fine carpet. There had been no offer of breakfast this morning, and now, after having been in the car for over six hours, she should be starving.

Apparently Mace thought so too and declared they'd be stopping anyway. Moments later, they pulled off the highway.

The throwback bar and grill was mirrored by the broken-down neighborhood surrounding it. The initial revolt against the vampires, and subsequent uprisings, had taken a toll on the smaller towns, devastating most and crippling others. Now, with a few exceptions, only the largest cities had access to electricity and treated water, which was why they were almost all overpopulated.

With the smaller towns cut off from such conveniences, each had devolved into its own country of sorts, governed independently from the rest of the world.

She'd recalled traveling through small towns with her parents when she was young. Almost too young to remember the roguish locals...almost. Vaguely, a memory of her father fighting off a gang of men, defending his wife and two children, entered her mind. Fuzzy as the memory was, it was one of the most frightening nights of Cora's young life, B.E. Before Edgar. She'd clung to her mother, fearing her father's imminent death. But then, just as the group had taken her father to the ground, surrounding and kicking him, her mother had done...something. At the time, Cora knew it had been extraordinary, but now she couldn't recall what it had been. In any case, the men had stopped hurting her father.

"Why are you so pensive?" Mace snapped.

"Hmm? Oh, I'm just worried about stopping in such a small town."

Mace humphed. "You think I can't protect you from a few uneducated humans?" He pulled into the lot, jerked the car into park, and shut off the engine.

There was that confounding attitude again. "That's not what I mean. But now that you mention it, we haven't had a whole lot of luck keeping out of trouble, and this place screams trouble."

The barred windows were bordered by peeling, bubbling brown paint that had probably been a vibrant red at one point. The parking lot was littered with debris: glass, torn paper, dirt clods, and such, with only two other cars taking up spots—a beater truck and a white Honda that wasn't in much better shape.

"*I* scream trouble," Mace growled and exited the car.

In his borrowed leather trench coat, he did look menacing. He started for the building without bothering to wait for her. After a cautionary glance around, Cora followed.

The inside was dimly lit, and her eyes took a moment to

adjust. The place was more packed than she'd initially assumed by the lack of cars in the parking lot. A U-shaped bar took up the center of the room and was crowded by patrons. Several tattered booths lined the perimeter, most filled as well. Mace headed for a free booth in one of the darkest corners. She trailed behind him, feeling rather like a well-trained puppy.

He claimed the seat that faced the room, his eyes scanning his surroundings. She perched opposite him. When he finished assessing the room, he met her gaze. If the coldness wafting from him was tangible, the blood in her veins would have frozen solid.

She pursed her lips and quirked a brow in question.

He smiled then, but it was more cruel than pleasant. "Only two days and you've no problem staring me down? I wonder if the whole thing was an act from the start."

That statement planted her back against the seat. "Excuse me?" She resisted the urge to cast her eyes down, suddenly and irrationally feeling exposed, but in what manner, she couldn't decide. What she did know was that Mace was looking more dangerous now than he ever had before.

Since the night of the crash, she had begun to think of him as no longer a menacing vampire, but a protector. A living nightmare turned benign. He was supposed to be safe, her savior, even if he was rough around the edges, but right now he seemed anything but.

Clearly, between last night and now, his attitude toward her had taken a swift dip into perilous waters. It was entirely possible—no, probable—she was no more safe with him than she had been with Edgar.

That thought chased away any lingering security that had gathered in her mind, and her eyes dropped solemnly to the table.

Mace snorted. She could still feel his gaze boring into her.

Before either of them broke the silence, a pretty blond waitress approached and set two large waters on the table, no ice. "You all ready to order?" She tapped her pen on a pad of paper in her hand.

Cora was even less hungry now than before, but she really should try to eat something. "What is your soup of the day?"

The waitress hooted out a sardonic laugh and proceeded in a nasally, mocking tone. "Well, we have a superb Italian Sausage Tortellini, and the chef is just raving about the Butternut Squash." She laughed again, shaking her head and adding to herself, "Soup of the day."

Cora stabbed the girl with a scathing look. "I suppose you don't offer salads either?"

"Aw, dang." The waitress snapped her finger in false dejection. "Just ran out."

Cora scowled. "Then what do you have?"

"Meat and beans," she replied, as if it should have been obvious.

"Then why didn't you ask us if we wanted meat and beans?"

The waitress looked aghast at Cora's raised tone, as if no one ever dared to challenge her.

Cora waved her on. "Go on, give it a try."

The waitress jostled her bottom teeth irritably. "You're clearly not from around here, sweetling, so let me tell you how it is. The men shoot the animals, the cook cooks the animals, and you eat the animals. If you want a salad, you can go pluck some leaves from the forest, and I'll get you a plate."

Infuriatingly, Mason laughed at that, drawing the woman's attention.

She smiled at him and purred, "You look like a meat and potatoes kind of guy to me."

"Look again," he replied darkly, flashing fang.

Her delicate brow turned up.

"But I promise I'll like anything you have to offer."

Her smile widened at the innuendo. "That so?"

When Mace returned her grin, the blood in Cora's veins heated to an uncomfortable level.

"Well, I'll just have to test that theory out." the waitress continued sweetly. "I'll bring you the chef's special." She turned and walked away then. By the sway of her hips, she was expecting Mason to watch her go. Cora gritted her teeth when she realized he was.

"Should I get a mop for all that drool?" she spat.

He turned an amused gaze on her. "Is that jealousy I hear in your tone? Couldn't be. Not after the way you woke me up this morning."

"Is that why you're in such a pissy mood? Because I awoke to your razor-sharp canines in my face, and naturally I freaked?"

"I'm not in a pissy mood. Women get pissy. I'm just pissed."

"What's the difference?"

"Testosterone."

She rolled her eyes.

"And no, your silly behavior this morning is not why I'm angry with you."

"Oh, please do enlighten me."

Mace cocked his head. "Such a brave little witch you're turning out to be."

"So now you're insulting me? What did I do to deserve this treatment? Might I remind you that I saved your ass yesterday."

He narrowed his gaze and leaned back as if she'd just presented him with a puzzle. "I spoke with Trent this morning. Your blood test results came back." There was an accusation in his tone.

Icy fingers of dread ran down her spine. Mace noted her trepidation with another tilt of his head.

"And?" she prompted. Was there even more vamp blood in her system than they'd expected?

"You must've known what we'd find."

She shook her head. "What do you mean? Is there something wrong with my blood?"

"No. Everything's fine. For a witch."

Cora stared at him blankly for a moment. "You're using that word in place of bitch, right?"

Instead of answering, he said, "There's no way you don't know what you are. It's impossible. It would be like a vampire not knowing he was a vampire. There are clear cut signs. Undeniable signs."

Against her will, her lips curled upwards. Then a laugh squeezed from her lungs. "You think I'm a witch? Like a real witch? As in hocus pocus and all that?" She laughed again. "And you called *me* silly?"

"This is no joke, Coraline."

"Of course it is. It's the stupidest thing I've ever heard."

"Then do you find this funny? Your blood is laced with dark cells."

—

At his revelation, Cora's smile faltered, and her skin paled to a disturbing shade of green.

And yet he couldn't believe she was ignorant of her lineage. No. She'd willfully kept this from him, and for some reason, was lying about it now. Maybe because she was damn near a pure blooded witch from one of the most ancient lines on record.

"You said the dark cells would dissipate," she said with a slight tremor in her voice.

"For humans that's true, but you have magic in your blood. Magic tends to seek out and assimilate power." As if she didn't already know that, Mace thought bitterly. "Trent believes you might be regenerating the dark cells on your own."

"But, but..." Cora looked as if she might say more, though no words followed. She merely looked lost.

"I should have known," he added absently. "What with your predilection for swearing to a goddess."

She snorted. "That means nothing. I was raised that way."

He gestured at her with his palm face-up to punctuate his point. "Because your parents were witches."

She gave him a withering stare, then leaned forward. "If I were a witch, as if they even exist, don't you think I would have used my *mystical powers* to get away from you...from Edgar?" She leaned back, eyes once more on the table as if bombarded by a barrage of harrowing memories.

Mason's gut twisted, and he wished he could have been the one to deal this Edgar the death blow.

The overly flirtatious waitress approached then, two identical dishes in hand. She placed the first in front of Mace: a large hunk of meat, a slop of brown beans with some sort of gravy, and a side of corn. The second, she dropped on Cora's side of the table.

Cora glared at the girl with uncharacteristic animosity. The waitress ignored her, instead appraising Mace suggestively.

He hadn't stopped only for Cora's sake. He needed sustenance too, and he was pretty sure he'd just found a willing donor. He would have preferred to feed from Cora, had she not such an aversion to it. He'd never tasted someone so sweet. So god dammed addictive.

This morning, with her startled pulse racing, he'd had to remove himself from the room just to get away from her delicious scent. And yet, it hadn't been enough. From sleeping so close to her, her feminine fragrance had latched onto his skin. A quick shower had eradicated her from his exterior, but his mind? His mind had been much more stubborn, reminding him of how she had tasted just two nights ago. He'd been a heartbeat away from fetching her from the other room and pulling her back into the shower with him.

A quick call to Trent wound up being the distraction he needed. After relaying what had happened the previous day, and warning Trent to keep an eye out for a traitorous mole, the news that Cora had been withholding her true nature had dampened his desire. Oddly, now his desire for her seemed to be flaring back up, prompted by the jealousy he was sensing from Cora's direction toward the waitress giving him come-hither glances. In a primitive way, that pleased him.

He swallowed, remembering his conversation with Trent. "I inadvertently initiated a blood bond with Cora. I crave her more than ever," he'd admitted.

Trent had groaned. Mace could just imagine him scrubbing a hand down his face in frustration. "That's not good, man."

"She's only human," Mace had gone on to say. "It won't last."

"Bad news," Trent had replied. "Her blood results indicate she's a witch from the Conwell bloodline."

It had taken Mace several moments to respond. His interest in her might be more than a mere infatuation or even a newly created blood bond. "Are you certain?"

"There's more...." Trent had proceeded to alarm him with news of the dark cells in her blood, nearly half of what constituted a healthy vampire...and possibly multiplying.

Mace gritted his teeth. If he'd known what she was from the start, he would have never fed her so much of his blood that first night. Or taken from her.

The waitress kept her attention on Mace as she spoke. "I've brought you the tender loin of an adult elk caught this morning. It's one of my favorite cuts," she preened.

"I'm partial to the neck," he replied.

Cora's lips parted on an outraged O.

The waitress didn't seem to notice, or maybe didn't care. One of her brows lifted in a delicate arch. "Hm. Intriguing. I'll have to give that a try. Is there anything else you need at the moment?" Her eyes sparkled with invitation.

"I think we're good, thank you," Cora interjected.

The waitress slipped a stony glare toward Cora and turned to leave. Mace glanced at Cora. Her jaw was tightly locked, eyes flashing with indignation.

She glanced down at her food with disgust. "She dumped salt all over it, and something else, I'm not sure what, but I'm not eating this."

Mace could smell the heaps of salt from where he sat, but was surprised Cora noticed without having tasted it first. The mystery ingredient was cumin, half a bottle's worth was his guess.

He shoved his plate across the table and pulled the ruined meat back towards him. "Mine is fine. Eat."

After a moment of hesitation, Cora sliced off a piece of meat and popped it in her mouth. For some reason, that made him relax a touch. He couldn't recall the last time she'd eaten. Had it been that coffee cake he'd brought her? It was his job to keep her safe and that meant well-fed.

As a vampire, he didn't require human food, hardly spared it a thought, though he often ate conventional food to blend in when necessary. Even though Cora was a witch, she needed meals as often as any human. He was actually surprised she hadn't bothered him to stop earlier.

His own stomach growled, but it didn't hunger for elk. His attention swept the room. The waitress stared at him from the entrance to a hall near the kitchen. A sign above read Restrooms. When she caught his eye, she smiled and backed into the hallway, out of sight.

"Stay here. I'll be right back," he told Cora.

Her eyes went wide. "What? Where are you going?"

"Don't worry, I'll be back before you finish your meal." He didn't wait for further protest, making his way across the bar.

Cora watched Mace head toward the facilities. Did vampires relieve themselves like everyone else? She supposed it was entirely possible, but Edgar had never once used the restroom that adjoined their living quarters, so she had assumed he didn't suffer from those needs.

She took a sip of water and eyed the hunk of meat that covered half the plate. The small bite she'd taken felt heavy in her stomach, the after flavor gamey. She'd never been fond of meat, but on the streets, she tolerated it whenever she'd managed to get her hands on fresh leftovers discarded by some of the classier restaurants. She's always chant to herself, "beggars can't be choosy," or some such nonsense meant to chase away the dreary reality of just trying to survive.

Right now, she should feel blessed for such a bounty, but her body felt off, her stomach churning. She took a gulp of water, hoping the cool liquid would calm her gut.

It didn't.

Her body's reaction was abnormal, almost foreign, to anything she'd encountered before. Nausea came sudden and with great violence. Her skin warmed to a feverish degree, and a light sheen of sweat developed over her flesh. On the heels of that came the taste of metal in her mouth, evoking an unexpected rage, oddly enough, and her heart slammed against her ribcage.

She pushed away from the table and rushed toward the ladies room. The good thing was, if she became sick, there wouldn't be much for her stomach to evacuate.

She barreled through the restroom doors and headed straight for the sink, seeking cold water to splash on her face. A feminine moan gave her pause.

A figure near the far wall caught her eye. Scratch that, two figures...embracing. For a brief moment, her cheeks burned with embarrassment as she assumed she'd walked in on a couple hooking up in the bathroom. But the familiarity of Mason's back turned her embarrassment in to molten fury.

"What are you doing?" she screeched.

Mace cringed and lifted his head from the woman's neck to glance back at her. Cora gasped as the female's face came into view—the snotty waitress, features rapturous in the wake of Mason's bite. Impossibly, Cora's ire deepened till she thought she might be swallowed whole by the darkening pit of rage.

"Her?" she spat accusingly.

"I told you to stay put," Mace growled.

The waitress whimpered and reached for him as if bereft.

Cora turned away with disgust and stomped out of the restroom, through the rowdy bar, and out the front entrance.

A strong hand clamped over her shoulder, staying her. "Where are you off to?" Mace asked.

"Let me go. I can't stand to look at you right now."

"Why. What's wrong?"

"Her? You had to...with her?" Cora kept her back to him. "She's such a...I just thought you had better taste?" In truth, she hadn't expected to see him feed at all, had been blessedly spared that burden back at Ever Nights.

Wait. Burden?

Why would she feel that way? It shouldn't matter to her where Mace found his food, even if said food was a small town skank-bag. Should it? No, of course not. But for some insane, irrational reason, it did...

As if his thoughts were trailing down the same path, Mace asked, "What do you care who I feed from? As long as it's not from you, what does it matter?"

"It doesn't." She ignored the false note in her tone.

Mace went silent for a moment before responding. "I need to eat, Cora, just like you. Only, my food source is different than yours. It has to come from a warm vein."

"I know." She hesitated, wondering why he was bothering to justify this to her. For that matter, why was *she* taking this so personally? "I...I was just surprised, is all. Go on back and finish so we can go."

He didn't move.

"Really. I just wasn't expecting to see—"

He turned her around to face him. "Are you...crying?"

"No!" Her eyes burned and she knew they were probably red, but she wasn't—a hot tear scorched a path down her cheek.

Mace looked horrified.

What the hell is wrong with me? "I'll wait in the car." She turned for the vehicle.

"Cora..." Mace sighed in an uncertain tone, then paused.

"That's them," an angry female voice called from the direction of the bar. "Fucker bit me while she watched."

Halfway to the car, Cora turned to see the waitress flanked by several burly men, all glaring at her and Mace.

Chapter 10

Mace sneered back at the four men spilling aggression from their pores. He recalled the waitress's hollered warning when he'd left her to chase after Cora. *Don't you dare leave! Get back here!* She hadn't liked that he'd left her to run after Cora. And in his haste, he hadn't thought to compel her to forget him.

"Cora, get in the car." Mace tossed the keys her way.

Her hand whipped out, snatching them out of the air. Wide eyed, she peered at the keys as if surprised she'd caught them.

To the waitress, Mace said, "Do you wish to get these men killed for your wounded pride?"

The girl lifted her chin.

One of the men growled, "Andy, get my gun."

"Mace," Cora called unsteadily from beside the car. "Let's just go."

Mace had never backed down from a fight. And if Cora wasn't here, vulnerable as she was, he wouldn't have now, but she'd been in enough danger over last couple of days.

He headed for the car. "I said get in, now."

She pressed the button to unlock the car, ripped open the passenger side door, and settled inside. As Mace took the driver seat, she handed him the keys. The men came forward, hissing vile slurs. By the smell wafting off the group, at least a couple of them were just this side of drunk.

Mace revved the engine and then sped out of the parking lot just as he caught the glint of a two barrel shotgun.

"Get down, Cora," he ordered.

She only slightly ducked her head and looked over at him. "Huh?"

He shoved her by the back of the neck, forcing her torso toward the floorboard seconds before a shot rang out. At the same time, he cornered a building. The thwarted bullet ricocheted off the edge of the brick.

Cora gasped and twisted to look behind them.

"Stay down," he growled.

"They aren't behind us. I don't even see...Shit."

Mace glanced in the rearview to see that beater from the parking lot lurch onto the street. He lowered his foot on the gas petal. Cora was now fully turned around in her seat on her knees, peeking around the headrest.

"Damn it, Cora, do as I say."

"They can't possibly catch us in that POS."

The road took a sharp turn, and Mace jerked the wheel at sixty miles per hour. Tires screeched. Cora toppled headfirst into his lap.

"I know you were jealous back there, love, but make it up to me later."

She righted herself, plopped her ass in the seat, and yanked the seatbelt around her torso, snapping it into place. "Ha! You wish." She gave him a caustic look. "Here's a thought. Why don't I use some of my *witchy* powers to pop their tires?"

"Anything you can do to help."

A second shot blasted out the back of the window. Cora screeched and covered her head with her arms.

Mace gritted his teeth and slammed the gas pedal down as far as it would go. "Do you know how to shoot a gun?"

"Not really."

He reached over her and opened the glove compartment, revealing a nine millimeter Glock.

"Holy mother..." Cora pushed back against the seat as if she could melt through it.

"Take it. It's loaded. Aim it out the back, *and only out the back*, preferably at the driver."

Another shot sounded from behind. It missed, but Cora screamed anyway and covered her head once more. The following shot took out the driver's side mirror.

"Dammit, Cora, this isn't a wait-till-you-feel-ready type of situation." He sighed at her horrified expression. "Would you rather drive then?"

"Yes. please!"

"Fine, be quick." They'd reached a long stretch of road with no other cars in sight. "Put your foot on the gas over mine."

She shimmied her leg into position, and they traded feet. The car lagged slightly. In a swift and proficient move, Mace lifted her and swung her body over his, while shifting under her to take the passenger seat and the gun.

Cora offered an astounded look at the ease with which they'd pulled off the maneuver. Then she faced the road, eyes narrowed in determination, and slammed the pedal to the floor.

The car jerked forward as if pulled by invisible cables.

"Try not to get us killed," Mace instructed.

To his surprise, she laughed. Either she was losing her mind, or the stress was getting to her.

Mace swiveled around to squeeze off several rounds at the truck. The driver ducked just in time to avoid a forehead bullseye. The passenger leaned out the window, brandishing the shotgun. He cocked it and aimed low, going for the tires.

"Swerve, now!" Mace yelled to Cora.

She did and the bullet took a chunk out of the aged asphalt on the road, sending the shattered debris flying. Mace aimed for the truck's engine and fired several more shots. The truck didn't slow. The outside might say piece of shit, but Mace suspected there was some real power under that hood.

"Fucking rednecks."

"Ah-ha!" Cora cried. Her expression twisted into something excitable.

Mason's bewilderment turned to anxiousness when he saw they were approaching a T intersection at almost seventy-five with a solid brick wall cutting their path short. Instead of easing off the gas, she sped up.

"Cora? What are you doing?"

"Hold on." Mere feet from the turn, she transferred her foot to the brake as she yanked the wheel to the left.

The car listed sideways, skidding loudly. The scent of burning rubber seared his nostrils.

Mace looked to his right, watching grey bricks rush toward him. At the last second, the car hooked, fishtailed, and then pitched forward in their new direction...nearly at speed. He looked back at the truck, which spewed smoke from the wheels as the driver slammed on the brakes. He hadn't acted soon enough and the front end of the vehicle crunched through the wall, bringing the truck to a drastic stop. The truck's bed settled off kilter with one wheel still spinning wildly.

Mace turned to Cora credulously.

She chortled at his expression. "Winston loved to race cars. He took me and his friends to the track all the time. I thought you'd've known that."

Mace put the Glock back in the glove compartment. "He paid a shit-load of money to rent it out privately. I couldn't get in without drawing unwanted attention."

"Oh. Well, it was exhilarating. I almost beat him a couple times, too," she preened, and then hit the gas again.

Mace smiled and leaned back in his chair to take her in. The sun was just starting to dip in the sky, and it gilded her blonde hair with an ethereal glow. Her face was flush with excitement, her smile radiant. Not for the first time, he thought she was the most beautiful creature he had ever seen.

She peeked at him from the corner of her eye, blushing at his scrutiny. "What?"

"You are unlike anyone I know."

"'Cause I'm a *witch*," she joked sardonically.

"You *are* a witch. And no, that's not why."

She rolled her eyes. "Whatever."

Could she truly not know? How would that be possible? True, she hadn't used magic in all the time he'd watched her. Not that he could tell anyway. But then, witches thrived by keeping to the shadows and staying inconspicuous.

He changed the subject. "Why were you angry earlier?"

Her mouth slipped into a frown. "I don't know. Vamp feeding on a human. Guess I just freaked."

"It was more than that. You were throwing off some serious pheromones."

She gasped. "What?"

"Possessiveness, jealousy, aggression. Do you see me as yours, Cora?" He teased. "Didn't like another woman touching me?"

"In your dreams, vampire."

"True."

Astonished eyes left the road for a second, searching him for a sign of humor. She swallowed, finding none. Her sweet scent changed to something like apprehension.

He frowned. "I was thinking of you, you know."

She didn't respond, but her fingers tightened around the wheel.

"I was imagining it was your body against mine, your scent all around me, your sweet blood giving me strength."

He could hear her heart speed up, and once more her scent changed...to arousal.

He stifled another smile at that. As he'd taken sustenance from that waitress, he'd imagined running his hand through sandy-blond, sun-kissed hair instead of dull, rusty brown. Imagined placing light kisses on Cora's neck till he had her begging for his bite. Rolling his pelvis against her core as she wrapped her lean legs around him.

The waitress's blood had tasted no better than motor oil compared to Cora's.

The scent of Cora's desire coated the vehicle's interior, causing his shaft to stiffen in response.

In a thick voice, he asked, "Would you have liked that?

Her hands tightened around the steering wheel. "No!"

—

Yes! Cora's mind corrected. She stifled a shiver as sudden warmth enveloped her.

"No?" Mace sounded surprised, and maybe a little disappointed.

But he was merely teasing her, right? Of course, because she knew he could scent her *pheromones* right now. She might as well have a ginormous In Heat sign flashing above her head.

Her cheeks flushed.

Stealthily, she glanced at him without turning her head. He was staring at her as though a bit confounded.

Not more confounded by me than I am.

His words had forced her to imagine herself as he'd described: folded in his strong arms, the vein in her neck presented.

A thrumming, almost like an electric current, raced through her body, so overwhelming, she had to use all her willpower to keep from pulling off the road and throwing herself onto his lap, crotch first.

Unconsciously, her tongue darted out to lick her lips, and she squirmed in her seat.

Mace grunted. "You can't lie to yourself for much longer."

"You think I'm lying?"

"I know you are."

"Well, you can think whatever you want, but I'm nobody's *blood bag*."

"That's a derogatory term. I'd never use it to describe the women I'm with."

"*Women*. As in the plural?" She snorted. "Well, just sign me right up."

"Don't be petty."

"I'm not being petty." *I am totally being petty*. "Besides, you're calling me petty when your *woman* back there just tried to get us killed because she wasn't satisfied."

"She's not my woman, she was just—"

"A blood bag?"

Mace glared at her for long while. "You're just trying to piss me off so I'll stop flirting with you."

That hadn't been the plan, but thankfully her anger had helped to siphon away some of her lust.

"Even though you like it," he added in a slightly roughened tone.

"I do not." *I so do*. She mentally shook that away, reminding herself that Mace was a vampire. A dangerous, sexy, dangerous vampire.

"Pull over," Mace ordered.

She tensed. "Why?"

"We're getting close to our turnoff. From there, the way to the safe house is windy, and I don't want to have to call out directions."

"Oh." She eased the car onto the side of the road and put the car in park. As she got out, she gauged which direction Mace would walk, and as he headed around the front, she started toward the back.

Before she made it a couple steps, his body pinned her against the car.

She gasped, going stiff. Yet he made no other move. She forced her eyes up, meeting his gaze. His expression was softer than she'd expected.

"I wasn't saying those things to be cruel, Coraline, or to

make you uncomfortable." His tone was gravely. The steel of his erection pressed against her lower belly.

She fought a renewed wave of desire.

"I said them because you turn me on so fucking much, and I can't keep it to myself anymore."

Her mouth dropped open. That infernal heat was back, full-force between her legs, this time dulling her mind. His eyes dipped to her lips, and she knew he was about to kiss her. Adrenalin flushed through her system, bringing with it cognition in the form of a pathetically tiny voice. "Mace, I'm scared."

"I know, baby. I don't want to scare you." He offered a crooked smile. "But you ruined my meal back there, and as detestable as that meal was, I think you owe me a boon."

"W-What do I owe?" Her mind turned to ravaged flesh and flowing blood. Her heart sped.

"A kiss," he said.

Though her body relaxed, her heart kept pace as fear was replaced by anticipation.

His eyes turned dark with lust, indicating he might want much more than just a kiss.

Her rebellious brain screamed, *I do too!* She had to get control of herself. "A regular kiss?"

He nodded.

"T-That's it?"

"For now."

She swallowed, finding no moisture in her throat. "Okay."

His hand slipped to her nape, and she struggled to breathe evenly.

He dipped his head, and their lips came into contact like a brand searing flesh—hot and, she feared, a little permanent.

Nobody kissed like Mace. He was the example to which all other males should be measured. His tongue expertly delved past her lips even though she hadn't planned on letting him in. His body was like warm pliable steel folded around her, making her aware of every corded muscle.

Instantly lost, she opened her mouth wider for him, and he growled with pleasure, taking the invitation. The feel of his tongue on hers caused a jolt that traveled straight to her clitoris. She let out a soft moan.

Determined not to be totally overtaken by the moment, she swirled her tongue in step with his, matching his every wicked thrust. A strong hand palmed her backside, giving an appreciative squeeze. His hips rolled forward, managing to stimulate her through her...panties?

Her skirt had somehow gotten hiked up past her upper thighs, and Mason's hand kneaded the soft flesh of her ass.

She pulled her head away and gasped for air. "This is more than a kiss."

"Not one of my kisses," he growled and claimed her mouth again, this time a little more urgently, a little more brutally, a little more perfectly.

Holy goddess, he could make her orgasm just with his tongue in her mouth.

The sound of honking interrupted them, and they both looked to see a car approaching. The young passengers laughed and leered at them as the car zoomed by, kicking up a fine cloud of dirt from the road.

Cora coughed as she worked to catch her breath. Then she noticed her fingers were digging into Mason's shoulders, and one of her legs was curled up by his hip.

She hurried to right her clothing.

Mace stepped back, his expression smug.

"Does that make you feel macho?" She turned to continue her trek around the car.

Mace slapped her lightly on the ass. "No, but that does." At her glare, he added, "I changed my mind. You're driving." With that, he reclaimed the passenger seat, leaving her dumfounded and fuming...and desperately wanting more.

Chapter 11

It soon became clear why Mason wanted her to drive. He wanted to continue flirting with her without any distractions. As he navigated, his voice dropped a couple of octaves and it made everything he said sound overtly sexy, even when telling something as simple as *make a right here*. It kept her off guard having to keep an eye on the road while contending with his every remark.

Aside from that, having her in the driver seat gave him leave to study her continuously. Having his eyes on her was almost physical, especially when he lowered them to examine her legs as she applied pressure to the gas or brakes, which he did regularly. It was both unnerving and titillating. The urge to take her hands from the wheel and tug down the hem of her skirt affected her often.

"You handle this vehicle masterfully," he commented after he directed her onto a dirt road banked by thick trees that screened out the setting sun. "I wonder what else you are able to handle so well."

She was inclined to believe he did it on purpose, but she wouldn't call him on it just to have him accuse her of being the one with a dirty mind.

What was worse than Mace coming on to her? Some rebellious part of her had taken over her vocal cords and was countering his every remark. "Oh, I can handle just about anything I get my hands on."

He grinned. "I've no doubt you'll demonstrate that for me later."

She stifled a flustered gasp. "Sorry, all demonstrations have been canceled until further notice."

"I have a feeling something will pop up."

Of their own accord, her lips curled upward. She forced a frown, but Mace noticed.

Torture by way of thick, husky voice and sexual innuendo; that was his plan.

And she was enjoying it.

A vamp was teasing her, and she was actually responding in kind? A vamp had kissed her, thoroughly, brutally, carnally, and she had kissed him back with equal fervor.

Was she mad?

How had things flipped on her so quickly?

"You're going to have to handle your own demonstrations for the time being," she responded, determined to keep her head.

The dirt road shallowed into something more of a trail. She eased off the gas slightly.

"Oh, I'm not one to work alone," Mace replied. "I prefer to have a helping hand."

"Don't sell yourself short. I bet you'd be quite proficient at it if you gave it a shot. Taking charge might even help to stroke your poor neglected ego."

"It's not my ego that needs stroking."

Cora swallowed. The innocent banter was moving uncomfortably toward something transparently tawdry. She attempted to derail the conversation. "Tell me more about this witch theory of yours."

From the corner of her eye, she thought she saw him frown. "It's not a theory. DNA tests confirm you're part of an ancient line of witches."

DNA? "I thought Trent was only checking for dark cells in my blood."

"At first, yes. But when he found such an abundance of dark cells, he ordered further testing."

"Alright. So when you say witch, you mean, like, a religion or something. Another word for gypsies, maybe? My family did travel a lot." The road took a wide turn and then crossed over a shallow stream.

"How is it you don't know any of this?" Mace asked. "Your parents never told you about your heritage?"

She shook her head.

"You sure they were your biological—"

"Of course," she interrupted irritably. "I mean...I'm pretty sure." Doubt suddenly plastered her mind and she slumped. "They must have been," she finished lamely.

"Doesn't matter. Something isn't right about your situation. That's for sure. I've never heard of a witch being born without some innate magical tendencies. Your powers should have come to fruition long ago." He gestured to the busted back window. "And no witch, no matter how inept, would have tolerated a shotgun blast practically up the rear."

"Have you ever seen a so-called witch use actual magic?"

His expression answered for him. "I was at a club a few years back, you know, one of those vamp-friendly blood donor joints. There was this attractive girl in tight black leather dress that showed more skin than it covered. Sleek blonde hair. Great eyes. Just my type. Smelled enticing."

Cora gritted her teeth and gripped the steering wheel tighter, concentrating hard on the road.

"You look fiercely agitated, Cora. Something bothering you?" He sounded amused.

"Nope, just trying to stay on the road." And fighting back a wicked case of jealousy! *What is that about?*

Mace chuckled. "Anyway, I solicited her. She was in the donor section of the club after all. But she wasn't having it. I ended up being slammed through a wall, just like our redneck friends in the truck back there, but without the armored shell. When I looked up to see which bruiser had pile-drived me sideways—it couldn't have been that wee thing—she vanished before my eyes."

"That's all circumstantial. She could've been really strong, and then you could have been blinded by a light or something and just imagined she'd vanished."

"Unnaturally strong. I'll agree to that, if she had *touched* me. But she hadn't laid a single finger on me, and neither had anyone else. As for a light blinding me? I know what I saw. Being tossed like a ragdoll by a creature that wouldn't weigh a hundred pounds sopping wet tends to stick in your mind."

Cora's brow furrowed. "A creature?"

"Witches are not human. Well, not fully."

She snorted. "So you believe I'm not even human?"

"Don't sound so offended. Being human isn't all that. I know from personal experience, and I don't recommend it. They die too easily, get sick, can barely heal a paper cut on their own. If you have some claim to the supernatural, embrace it and milk it for all it's worth, I say."

Cora went quiet. Supernatural? Inhuman? Creature? She didn't feel like any of those things. There must be some sort of mistake. More likely, her blood sample had somehow been tainted, or tampered with. "I don't know if I trust that blood test. I need a second opinion."

"Agreed."

Cora's head snapped toward him. "Really?"

"You were expecting an argument? I'd like to be sure as well. Especially since you've displayed no magical abilities whatsoever." He pointed ahead. "Slow down, there's another turn coming up."

She made a left onto an even more compact pathway with a rocky terrain and thick overgrowth. She had to push the car along at a whopping two miles an hour for fear of bottoming out on a sharp rock or dip. As they went, low branches scratched loudly along the side of the car. Cortez's paint job would be screwed at this rate. Mace didn't seem concerned.

"As soon as we're settled, I'll report to Trent and have him send someone trustworthy to gather another sample."

"Settled where?" she asked, just before the forest gave way to a picturesque, grey stone cottage. The irregular stones that made up the walls were marked by time, discolored and weather-stained. Thick wooded shutters, bleached by the sun, closed in several of the windows. A dark slate roof topped off the one-story building, adding a foreign aesthetic. It appeared to be very old, yet built to last the ages.

"When was this built? Seventeen-oh-ancient?"

Mace snorted. "It's not that old."

"Older than me, I'd wager."

"Most everything is older than you." He smirked. "And be glad it is. Almost everyone who knew of its secrets is long dead."

"That sounds ominous. What secrets?"

He pursed his lips, indicating he wasn't about to speak on the subject. Instead, he replied, "We'll be safe here."

Okay... "So..." She hesitated as she parked the car in front of the cottage. "How old are *you*?"

His smile widened. "Older than you."

She rolled her eyes and stepped out of the car. Her feet sank into layer upon layer of dampened leaves, shielding her against the muddy earth below. The aroma of freshly fallen rain hung in the air.

An eerie sensation crept along her skin, raising the hairs on her arms and back of her neck. She shivered and glanced around.

The surrounding forest appeared thick with life, the tall trees probably hundreds of years old. Movement caught her eye. A shadow scurried behind a bulky shrub. Just an animal, she told herself.

Mace was already to the door, seemingly unaware of her unease as he prepared to enter that fossil of a building and leave her out here alone. She rushed after him.

The main living room was twice the expected size, and the stone design, which resembled the exterior, reminded her of what the interior of a medieval castle might look like, complete with a set of buck heads mounted on the wall ahead of her and deer antlers to her left.

As she walked farther into the room, she expected the wood floor to creak under her feet, but it remained silent. An ornate Chesterfield sofa and matching love seat with flared arms fronted a hearth that boasted a flat-screen television directly overhead.

"No bear skinned rug?" she said. "I'm disappointed."

Mace gave her a wry look.

An archway on the opposite end of the room led to a large dining area and kitchen combination. The kitchen occupied most of the room with the fridge directly against the back wall in front of her. To the left of that, dark wooden cupboards lined the two adjoining walls. Underneath the cupboards, a black marbled countertop wrapped those same walls and then broke away into a J shape, creating a small bar. There was also an island counter situated near the center of the room and angled toward the smaller dining space to the right where an antique-ish iron chandelier hung from the ceiling just above a thick square wooden table and chair set.

When she returned to Mace in the living room, something caught her eye that she hadn't noticed upon entering.

A set of stairs decorated by an ornate wooden banister rounded its way to a second floor, disappearing behind the wall that housed the hearth.

She paused and looked a Mace. "A second story?" From the outside she'd assumed there was only one story to the cottage.

Mace just shrugged. When she realized she would receive no explanation, she climbed the stairs.

Seemingly content to let her explore, Mace waited on the first floor.

As her foot landed on the top step, that odd sensation crept over her again; an almost cool feeling yet warm at the same time, as if her body couldn't decide between the two.

She rubbed her arms in an attempt to get rid of it.

Down the lengthy hall that was only decorated by a small, square table under an old-looking mirror, she found four rooms, two on either side and each with a bed, writing desk, closet and dresser, and a set of large windows she hadn't seen from the outside. She peeked out of one, spotting the car where she'd parked it. Weird.

All four rooms had their own bathrooms as well with a sink, tub, and separate walk-in shower. It was as if the top floor had been designed to be rented out. Maybe Mace's "safehouse" was, in fact, a quaint lodge. Probably for high-class patrons with a taste for skiing who like to get away for a weekend. Though it was summer now, in a few months, snow would cover the surrounding hills and mountains.

That cold/warm sensation hit her again. After it passed, she rejoined Mace downstairs. "It feels weird up there. Is this place haunted or something?"

One corner of his mouth lifted. "Not haunted, no."

"Well something's giving me the shivers."

He studied her for a moment, then headed into the kitchen, gesturing for her to follow. "Like I said, this place holds a lot of secrets." He pressed his palm into a section of the wall, and a panel shifted sideways, revealing an opening the size of a door. She stepped forward to peer inside. A darkened staircase led down to a gravel covered floor.

A hidden cellar?

She gulped.

Chapter 12

"Don't tell me there's a dungeon down there and that's where you plan to kill me," Cora said to Mace as she stared bleakly into the darkened cellar. "Oh, man. I knew it. A vampire that wants to protect me?" She snorted. "How stupid am I?"

Mace sighed. "Don't be so melodramatic. The staircase leads to an underground tunnel which in turn leads to the closest town. It's an escape route in case...well, in case of anything. It was installed just after the volatile revelation of my kind."

"Oh." Cora offered a small smile. "That's...convenient. And a little freaky, actually. How long is it?"

"Miles. Eight to be exact."

She whistled. "That's a heck of a jog."

"Not if you're properly motivated."

She conceded that point with a tight nod as she gazed down into the darkness. "What if someone were to come here from the other end?"

"No one but a well-trained witch, who knew what to be looking for and where, would be able to find the tunnel's end."

"Why's that?"

"Because it's magically hidden, just like the top floor."

She blinked up at him. "No way." As if needing confirmation of his claim, Cora sprinted back through the dining room and out the front door. Mace followed, finding her gawking up at the spot where the second story should be.

Backing up for a better view, she bumped into the sedan. "You've got to be shitting me."

She raced back into the house, and Mace heard her bound up the stairs. Then all sound of her disappeared, smothered by the spell that had been placed upon the cottage so long ago.

He crossed his arms and leaned against the hood of the car, waiting patiently for her to reemerge.

When she did, she appeared a bit dumfounded. "Mace, I was yelling at you from the window. Didn't you hear me?"

When Mace explained the sound dampening effects of the spell, her expression became a mix of amazement and fascination.

"Being a witch is starting to look a little better now, yeah?"

She frowned. "I still don't think you're right about me, but if magic exists, real magic...well, that's just incredible, isn't it?"

He shrugged. "Incredible for some, bothersome for others."

She cocked her head.

"Witches and vampires aren't exactly BFFs of the supernatural world. We've had our...disagreements over the years. Imagine going up against a being that can overpower you with the flick of a finger, strip your will with a word. Imaging how disconcerting that can be."

"I don't have to imagine that. It's how humans feel every single day with you vamps walking around."

Mace lifted a brow. "Touché." He strolled back into the house, and Cora followed. "There's some non-perishable food in the pantry," he told her. "Make yourself something to eat while I'm gone, and promise me you'll stay inside till I return."

"Where are you going?"

He hesitated. "I need to check the tunnel, make sure there've been no cave-ins. I'll pick up some fresh produce while I'm at it." He intentionally left out the main reason he needed to go; his hunger was not sated.

Cora might be opening up to a little flirtatious banter, but she was far from ready to allow a vampire, even him, feed from her. Plus, if the blood test was correct and she was indeed a witch, it would be wise for him to avoid sharing any more blood with her anyway.

The bond between them, he could tell, was already strong, making the idea of taking from another utterly repulsive.

He swore under his breath and headed out.

"Alright," Cora replied, even as anxiety crawled up her spine. Was it because she knew she'd soon be alone here in this eerie cottage, or because she suspected the real reason Mason wanted to leave? And it wasn't to get fresh produce. Her stomach turned at the thought of food. Was she getting sick? She was feeling a bit achy, but figured that was from driving for so long. She decided not to mention her nausea to Mason, worried he might suggest she take some of his blood to heal.

At the notion, a jolt, almost like anticipation, shot through her. Why did it suddenly sound so appealing? She stubbornly buried that idea.

After Mace vanished down the dark staircase, the panel slid closed behind him.

Curious if the secret entrance opened only for Mace, she placed her palm on the wall in the same spot he had. The panel shifted once more.

As if expecting her, Mace stood facing her with his arms crossed tightly over his chest and a censuring brow raised.

She frowned. "I was just checking."

"Unless your life's in danger, you're not to step foot down here. Understand?"

She mimicked his stance. "I got it."

He nodded once and then pushed the panel back in place.

For the next hour, Cora took it upon herself to explore the cottage, opening dresser drawers, closets, and any other noticeable compartments, finding nothing of much interest. In the dressers, there were a few folded shirts and pants, predominantly for males. The closets held a couple nice suits and jackets and empty hangers. There was a line of books on a shelf in the main room of the first floor, some of them ancient looking. One of the covers was so worn the title was no longer readable. She idly glanced at a few of the others: The Art of War, Gods and Generals, A Comprehensive Guide to Body Language. But the two that surprised her the most: Wuthering Heights, and Pride and Prejudice. Both well preserved, but aged so thoroughly they could pass for first editions.

Vamps reading for pleasure? Who knew?

Growing bored with her unfruitful snooping, she found a linen closet and claimed a fluffy orange towel, then snatched a T-shirt and pair of sweats with a string-tie waist from one of the dressers.

She was ready to test out the shower.

* * *

The sun slowly melted into the horizon, and the sky morphed from blue to navy. Mace strolled through the main street of the small seaside town with the strut of a man who belonged without question, drawing little attention.

The heavy, pungent fragrance distinctive to ocean water filled his nostrils and could almost be felt gliding over his skin. He wondered if Cora had ever seen the ocean up close and imagined what expression she might take if he brought her here. Would she smile as brightly as she used to when she'd been under the illusion the rough parts of her life were behind her? Would she offer that same smile to him in gratitude? Maybe allow him to hold her as they watched a sunset over the water?

He mentally scoffed at himself. When in the hell had he become a namby-pamby romantic?

Yet he couldn't corral his thoughts. He moved on to how she might display her gratitude for such an evening. Perhaps later in the night she would thank him with a kiss. A touch. Perhaps allow him to pet that pretty body of hers.

He ran a hand down his face and cleared his mind so he could focus on his current objective. He was supposed to be hunting, not fabricating ridiculous fantasies...with an alleged witch no less. Thinking of Cora like that—as his—was rousing his hunger, while making that dark-haired female on the corner just up ahead appear less than appealing.

The woman watched him as he approached. He made no attempt to hide his lengthening fangs. She smiled and arched her body, visibly accentuating her curves, clad in a tight pair of plastic orange shorts and thin, white gauzy top, sans bra.

A blood hooker.

The town was full of them. In fact, most of the towns that lined the Pacific had their share of blood hookers to accommodate the large population of vampires resided along this coveted stretch of land.

In a breathy voice, she introduced herself and Mace subsequently forgot her name. She leaned into him, rubbing herself against his chest. She smelled of sex and blood. Another vampire had been here shortly before him.

Repelled, he set her at arm's length.

Her brow furrowed at the abruptness. "What's the matter, baby?"

In all his time as a vampire, he had never experienced such a strong aversion to a potential blood donor. If he fed from this woman, he might literally retch. "I'm sorry," he muttered. "I thought you were someone else."

As he walked away, she called after him, "I can be anyone you want."

No, she couldn't. No one could mimic the obstinate, strong spirited, sometimes coy, and always sexy Coraline.

Mace scrubbed his palm down his face. Seriously? When the fuck had he become such a pansy? And when the hell had Coraline become his version of ideal? Dammit! He was going to be screwed six ways to Sunday if he didn't force her from his mind.

His phone buzzed in his pocket.

He retrieved it and glanced at the name before greeting, "Hey, Trent. I was going to call you shortly. Any leads on the mole?"

"None yet, but I have many feelers out at the moment. If there's a traitor in our midst or among the humans, I'll find him. How goes it with you? Have you decided on a location yet?"

"Is this line secure?"

"It is."

Mace glanced around, making sure no one was within hearing distance. "I've taken her to the enchanted cottage."

"No shit? You think she needs that much defense?"

"After the attempts on both our lives, don't you agree?"

"I suppose. It's just a surprising place to bring a witch. What if she manages to dip into the centuries-old magic surrounding that place? She could use it against you."

"About that. I think we should do another blood test on Cora, with a fresh sample. She denies any knowledge of being a witch."

Trent snorted. "And you believe her?"

"I...I'm not sure. All I know is that she has yet to use magic, even when her life might have depended on it."

Trent sighed. "Very well. I'll see if I can spare someone in the morning."

"I'd prefer it if you came yourself."

"I'm a little busy here, Mason. I might have uncovered a new lead into Brayden's disappearance. I need to keep on it."

"Fine then. Just be sure whoever you send is trustworthy."

Pause.

Trent's voice hardened. "Watch yourself, Mason. That was just shy of an order."

Mace cringed, glad that Trent couldn't see it. "Apologies, sire. You know I trust your judgment."

The line went quiet for another moment. Then Trent replied, "If I can spare the extra hand, I'll have someone there by tomorrow."

Without another word, he hung up.

Great. What a perfect time to piss off his maker.

* * *

With her hair wrapped in a towel, Cora stretched out on the sofa, stomach down, knees bent with her feet hovering over her behind, and a copy of Pride and Prejudice open to chapter four. Elizabeth Bennet had just had her first run-in with Mr. Darcy.

When she heard the front door creek open behind her, she decided to tease Mace a little. "I never would have taken you for a closet romance novel junkie." She laughed.

"'fraid those don't belong to me, *cher*."

Cora froze. That was not Mason's voice. She swiveled around. The book slipped from her grasp and fell to the floor with a dull thud.

In the doorway, thick arms sheathed in a black leather jacket folded over a broad, powerful chest. Light, grey-blue eyes contrasted drastically with the dark, raven hair that was pulled back in a tight braid that cascaded down his back. The sides of his head were sheered to within an inch of his scalp.

Cora's heart began to thud in her chest.

The wild-looking vampire twisted his features into a predatory grin, fangs prominent. "I thought I smelled something sweet."

Her throat worked overtime to suck in air, but the essential muscles seemed to be malfunctioning. The vampire's eyes flashed, and she realized he was reacting to the furious spike in her pulse.

Whereas her brain demanded she stay calm, stay still, and slow her heart rate, her body reacted on animal instinct.

She flew off the sofa toward the dining room, but the vampire's fingers threaded through the hair at her nape. Caught so easily.

"I wouldn't recommend running from me, pet. Not unless you want me to chase you?"

He forced her around to face him. She knew he would attempt to compel her, but her eyes were frozen wide.

"Now settle down and come back to the couch, *cher*." His tone dropped an octave. "You can sit on my lap." When she resisted, he arched a brow as intuition sparked behind his grey eyes. "Intriguing. You have a name, sweet girl?"

She shook her head, intending not to answer, but her mind and body were still separated by an ocean of terror. "C-Coraline."

"Coraline." With his accent, he rolled the last syllable. "Lovely, frightened Coraline. I don't usually enjoy the smell of fear on a woman. This will be better if you relax."

"W-What will be better?"

"When I feed from you," he replied, then gestured to her body. "These loose clothing? Usually I prefer more form-fitting attire, but I have to admit, this is actually working for me."

He pushed her up against the wall, crowding her with his massive frame. Fist still tight in her hair, he pulled her head to the side, revealing her neck to him.

The moment she felt fangs brush flesh, her fright amplified into something savage and unruly. Without thinking, she slammed her knee into his crotch.

He released her and hunched over, gurgling an unintelligible curse.

Bracing herself on the wall, she brought her right leg up and then punched her heel into his chest. He tumbled backwards.

Before he could right himself, she was to the dining room and planted her hand on the secret panel. It seemed to take forever to open.

The vampire grunted angrily in the other room.

As soon as the panel offered enough room for her to squeeze through, she stumbled down the steps, nearly tripping on her way.

The tunnel instantly illuminated with torches as she hit the landing. Ignoring the rough terrain under her bare feet, she raced into the unknown, powered by concentrated adrenaline.

Chapter 13

Mace stepped off the rocky ledge and dropped the twenty feet into the sea. His jacket flared up before he breached the cool choppy water. He allowed the weight of his clothing to drag him down. When he felt the pressure build in his lungs, he swam for the fissure that sliced an opening into the wall of stone.

He followed the familiar path to the hidden cavern and broke the surface, taking in the stagnant air that smelled of moist earth, salt, and aged metal. After trudging out of the water, he reached for one of the old towels that had been left hanging over a short stalagmite and haphazardly dried his face and hair.

Not a single drop of blood had satiated him tonight, though he'd forced himself to feed twice. Both females had walked away satisfied, while he only felt empty and unfulfilled.

His craving for Cora was too great. The bond was set.

She had to be a fucking witch. No human could have done this to him with only one blood exchange.

He glanced down at the tome and assorted items in his hand,

protected from the water by a clear plastic sheath. Purchasing them had been an ordeal. The elderly, salt-and-pepper haired witch sitting behind the counter of the specialty shop had eyed his every move as he'd perused her store, as if she were ready to hex him. He'd entered the place on a whim, thinking of Cora.

When he'd approached the witch with one of the silly stones her kind coveted, she'd practically interrogated him. "Wa'chu be wanting that fo', vampire?"

Her tone instantly grated on his nerves. "That's really none of your business." He didn't bother asking how she knew he was a vamp. Witches had their ways of knowing things like that.

She merely stared at him with a bored expression, waiting.

"Is it for sale or not, old woman?"

Faster than he had assumed she could move, she swiped the stone out of his hand. "Depends on wa'chu using it for. You can't be suckin' magic out of it with your teeth."

He rolled his eyes. "It's not for me."

"Oh, it ain't, ain't it? You even know what it's fo'?"

"Honestly, I don't really care."

She leaned back in her chair and humphed. "This is used to enhance energy and sexuality."

"Well, then everyone should carry one." He pulled out his wallet. "Ring me up."

She grabbed his left wrist yanked his hand toward her.

"Hey!"

"Shush, you." She examined his palm, turning it this way and that. Periodically, she raised a brow and met his gaze before going back to her task.

Growing impatient, "Look, woman—"

"Shush!" She tugged him to bend forward to her height and

invaded his personal space by pinching his chin between her thumb and forefinger while staring invasively into his eyes.

"You nutty..."

She waved her free hand, and his vocal cords seized. He experienced a moment of panic before she waved her palm again, and a sense of ease relaxed his muscles. A part of him resisted the intrusive magic.

"Release me, or I will end you, witch."

With her face still too close to his as she continued her examination, she commented, "I've a tonic that'll cool your aggression, another that'll open your heart, and you've a problem with blood, no?"

"I don't need your magic, witch."

Placing her palms on either side of his face, she tilted his head and used her thumbs to push his eyelids up. Her tone became contemplative. "Mayhap, if you can accept the lady..."

"Enough!" He jerked away, preparing to leave.

"Wait. I've things she needs if she's to discover her past."

He paused in the doorway, grinding his teeth.

"She's lost. You cannot help her. That much is clear."

He turned back. "My patience is gone, old woman. If you're serious, then make this quick."

For the next few moments, he'd followed her around the shop as she'd picked up various items, pausing periodically to consider their usefulness. He had no idea if she was screwing with him or if she truly had some sort of mystical insight into Cora's situation, but his wallet was now nearly empty. To top it off, when he thought the witch had finally finished with him, she'd slipped a Celtic woven pendant over his head and made him promise never to take it off.

"Yeah, sure," he'd boldly lied.

Now, in the brightly lit cave, he reached for the silly thing, ready to rip it away and toss it into the ocean.

Before he could, the necklace, pendant and all, turned as hot as heated iron, burning his skin underneath. He flinched and hurried to yank it off, but only found tender, blistered skin where the necklace should have been.

He swore out loud. *Damn shifty witches.*

Unfortunately, he couldn't return to demand to know what spell the witch had just cursed him with. Not now, anyway. Shortly after he'd left the witch's abode, an eerie sense of urgency had him rushing back to this tunnel rather than quenching the last of his thirst.

He flung the towel back over the stalagmite and started through the tunnel. He halted, noticing that all the torches were lit.

Anxiety prickled his skin.

His night vision was superior to humans, so he'd never required the light to maneuver the tunnels. Who would have lit them? Cora? Or had someone witnessed his exiting the cavern through the ocean and managed to find their way here?

Instinctively, he knew it must be the blood bond with Cora that drove his disquiet.

She was in trouble...and he'd left her alone!

Fear gouged its way through his chest. He took off at a sprint, but the sound of footsteps beating the ground toward him had him slowing with caution.

A figure came around the bend.

"Cora?"

She was barefoot and dressed in loose clothing, which

should've appeared ill fitting and frumpy, but on her, it was just as sexy as that outfit in the hotel that had nearly made him spill his seed on the spot.

"Mason! Thank the goddess!" She launched herself into his arms, gasping heavily as though she'd run the entire eight miles of the cave without a break.

Her hair was damp and smelled ambrosial. Her fierce pulse smelled even better. If she weren't exuding the aroma of pure fright, he might not have been able to keep his head. The scent of her racing blood was prominent, and his fangs descended. His stomach churned with renewed hunger as though he hadn't had a drop tonight.

"What's happened?" he demanded.

She pointed behind her. "There's a vampire. He tried to attack me."

Mace adjusted her head to see two small marks dotting her neck. Every muscle tensed with the need to mutilate whoever had dared touch her.

"I think he followed me down here."

Aggression rippled, sloshing through his mind. And yet, what she suggested made no sense. For one, Cora could never have outrun a vampire. Two, no one but Trent and those he'd sired knew of the enchanted cottage. Three, if anyone besides them *did* know of the cottage, none should be able to cross the property line without having been invited by himself, Trent, Brayden, or...

"Knox."

"Mace," Knox greeted, stepping from behind the bend.

Cora began to shake, and Mace placed himself between her and Knox. Then he exchanged a sequence of meaningful looks with the other vampire, hidden from Cora's view. Knox knew him well enough to read the warnings that ran across his face, and vice versa. The first stony expression asserted his claim over Cora. The second threatened death if Knox so much as pointed a fang in her direction again. Knox responded with an expression that said he was not impressed and he'd do whatever the fuck he wanted.

We'll see about that.

"What the hell are you doing here?" Mace growled.

Knox crossed his arms and leaned a shoulder against a protruding rock. "Why do any of us come here?"

"So the fearless Knox is hiding out?"

"Lying low," Knox corrected.

"Why?"

"None of your business. And I don't care why you're here with a human either."

"You're lucky I don't kill you for touching her. It won't happen again, understand?"

Knox shot Cora a fang-filled smile. Cora inched closer to Mace.

A patch in Mason's chest bloomed with pride that she trusted him to protect her, even if only a little. He ignored the dark thought that she was shrewdly taking advantage of her situation for her best chances at survival—a tactic she excelled at. He was the only thing standing between her and Knox, and given the choice, she'd no doubt prefer to be rid of them both.

He glanced down at her, selfishly grateful that she needed him.

—

After having raced through the lengthy, unfamiliar cave, Cora had nearly collapsed at seeing Mace—partly from exhaustion, and partly from the indescribable relief that had smothered the better half of her terror. She'd be safe with him.

Now, as he gazed down at her with concern, something warm joined the beating of her heart, something unfathomable, unintelligible, inexplicable...a perfect blend of overwhelming wonder and unmitigated tepidity. Something that was equally as frightening as being pursued by a hungry vampire, yet every cell in her body fired with a carnal craving.

Mace threaded his fingers through her hair and used his thumb to caress her cheek. Almost unconsciously, she leaned her face into his palm and allowed this newly recognized feeling to settle in and calm her nerves, even as it choked words from her throat.

His eyes glowed the color of dense clouds ready to storm, as if his emotions mirrored hers. Every fiber in her wanted to reach for him, but she somehow managed to keep her muscles in place. The effort was maddening.

"Ugh," Knox spat, looking aghast. "You're not blood bonded, are you? With a human? That's rich."

Cora's euphoric feeling sank like a stone in her stomach. Mason shot Knox a murderous look.

"Blood bonded?" she asked. "What's that?"

"And she doesn't even know about it?" Knox belted out a laugh. "What are you playing at, Mace?"

Cora gulped down a lump that had developed in her throat.

Mace swiped his hand through the air in Knox's direction. The gesture seemed almost desperate. "Shut the fuck up, Knox, and go away. In fact, I want you out of the cottage. Find somewhere else to loiter."

"Fuck that. I was here first. You leave."

He glanced back toward Cora. "We can't."

"Sure you can. Do you need me to shove you out the door?"

"Only if you'd like a blade in one of your vital organs."

"What is blood bonded?" Cora interrupted with stress soaked words.

She went ignored.

"You want to play house with your little human, then you can do it down here." Knox gestured to the dark and damp cavern. "The cottage is mine."

"The hell it is. And as far as I can tell, you arrived after we did. The cottage was empty when we got here, so you have no claim to it."

Cora's chest sank with every second as her mind slowly, reluctantly piece together its own conclusion, but she needed to hear Mason say it. She placed her hand on his shoulder, hoping to claim his attention. "What is blood bonded?"

He continued to glare at Knox, muscles tensed.

Knox shook his head. "You know our scents are as good as erased if we're gone long enough. I've been out hunting all night. But if you need some form of evidence, I'll go back there and piss all over everything for you."

A twinge of anger seeped into Cora. Both of them refused to acknowledge her.

Mace sneered. "What are you hiding from, Knox? Did you finally hustle someone bigger and badder than you?"

Knox crossed his arms. "Impossible. There's no one that fits that description."

Her patience plummeted, and fury notched up her temperature. Her fist clenched. "What is blood bonded?" The scream echoed through the cavern, bouncing back at them several times.

Mace looked at her. Her expression said she was on the verge of a full-on panic.

"Let's go back to the cottage," he said calmly, reaching for her.

She jerked away.

He pulled his hand back. A dull pain, coated by sadness and salted by betrayal, twisted in his chest. It took him a moment to realize he was gleaning Cora's emotions.

Her lips curled into a deep frown. Distrusting eyes appraised him as though he'd been exposed as a villain.

Damn you, Knox.

He'd been looking for the right time to tell her about the bond and what it meant. Unfortunately, Knox had beaten him to it.

"Cora, it's not as bad as you're thinking," he said, attempting to dull her ire. He wished he had explained everything to her earlier, like in the car where she couldn't run away.

She took another step back, and Knox let out a dark chuckle. Mace turned to pin him with a threatening stare. Knox merely smiled wider, enjoying the show.

Mace faced Cora again, softening his features. "I hadn't intended for it to happen. That first night when we shared blood, we sparked a bond between us—"

"We?" she snapped. An accusatory finger landed on him. "No, *we* didn't do anything. It was you." She shook slightly as she backed up until she met the cavern wall.

Mace kept his tone light. "It's not so bad, I swear. It makes it easier to sense each other's moods, but that's about it..." *Roughly*. "And it's not permanent."

At the last part of his speech, her expression relaxed a touch. He tried not to feel affronted by that. Before Knox's interruption, he thought he'd seen strong desire behind her eyes. Would it be so bad if it *were* permanent? He mentally shook that errant thought out of his head. Of course it would be.

"It'll go away?" she asked shakily.

He nodded.

She turned suspicious once more. "Just like you said the dark cells would go away?"

"What's this now?" Knox asked, dropping his arms. "Dark cells?"

"None of your business," Mace snapped. He reached out for Cora again, and she only slightly flinched. He gritted his teeth. "Come back to the cottage with me. We should speak of this in private."

She glanced toward Knox, hesitating. Then she nodded.

"Your drama bores me anyway." Knox waved a negligent hand at them and then headed back down the tunnel, calling back, "Stay in the cottage or don't. I don't care, but I'm not leaving."

Mace cursed under his breath and then waited till Knox was out of earshot before leading Cora down the same path. She no longer clung to him in fright...or in trust. Any hint of desire was now dead and possibly buried. Forever.

The moment they'd shared before Knox's callous revelation had been strong, heavy, almost tangible, and so heady he'd nearly dropped to his knees…undone by a look.

Was it because of the bond? Or something else?

Whatever it was, it was gone now. And he wanted it back.

Chapter 14

Cora walked next to Mace, though more than a few feet separated them. It was necessary. She was unnerved by his explanation of the blood bond.

For a moment, for one crazy second, she'd imagined she had feelings for Mace. To hear that it was caused by this unwanted bond was a relief—

Not disappointing at all.

"Did you hear me, Cora?" Mace asked

"Hmm?"

He peered down at her. "I asked if you were okay. You're taking this better than expected. Would you like to talk about it? Or are you sparing the ire for later?"

As they had made their way through the hidden passage, she remained quiet, contemplative, as Mason attempted to play down the *bond*. She could tell he was playing it down because he would follow sentences with, "But it'll fade," and "It's only temporary," and worst of all, "This was the last thing I wanted." Why the latter brought a pang into her chest, she couldn't say. Then he would look at her, as if to gauge whether she was buying it.

She wasn't.

And eventually she had stopped listening.

Not because she didn't want to know everything. But because the implications of being tied to a vampire—by freaking blood—if even for a short time, had completely overwhelmed her ability to pay attention to what was happening around her. Even her lingering fear of Knox had been diminished by it.

However, she had managed to mentally file away a few facts. Blood bond: a semi-permanent bond with a vampire born of a blood exchange with side effects such as telegraphing one's emotional state and unwarranted feelings of trust. Sounded like the makings of a perfect snare; a captive treated to a solid dose of Stockholm syndrome.

She thought back to when she might have reacted out of character because of this so-called bond. In the tunnel just now, for sure. And no wonder she'd helped him on the mountain pass. Would she have left him there without this bond guiding her actions? Left him to die?

She shivered. Mace cocked a quizzical brow at her, but said nothing.

It wasn't that she thought Mace was outright lying to her, but she could tell—whether it was from having gotten to know him over the last few days, or from his bond—there was something more he wasn't saying.

And yet he was trying to explain things as gently as possible, trying to reassure her that she was safe with him. She imagined when he'd said that, he was thinking of Edgar, just as she was. If nothing else, it was sweet of him. And it did manage to ease some of her irritation.

That didn't mean she wasn't pissed at having been corralled into a bond she never asked for.

Nevertheless, she wasn't in the mood to take it out on Mace at the moment. "Later would be better," she finally replied.

He gave her a small smile. "Any time you're ready, then."

They ascended the stairs into the cottage, finding Knox had taken command of the sofa in front of the flat-screen. The movie he watched was something Cora didn't recognize, which wasn't surprising considering it was kung-fu, starring an all vampire cast. She'd seen a few movies before, but mainly the only television she'd watched was with Winston, and that was mostly stock market analysis and twenty-four-hour news networks.

Without taking his eyes from the screen, Knox said, "Check it out, this guy's about to have his head taken clean off."

"I've had enough of blood," Cora muttered under her breath, ignoring the action on the screen. If she could help it, no vampire would pierce her vein again.

Knox made a sound that was half laugh, half condescending scoff. "You'd better get over that real quick. You're bonded to a vampire, *cher*."

She raised a brow, wondering, dreading, fearing she already knew, what Knox meant. But she clung to a small thread of denial with an enforcing desperation. Mace could drink from others. That was one of his reassurances. She didn't need to feed him, right?

She looked to Mace.

He just shook his head. "Don't mind him. If he could age, he'd be one of those crotchety old men who throw their canes at children. He's an expert at causing trouble." He handed her a parcel she hadn't noticed him carrying before and then averted his gaze too quickly.

Now that she was aware of it, she thought she sensed anxiety and guilt coming from Mace.

She pursed her lips and started up the stairs, convinced he wasn't offering her the entire truth about this bond thing. Knox might be more forthcoming, but she wasn't about to try and get him alone to find out.

"I'll be up in a moment," Mace called after her.

She shot him a surprised look. Then her eyes darted to Knox and back as if comprehending his meaning. Mace wasn't about to leave her in a room alone through the night with another vampire in the house. He could tell she was confused and scared. Most of all pissed. He'd address that later. Right now, he needed to set some ground rules with Knox.

Impossibly, her lips thinned further.

He expected a protest. Instead, she replied with a curt nod before disappearing to the second floor. Though he didn't hear any noise, he imagined her cursing them both.

He couldn't blame her. Even though it was for her own good, she was essentially a prisoner. In more ways than she was fully aware.

Mace turned back to where Knox lounged carelessly. "Get the fuck out of here."

Knox rolled his eyes. "I thought we had this conversation already, and it ended with go fuck yourself."

"You selfish prick!" he snarled. "When will you ever choose the clan over yourself?"

Knox's expression turned dark. "You don't want to go

there."

"We used to be like brothers. How many times have I risked my life for you—"

"I never asked you—"

"—and you can't even do me a solid?"

"—for shit! Fuck you!"

Mace lunged for Knox's throat, but Knox saw it coming.

Without getting up, the heel of Knox's boot kissed Mason's chin with all the power of a grand slam hitter. Mace stumbled back, stunned, tasting blood.

Knox lowered his leg and relaxed into the couch once more, one arm over the back. "Seriously, Mason? Are we really going to do this?"

Mace spit out a mouthful of blood. "Yeah."

Tension crept through the air as they both waited for the other to move.

Knox swiped his finger under his nose, sniffing. A baneful smile crept over his face.

* * *

Cora dropped the clear plastic pack Mace had handed off to her on the mattress and plopped down beside it. She was tired and wired at the same time, feeling like she should be doing something, but hadn't the energy. She should be running as far and as fast from this place as she could manage.

She fell back onto the mattress, her arms sprawled out and legs dangling over the edge, staring up at the ceiling.

The notion that she could escape Mace was laughable at this point. Not only was she in the middle of nowhere—a forest no less, a vampire's ideal hunting ground—but she wasn't entirely sure she wanted to escape him. Which was infuriating in and of itself.

She glanced down at the package. There were several items within: Two books, a set of candles, a smaller item that looked like a jewelry box, and some fresh fruit—peaches and strawberries. Her favorites, naturally. What else had he discovered while he'd watched her for so many months?

She pulled out a peach, suddenly reminded of her total lack of appetite. She should be ravenous. Was it wise to be concerned?

Determined, she bit through the soft skin, finding the center juicy and ripe. She knew it had to taste wonderful. However, her taste buds were of a different opinion. Nonetheless, she took another bite, and another, till only the pit remained. Her stomach gurgled uncomfortably and then settled with a heaviness as though she'd eaten an entire feast.

Definitely not right.

To distract herself, she rummaged through the rest of the items. The candles were thick and waxy, as if homemade, and perfumed by an array of scents: rosemary, jasmine, burnt wood, floral, and other fragrances she couldn't identify. There were over a dozen candles all together of different colors, shapes, and sizes.

She retrieved the book next and read the cover: A Witch's Guide to Demons, Vampires, and Other Supernatural Entities.

Another, smaller book, read Quick Spells for the Witch on the Go: Pocket Edition.

In the jewelry box, there was a beautiful pendant—a transparent, yet deeply purple gemstone attached to a silver chain.

Lifting the chain, she allowed the stone to dangle freely as she examined its many facets. She could understand the fruit, the books, but why would Mace buy the candles and this necklace?

A loud crash drew her to the window. Yellow light from the front door cut through the darkness and stretched over the yard, revealing Knox and Mace below. Knox landed several punches to Mace's face, backing him up against the car. Mace gripped the side of Knox's head and then slammed his skull down through the passenger side window. Glass shattered. The harsh blow didn't slow Knox down. He responded by head-butting Mace, following it up with another swift punch.

Both males were alarmingly bloody. How long had this been going on? What were they fighting over? Oh, goddess! What if Mace lost?

She banged on the window, yelling for them to stop. Then she remembered they couldn't hear her. She opened the window and leaned out, preparing her lungs for a screech that would not go unheard. Instead, she found herself staring into a small, dimly lit room.

Against the far wall, a reading lamp sat atop a desk. All color but that of the lamp seemed to have been leached away. There were no windows, and she instantly felt confined. A hallow kind of depression hung heavy in her heart. That depression transformed to terror when she realized the room was populated by a single shadowy figure seated at the desk. Its dark head seemed to look her way. Then the figure slowly stood, reaching out for her.

Cora sucked in a painful gasp that filled her lungs too full and screamed.

Chapter 15

Mace kneed Knox in the face, breaking his nose. Knox stumbled back with a curse before redoubling his attack. Mace took another set of knuckle blows, countering with a quick succession of body shots to Knox's ribcage.

The sound of Cora screaming had them breaking apart. Moments later, she burst through the door. At first, he thought she was worried for him, but her expression was much too panicked for that.

"What's happened?" Forgetting the fight, he hurried to Cora's side.

Just as in the tunnel, she threw herself into his arms, uncaring that he was covered in blood. For a fraction of a second, his concern was overshadowed by an inappropriate bout of satisfaction.

"There's something in the house...through the window...a shadow..."

Her words were separated by heavy gasps. Mace feared she was just shy of hyperventilating.

"Clam down and breathe," he said. "You're safe now."

"Where was it?" Knox demanded. He reached for Cora's arm.

Mace gripped her tighter to his chest and sent Knox a look of warning. If he touched her now, their little disagreement would turn life threatening.

Wisely, Knox backed off. Then, checking his tone, he said to Cora, "Tell me where you saw this shadow."

After a moment of catching her breath, she replied, "The bedroom at the end of the hall. I leaned through the window to shout at the two of you. There was another room, though, and a thing reached for me."

She shuddered. Mason's already aggressed blood fired with fury, mostly directed at himself. How could it be so difficult to keep one mortal safe?

"Do you know anything about this?" he asked Knox.

Knox shrugged. "I suspected something was here."

"And you didn't tell me?"

"You weren't exactly booting up for a chat."

"Dammit, Knox—"

"I don't think it's anything to worry about. Just a ghost or something." He glanced between them, and then added, "I'll take that room tonight."

Mace raised a brow. "What are you playing at?"

Knox glared at him. "I'm not playing at anything. Like I said before, stay if you want, or go. I don't care. But the apparition won't harm your female."

"What makes you so sure?" And why even add that little bit of reassurance. Knox might have them out of his hair tonight if he'd suggested the thing was dangerous.

Knox swiped a bit of blood from his mouth. "I just am." Without another word, he turned and headed back inside.

* * *

"Just say the word and we'll leave tonight," Mace repeated for the fifth time, and again, Cora merely shook her head.

He sat on the edge of the bed with a towel around his waist, fresh from a lightning fast shower. Clearly, he was loath to leave her alone again, which she appreciated. Even though she was still mad at him, it was reassuring having a vampire as a protector. Except when he'd insisted on standing guard in the bathroom while she'd washed up. It had taken some finagling on her part to keep him out. Per his request, she'd left the door open "just in case."

After drying and dressing in a fresh set of loose men's clothing found in the closet, she curled up on a plush chair across the room, the larger of the two books from Mace open in her lap. She'd immediately flipped to a section about ghosts, but she was finding it difficult to concentrate on reading with a shirtless Mace just feet away.

"I'm okay with staying," she replied. She'd long believed in the afterlife and spirits, and didn't think the spirit had meant to frighten her. "I was just startled by whatever that thing was," she continued. "I wasn't expecting it. Besides, I'm too tired to run off somewhere else, and there's glass all over the seats in the car from your fight with Knox. What was that about, anyway?"

"Old stuff, really. Not important. Sorry if I worried you."

"Could you tell I was worried? Because of the bond?"

Mace nodded. "You were afraid Knox would beat me and

then claim you as his, right?"

She shrugged.

"I would never let that happen."

"I know." She paused. One of her shoulders hiked up. "What am I feeling now?"

"Several things, I think. It's easier to tell when an emotion becomes sharp, or singularly, like when you're frightened. I could've pin pointed the exact moment Knox showed up."

"Really?"

Another nod. "It was frustrating not knowing the cause of your alarm, and not being able to get to you quickly. I don't think I'll ever go so far from you again."

Cora couldn't formulate a response because she was both terrified and relieved by his statement. The opposing emotions wreaked havoc on her mental balance.

Mace studied her a little too closely, and she went back to reading the same paragraph she'd been examining for the last twenty minutes. After going over the first few words, she zoned out again. Mace could sense that she was worried before, and she had been, but not for the reason he'd assumed. Looking back, it hadn't dawned on her that Knox might be fighting for the rights to her blood, although it should have.

She'd only feared losing Mace.

Another knock to her mental balance. It tipped wildly.

When neither one of them spoke for several moments, Mace found a pair of sweats to wear and relaxed against the left side of the mattress with his eyes closed and his arms folded behind his head. Cora ran her gaze over his thickly corded arms, sculpted chest, and six-pack abs. A thin line of hair just below his belly button trailed down past his waistband, directing her eyes even lower.

She swallowed.

Vampire or not, the man was beautiful.

When the urge to touch him assailed her, she blamed it on the bond.

Mace peeked an eye open.

She flushed and dipped her head back down to the book.

"Something I can help you with, Coraline?"

Without looking up, she replied curtly, "No, there isn't, Mason."

He let out a low chuckle. Stubbornly, she endeavored not to look his way again.

Reclaiming her cognitive functions, she abandoned her study of ghosts and flipped to the section on vamps. The first chapter was aptly named Vampires: A Quick Overview.

Vampires, otherwise known as creatures of the night, creatures of darkness, or the derogatory: leaches, bloodsuckers, and fangers, were once thought to be living corpses. The undead, brought back to life to prey on the living. As superstitions fell by the wayside, so did the archaic mythologies behind vampires.

Although their origins are still speculated about, it is widely believed that vampires evolved in the same manner as humans and witches alike. Originally thought to be cold-blooded, their blood runs red and as warm as any mammal. This opinion, however, has only been popularized in the last century, and is still disputed by many older officials in the witch and human communities.

Another myth that is still heatedly disputed is that vampires cannot tolerate the sun. Although vampires in daytime are commonplace now, it was not the case several years ago, before their rev-

elation to the human race. One could say that's because they were in hiding, but others have put forth the theory that the scientists of the vampire nation have discovered a way to nullify the sun's harmful rays.

Cora looked up at Mason. His eyes were closed again, but she didn't think he was asleep. She could attest that he felt warm to the touch and walked in the sun, but she too had heard the old myths: vampires burning in the sun, hunters seeking them in daylight. She recalled her parents debating such things once.

"Mason?"

"Mm?"

"How old are you?"

His face scrunched in confusion, but he kept his eyes closed. "Why do you ask?"

"I was just wondering if there was any truth to the old vampire myths."

He gave a conspiratorial grin. "Is that book filling your mind with questions?"

She didn't answer, and neither did he. She went back to reading.

Throughout history, witches and vampires have had a tumultuous relationship and generally do not associate. However, some exceptions bear mentioning. In the early 16th century, large clan of vampires and several covens of witches attempted to cohabitate Europe after both had simultaneously claimed the territory and refused to leave.

During this tense peace, the vampire/witch bond was discovered, which will be covered in more detail in later chapters.

Cora's heart spiked. She tried to slow it, but Mace took note.

"Something interesting?"

"Just reading about witches. It's fascinating," she replied, adding a bit of truth to the fib.

He chuckled. "Soon enough you'll be casting spells on me, I bet."

"Why did you pick this particular book?"

He cracked his eyes open. "I didn't. The shop owner did. Why?"

"Just curious if you had read it."

"Nah," he said, closing his lids once more. "Never made it a habit to study up on witches."

Cora read on.

This discovery is thought to have been a catalyst behind the Wiccan Wars. Several witches, in a pursuit of power, bound themselves to multiple vampires, essentially creating personal armies. Fearing the opposition, a race was sparked between rival covens to acquire more and more vampires. History books suggest the numbers eventually grew out of control, and as war broke out between covens, vampires rebelled. It was a brutal time.

As the war died down, vampires faded back into the darkness, and were thought to have left Europe for more secluded parts of the world.

The book went on to document other milestones in vampire history, including their revelation. Cora skipped ahead till she came to what she was most interested in.

A vampire's bond, also referred to as a blood bond or dark bond, is created when a vampire exchanges blood with another individual. Although there have been no scientific studies on the effect of a vampire's bond on witches, the Wiccan Wars, and other isolated events throughout history, urges any witch considering such a course to err on the side of caution. Through many accounts by those who have experienced the bond first hand, it's strongly believed there to be a transfer of essence during the exchange of blood, the effects (listed below) have been documented to last for several—and in some cases, hundreds of—years.

Cora gasped.

Mace sat up, fully alert. "What is it?" He glanced around the room till his gaze landed on the book that was now flattened to her chest.

"Nothing," she insisted with an intentionally muted tone. "I just—" She thought quickly. "—thought I saw a shadow. Guess I'm still a little spooked from before."

Mace quirked a dubious brow, and she wondered if he'd heard the false note. "The offer still stands. We can leave here any time—"

"No. It's fine. Please go back to sleep. I won't be startled again."

She had to control her reactions!

After a skeptical moment, Mace returned to lying in the bed, but didn't seem as relaxed as he had been before.

Dying to read on, she lowered the book back to her lap.

The most common effects of the bond include (but are not in-

clusive) clairvoyance between the affected individuals, a feeling of closeness or understanding, and a strong sense of loyalty.

Some less common cases reported telepathy, while others claimed to have gained physical strength and longevity from their counterparts. Aside from those benefits, there are perhaps more that have not yet been documented.

The drawbacks of bonding with one or more vampires: Our history suggests binding with more than one vampire at a time can tempt even the strongest mind down a power-hungry path that more often than not ends in destruction and sorrow. For this reason, binding with more than three vampires at a time it is prohibited by most coven authorities today.

Another drawback to binding a vampire is the constant need for a vampire to feed. Once a bond is sparked, the vampire(s) must take nourishment only from their bonded partner. No other can quench his/her hunger—

Cora shot to her feet. The book slid off her lap, flopping to the ground.

Mace leapt up as well. "Damn it, Cora! That's it, we're leaving."

He reached for her, but she jerked away.

He pulled back. "What's wrong?"

"You...You *have* to feed from me?"

For an unguarded moment, Mace was shocked. "What?" Then his eyes darted to the book in accusation. "What did you read?"

"It said you have to feed from me. No one else can satisfy your hunger now that we're bonded." Betrayal stained each word. "Is it true?"

He didn't speak for several seconds, which was answer enough. "Cora..."

"When were you going to inform me of this little stipulation? When your fangs were in my neck?" Her hand went to her collarbone as if protectively.

"No. It's not like that. I won't feed from you."

"You deliberately kept this from me. How can I trust anything you say?" Even as she said it, the bond had her *wanting* to trust him, infuriating her further. "You forced me into this against my will. You stole my essence!"

"What? What does that mean?"

Ignoring him, she continued. "You're making me want to trust you when I know that I can't possibly."

"You *can* trust me—"

"What else are you keeping from me? Why am I really here? What are your plans for me?" She paused as suspicions turned cancerous. "Is Knox in on this?"

"Now you're being ridiculous."

"Do you both plan to bond me and feed from me? To keep me forever, against my will?"

Mason's expression turned dark, dangerous, and he crossed the distance between them, looming over her. It took all her courage to stand her ground. Still, her throat closed up with trepidation.

"I've let you insult me enough for one night. To hear you speak, I am a depraved kidnapper with heinous intentions toward you. Have I abused you? Harmed you in any way? Left you to die when my blood could heal you?"

Cora flinched.

"No. I used it to save you. I've risked my life to spirit you to safety." His lip curled. "And you accuse me thusly? Merely because I kept something from you that I knew would cause you anxiety? I've fed several times since we've been bonded, by the way. Sure it has left me unsatisfied, but I can tolerate it till our bond fades. I'll survive. And without taking another drop from you, if that is your wish."

He turned away and ran his hands through this hair before continuing. "What I can't tolerate is your continued disdain."

She dropped her hand, regretting her outburst. He was right. He'd been the very antithesis of her every expectation. An apology was on the tip of her tongue when he faced her again.

Grey eyes flashed with a dark warning, and he added in a menacing tone, "Don't ever suggest that I would share you again."

Chapter 16

Cora lay awake next to Mace on the bed. He had his back to her, and though he was sleeping now, it still felt like he was giving her the cold shoulder.

How was it he had managed to make *her* feel guilty? *He* was the one who had lied through omission. Though his reason for doing so was somewhat touching.

Still, he had bonded her against her will!

However, if she were being honest, she didn't believe he intended to do that.

On the flip side, he *had* taken her blood without permission. He'd certainly intended to do that.

And yet, to be fair, she'd been begging for more than his fangs at the time...and he'd resisted. Had acted *mostly* honorable.

She recalled the less-than-honorable part, and her mind brought forth tempting images of sweaty bodies merging as one, moans in the night, Mason's talented tongue caressing her skin.

A delirious and deeply primitive hunger roused in her core,

raising the temperature of her body.

Her heart jerked just as Mason's body did.

He lifted his head off the pillow with a drowsy, "Cora?"

She couldn't form a response aside from the rapid increase of her pulse. Embarrassment surged. There was no doubt in her mind that through the darkness, he could tell her body was drowning in desire.

After a moment of intense silence from both of them, he put his head back down, muttering, "You'll drive me insane before long, woman. You know I would tend you if you asked it of me."

"I don't need tending," she whispered back.

"I've never met anyone who needed tending more."

She swallowed, mentally denying it.

After another bout of silence, he added so low she wasn't sure she'd heard correctly, "Or anyone more lovely."

About the time she regained control of her body, Mace had slipped back into slumber, his breath coming in light snores. She had no hopes of finding that peaceful, unconscious place, and the information still left in the book called to her. Giving in, she rose and snatched the book from where she'd left it on the floor.

Not wanting to disturb Mace further, she decided to take herself downstairs. Before she slipped into the hall, she caught the glimmer of the necklace he'd purchased for her on the desk. She slipped it on, enjoying the weight of it around her neck.

The living room was empty, thank the goddess. Knox must be in his own room, hopefully sleeping as well, although she didn't expect either Knox or Mace to remain in bed much longer. The sky was already bleeding from black into navy. Soon enough it would be cobalt and then baby blue.

She plopped onto the couch and cracked open the book. Emotionally preparing for what she might discover next, she started where she'd left off.

Once a bond is sparked, the vampire(s) must take nourishment only from their bonded partner. No other can quell his/her hunger. Bonded vampires that do not take nourishment from his/her bonded partner will noticeably weaken over time. It has been described as the equivalent of malnourishment in humans. A vampire can survive by feeding from alternative sources, but would experience the constant sensation of starvation. Witches who take on multiple bonds must be conscious of this phenomenon and consider creating a clear feeding schedule.

Managing multiple bonds: When taking on more than one—

Cora skipped past that section. "Not happening," she mumbled.

She dropped her head back against the sofa. Mace would starve if he didn't feed from her. He'd certainly attempted to feed from others already. Said he could manage. But he'd also said he hadn't been satisfied. Did that mean he was suffering? Was he starving even now? Would he prefer to feed from her? Of course he would. What had he said after taking her blood that first night? She was like heaven on his tongue?

She shivered.

He'd commented about already being addicted.

It was surely the bond causing a tiny smile to play along her lips. She mentally shook herself. Could she consent to feeding Mace and still keep her head? Did she even want to keep her head?

Oh, this was so confusing!

Frustrated, she scanned the next few pages till something stole her interest and killed her wayward thoughts.

With all the drawbacks of bonding a vampire, why, then, do some witches stand by the practice? Even taking on more than the conventionally accepted amount? In an interview, I posed this very question to a witch who, naturally, preferred to remain anonymous. Her response was enlightening.

"Better than a bodyguard," she'd said smugly.

She claimed the loyalty of a bonded vampire was equal to none, and that her brood, as she called them, would do anything she asked, even sacrifice themselves. She wouldn't admit to how many vampires she'd bonded and merely smiled when asked if it was over three.

Other witches, who have been asked similar questions, also boasted about the unwavering devotion they'd received while bonded to a vampire. It is not clear whether this devotion goes both ways.

Cora frowned.

Is that why Mace had commented more than once about their bond fading. Was he eager for it? Did he feel trapped...*by her*?

Revulsion twisted her gut. She couldn't imagine using him, or anyone, like that. Yet, hadn't he already risked his life for hers? Nausea threatened. Did this blood bond take his will and make it hers?

Voices filtering in from the porch brought her out of her

head. The front door opened, allowing in dawn's light.

"You're up early," Knox said, actually offering her a smile as he knocked mud off his boots before entering.

Cora set the book aside and stood, debating whether it would be more prudent to be amicable or to escape upstairs. Before she could decide, another figure stepped past the threshold, a shorter light-haired male.

Knox eyed the book she'd been reading. His brow rose ever so slightly. "I found Mr. Tucker here wandering the woods, trying to find the cottage. Apparently, he's here to test your blood?"

"Oh, yes," Cora said, relieved. She added for Mr. Tucker's benefit, "Hopefully there had been a mistake with the first test."

Mr. Tucker returned her smile with a small facsimile, his eyes darting back at Knox. He appeared a little intimidated by Knox's larger stature. He must be human. The poor guy probably hadn't anticipated being approached by a strange vamp in the woods first thing in the morning. She could relate.

She smiled at the man, feeling an instant sense of camaraderie, and then crossed the room to offer her hand as if it were her duty to put him at ease. "I'm Cora. It's nice to meet you."

He reached out and gripped her hand too tightly. His other hand disappeared behind the lining of his coat.

After everything she'd been through over the last few days, she really should have seen it coming. Yet, even after the gun she spied in Mr. Tucker's possession fired, even after Knox's foul curse and then witnessing him snap her attacker's neck, she was flabbergasted. It happened so fast, she hadn't even registered the pain in her chest.

"Motherfucker," she cursed.

Blood gurgled from her lungs. She toppled backwards to the floor, gripping her wound. As she stared at the ceiling, a hot tear trickled down to her temple and dripped onto her ear.

Knox appeared over her, looking appalled. He was speaking, but she couldn't hear a word.

He bit his wrist open and shoved the seeping wound to her mouth. His blood mingled with hers, finding its way down her throat.

* * *

Mace woke to the sound of a gunshot. The increasingly recognizable sensation of Cora's horror blasted through him. He hurled himself out of bed, and was down the stairs in an instant.

His jaw dropped at the scene. An unfamiliar man lay lifeless by the open doorway. A few feet away from that, Knox was hunched over a bloodied Cora!

Fury blanked his mind and he lunged for Knox, barreling him to the ground. Between the double-fisted, bone-jarring punches Mace mindlessly dealt out, Knox tried to speak.

Mace was too far past savage to listen. Knox had been touching Cora! Feeding her his blood! What else had he done to her?

It was only because Knox refused to put up much of a fight that a bit of reason filtered in, and he finally heard Knox shout through a newly broken jaw, "It was the human!"

Mace glanced up at the body by the door, a small human male with a gun lying next to his limp hand. Taking advantage of Mason's distraction, Knox rushed out an explanation. "He said he was here to test Cora's blood. Said Trent sent him, and you were expecting him." He added quickly, "I had to feed her my blood or she'd have died."

The sound of Cora's slow heartbeat eclipsed all else. She was pale, almost white. Blood seeped from her mouth. Had Knox given her enough? Mace hurried to her side, opened his vein for her, and pressed his wrist to her lips. As he lifted her torso, her eyes rolled back in her head.

"Cora, love, drink."

He cursed violently when he looked down at the large red stain coating the front of her shirt. He ripped open the fabric enough to keep her covered but reveal the gaping wound in her chest. A ravenous terror ate at his insides like acid on steroids. He could lose her yet.

"Coraline, baby, drink," he pleaded, disregarding the dampness on his cheek. "Come back. I'm sorry I got in your face last night. You can accuse me of anything you want. Hate me. Just don't die on me."

"Man, I'm sorry," Knox said, sounding sincere.

"I'll kill you if she dies," Mace hissed back.

"I know." Knox replied, watching with a kind of morbid fascination.

Through gritted teeth, Mace demanded, "Tell me she got some of your blood down."

"I think she did before she passed out."

For now, Mace was relieved by that. Later, he would deal with the confounding resentment that threatened to surge. More relief washed over him when Cora's wound began to knit itself closed. Her breathing became less labored. Her throat started to work as she swallowed his blood.

"That's it, love."

Her eyelids opened, and she looked up at him blearily. He expected her to grow angry, disgusted, maybe slap his hand away once she gained enough strength. Instead, she manacled her hand around his wrist, her grip like a vice as she pulled deeply from his vein, swallowed, then did it again.

"Careful," he cooed. "You remember what happened last time."

Her chest wound now looked more like a small gash. She was healing faster than expected. The residual dark cells in her system must be speeding the process. Uncaring, she drew from his vein again, and then again. Her pulls were starting to have a strange effect on him, a carnal effect, as if she were sucking him off rather than taking sustenance from him. It was both disturbing and erotic. He gently tugged his arm away, extracting it from her eager grip.

She appeared unhappy by that, but was still too weak to protest.

He scooped her up in his arms and carried her back to their room, calling to Knox, "No one else comes near this place."

Mace didn't wait for Knox to affirm the order.

* * *

The pain in Cora's chest began to ease. She realized she'd been transferred to the bed, but couldn't recall how she'd gotten there. Her fuzzy mind told her she'd nearly died yet again. Mace must be pissed. She tried to force her eyes open, but they felt like a million pounds each.

Mace's voice came as if from far away, offering soft words,

lulling her, assuring her. She was safe now, he said. He would take care of her. This absolute truth echoed through to her bones. He would always take care of her. He was the kindest, most generous vampire—no, person—she had ever known. He deserved to be taken care of with equal ardor. How could she deny him what he needed to survive? Merely out of fear? Life was too short for fear any longer.

Especially for her.

She knew that single grain of sand was teetering on the edge. It might have been thwarted this time, but eventually it would find its way down the hourglass. Like her, its final demise had been stayed off another day.

Her most recent brush with death had managed to kill something, however.

Her unnecessary mistrust of Mason.

Finally, she cracked her eyes open. Mace hovered over her.

"Hi," he said in a low voice.

"Hi," she replied a little shaky.

His lips spread into a small grin, but his eyes continued to show a deep chasm of worry. He wiped her forehead with a cool damp cloth. Her heart warmed at his tenderness, healing it in a way that had nothing to do with the bullet that had nearly carved a thoroughfare in her chest.

She felt no embarrassment when he ripped her shirt a little more and cleaned around her wound. In fact, she didn't want him to stop. Her skin was growing hot, like electricity surged through her. She recalled this feeling from when she'd first taken Mason's blood. At that time, she'd been appalled at her staggering desire. Now she embraced it.

Seemingly satisfied with his work, Mace set the damp cloth

aside, stood, and snatched his phone from off the bedside table. He scrolled through the screen and then lifted it to his ear. A moment later he yelled, "You fucker! How dare you send an assassin after Cora! You're fucking dead to me. And if I ever see you again, you'll be dead for real!"

Assassin? Who was he speaking to? Her curiosity was snuffed out by a maddening surge of desire that rolled through her like a bathtub of sloshing water. Her shirt felt confining, sticking to her uncomfortably. She pulled at the fabric, ridding herself of it and tossing it to the floor. Cool air washed over her heated skin.

Mace continued speaking into the phone with his back to her. "You might be my maker, but you just shit on any trust we once had. I'm not kidding. You and I are done from this point on. And by the way, the shithead you sent is dead, and Cora still lives, so fuck you."

Mace paused as if the person on the other end were talking. To Cora, those few seconds were like an eternity of sexual torture. Why had he stopped touching her? Her body burned with an agonizing need, worse than the first night Mace had healed her. In the back of her mind, she suspected the cause to be the mixture of blood from two vampires, but at the moment, she didn't care about anything but her body's salacious demands.

Couldn't he feel her pain?

Chapter 17

Using the same low, dangerous timbre he'd been using throughout the conversation, Trent ordered, "Mason, you need to relax."

"Relax? Relax!" Mace grew more outraged with every syllable. "I suspected you, but...fuck...I never wanted to believe you'd betray me like..." He froze as the sweet scent of Cora's arousal saturated the room.

He turned to see her in the middle of the mattress, perched on her knees, fully healed, and topless. Her eyes flashed with undisguised lust.

It was the sexiest fucking image he could ever imagine.

Trent continued speaking on the other end of the line, but Mace was no longer listening.

"Gotta go," he muttered absently before hanging up and tossing the phone aside. "Uh, Cora, are you alright?"

Her tongue darted out to lick her lips as she raked a hungry gaze over his body. "I need you."

Dammit all! She'd taken too much.

He raised his palms in a halting gesture, knowing it was going to take all his willpower to enforce a bit of restraint for her own good. She would despise him even more than she already did if he allowed her to succumb to unwanted lust yet again, even if it was his greatest fantasy to have her looking at him the way she was now.

"Cora, just lie down. It's going to take some time, but you'll be back to normal in a few hours."

Even as he said it, his mouth watered at the thought of sating her as he had the last time. But even that compromise had angered her before.

With the eyes of a feline targeting prey, she crawled toward him till she came to the edge of the bed. Mace swallowed hard and then gritted his teeth, mentally reinforcing his resolve.

"I won't take advantage of you like this. You'd hate me forever if I did."

As she lowered one foot over the edge of the mattress, then the other, Mace crossed his arms and leaned back against the reading desk, shaking his head. He didn't even trust himself to touch her right now, even to stay her.

Already he was stiff as a rod.

"I won't hate you," she purred, coming closer. Her soft hands ran over his folded arms, his shoulders, tempting him to reach for her.

He made himself like stone, freezing in place.

"Please, Mace. I feel like I'll die if you don't touch me."

"You'll kill me if I do," he ground out.

"I won't. Please."

"Sorry, love, you can beg all you want. It's not going to ha—
"

Cora reached past the waistband of his pants, surprising him with her grip. He hissed in a breath.

Her features turned sly with a sexy grin. "You're hard for me."

He should have known then that he wasn't going to win this one. "I'm always hard for you," he replied, his voice going rough. "But I'm still not going to—What are you doing?"

She tugged the drawstring of his pants loose and freed his shaft as she stroked him. Then, going to her knees, she sucked him deep into her slick mouth.

Mace cursed, his body jerking with exquisite pleasure. "You wicked woman."

As if on a mission, she licked her way to the tip and then sucked him down again. His head fell back on a groan. He gripped the edge of the desk, telling himself he should stop her. She would want him to stop her. He really should—

She swirled her tongue around the head of his cock and gave a small moan. Unable to miss a minute of this, he inclined his head to watch her. She gazed at him with the most exquisite teasing glint in her eyes.

"God, Cora, you're going to make me come from that look alone."

She appeared pleased by that, eager for it. Of course she was. She was out of her mind with lust. And *I am such a shit.*

Her mouth on him was like a blissful assault that he couldn't bring himself to fight off. Didn't want to. Guilt agonized him, but not enough to do what was right.

His muscles tensed as her hot tongue laved him mercilessly. His hips pumped forward and she drew him in once more, taking him deeper. He shuddered, threading his fingers through her hair to help set a rhythm and cursing himself while he drowned in selfish, hedonistic pleasure.

How many nights had he dreamed of her like this? Except in his dreams she was lucid. Dammit, he wanted her lucid!

He mourned for her; for his depraved selfishness.

Because there was no stopping this.

And if he was going to ruin all the progress he'd made with her over a single licentious act, the least he could do was offer himself to her fully, to reveal the truth of his feelings. To rip himself open by the heart and let her see it all, and to provide her with a fervent, impassioned night to remember him by years after she'd left him.

He lifted her by the arms to stand. "I want it noted that I attempted to resist, but you are irresistible." He scooped her legs out from under her and tossed her back onto the mattress. She gave a delighted laugh. He drank it in and committed the sound to memory, because it would be the last delighted sound he would hear from her. There'd be no sweet smiles for him later.

His heart broke a little.

And still he couldn't stop himself.

As he joined her, she urgently tugged his pants down his hips, and he kicked them to the floor. Hers were gone just as swiftly. His mouth took hers, finding it eager for whatever he had to offer. His tongue swirled with hers recklessly. Their teeth gnashed together from sheer enthusiasm.

With his palm, he luxuriated over her pert breasts, squeezing and fondling them softly. When he managed to pull his lips from hers, he transferred them to one taut peak, caressing it with his tongue. Her back arched as her breath came on a sharp mew. His right hand traveled down her side and over her hip to grip her backside. A dark part of him wanted to squeeze her there so tightly that he would leave a mark—something to announce his sordid claim on her—but he only kneaded her, stamping the merciless shape of her womanly curves into his brain. Memories would be all he'd have left of her.

He shook with the effort of taking this slow, when all he wanted was to shove into her and ride her till they both collapsed from excess.

His fingers painted a path around her hip, and he dipped into her warmth. A carnal growl escaped him.

She gasped on contact, nearly whimpering as though tormented, and undulated her hips. "Yes, Mason."

While he teased her there, his tongue returned to her breast with relish.

"I need more, Mace. Please."

"Tell me what you need, baby."

"You," she groaned as he penetrated her with his thick finger. Her head lulled, and her hips lifted off the bed.

"You need this?" he said in a dark, teasing voice.

"More." To emphasize her point, she dug her nails into this back. Or maybe that was from the second finger sliding into her silky sheath. He wanted her to drag those nails down his skin till she drew blood, both for punishment, which he wholeheartedly deserved, but also so that he could walk away from this with *her* mark on him.

Disappointment was all he received. Her hand returned to the mattress to grip the sheets. She was close to coming already.

He removed his fingers, ignoring her groaned protest. He would not accept disappointment, not from their one and only time together. He would take with him every kiss, every touch, every pilfered taste. Positioning himself between her legs, he dipped his head and took her clitoris between his lips, drowning in her sweet flavor. They both shuddered with bliss as his tongue ravaged her. Her hips writhed for him, silently begging for all he had to offer.

Through halting breaths, she moaned, "Don't tease me, Mace. I need more than that this time."

"Patience, love. You'll get everything you want. Right now, I'm taking what I want."

She gazed down at him, her expression unsure. "Are you going to bite me again?"

He paused, surprised by the question. After a moment of hesitation, he replied, "No," then returned to his task.

Soon enough she was writhing again, gifting him with the sweetest feminine sounds. Those sounds turned urgent, nearly brutal in their intensity.

When she came, she came hard, her head thrashing. All the while, he deliriously laved her tender folds, only stopping after she went completely limp.

He crawled over her and gently kissed the place where her wound had been. She sighed, and his eyes trained on her breasts as they rose and fell from her deliciously rapid heartbeat. He tried to hide his elongating fangs, but she noticed all the same.

She didn't flinch as he expected, didn't look horrified as she had when she'd woken up next to him that morning at Cortez's. No, her eyes were smoldering, zealous, voracious—yet another indication that she was out of her mind with lust.

He felt insidious for wanting his fangs deep in her flesh, for imagining the taste of her delectable blood, but he restrained himself, relying on guilt to temper his desire. He was already taking so much from her. Once more, he brushed the guilt aside, leaving it to eat at him later. He would dedicate centuries to it.

He gazed down at her, taking in the beauty of her under him, ready for his taking. Another mental snapshot to torment him later.

She fussed impatiently, squirming uncomfortably. Her pained expression demanded his immediate compliance. His shaft found her entrance, and he pressed his hips forward. As she took him to the hilt, she threw her head back on a gasp and clawed his back. Mace growled at the glorious pain of her nails. His fangs throbbed, but he would not soil this moment further by taking her blood.

He began a steady rhythm, dazed by the rapturous feel of her warmth convulsing around him. His pace increased, and as she took pleasure from him, he admired her beauty with a reverence that bordered on worship.

As their bodies collided ruthlessly, he found himself admitting, "I love you, Cora. I will love you even when you're hating me for this."

Her eyes snapped to his, going wide. Her mouth opened, then closed, as if she wasn't sure how to respond. Mace didn't need her to. Her expression softened. "I won't hate you," she assured through heavy breaths. "I could never hate you. Not anymore."

"You will. And I won't fault you for it."

She shook her head. "You're wrong."

He allowed the beautiful lie to surround him like the most gorgeous symphony. "Then tell me you're mine," he growled, giving a hard thrust of his hips.

She complied without hesitation. "I'm yours."

He gripped her nape in his fist and increased his pace. "There will be no one else for you but me." His thrusts became frantic to accentuate his words.

"No one," she moaned, arching into his frenzied onslaught.

He knew he couldn't hold her to it, a promise born of coercion and blood-drunk lust, but he reveled in her hasty response anyway.

Their bodies settled in a carnal dance, skin slapping against skin with brutal fervor, breaths mingling, ecstasy burgeoning. She clung to him so sweetly, her legs tightening around his thighs as he sensed her on the verge. Crying his name, she gouged her nails into his back again, urging him on. White-hot pleasure bounced between them, licking its way over every inch of skin.

A rumbling sound ripped free of his throat as his release dulled his mind and tensed his body. Cora cried out once more, joining him in a place where ecstasy ruled.

When it was over, all that remained was their exhausted bodies, clasped by tangled limbs. After a moment, he rolled onto his back, pulling Cora over him. Her arm came around his torso, and her fingers hooked his opposite shoulder blade. To his utter surprise, before she fell into adorable slumber, she kissed his chest.

His heart broke into thousands of jagged shards. He wondered how long it would take for those harsh edges to dull enough to stop cutting.

Chapter 18

Cora stretched with satisfaction, all the tormenting voracious needs of her body sated by a thorough, mind-shattering, deliciously brutal taking. She let out a soft sigh, reaching for Mace. She went still when she found herself alone on the mattress. The covers had been tucked around her.

Across the room, a fully clothed Mace occupied the arm chair in the corner watching her. She got the impression he'd been watching her for some time.

Aspects from recent memory had her lips curling into a lazy smile. That is, until she caught his expression, or lack thereof. His features were forbidding yet pained. If auras were a tangible thing, his would be darker than black.

She frowned, then pushed upright, holding the blanket to her chest. She tilted her head at him quizzically. For a set of agonizing moments, neither of them spoke. She took the opportunity to play over the events that inspired this awkward morning...or was it afternoon now? The light flooding through the window suggested it might be.

She tried to recall if she had done something to displease him. Her cheeks burned at the memory of all she had transpired between them. She'd been so persistent.

Mace took note of her reaction with a raised brow, but said nothing. He was pensive now, his eyes tight. Almost with a kind of sadness she couldn't understand.

Unsure what was wrong and completely self-conscious, she broke the silence with a sincere yet whispered apology for whatever she might have done wrong. What else could she say to a greeting like this?

He shot to his feet, expression murderous. "You're apologizing to *me*?"

She shrank back, eyes going wide. "Why are you angry?"

Dumfounded, he repeated her statement, as though he couldn't believe the words coming out of her mouth. "Why aren't *you* angry?"

She shook her head, not understanding.

He waited, as though she was expected to say something more.

Growing increasingly uncomfortable with her nakedness, she slid off the bed and crossed to the closet, taking the thick bedspread with her. In her haste, she hadn't secured the bedspread properly, and a stream of air whispered along her back.

He hissed in a breath and turned away. That made her even more self-conscious. Did he find her unappealing all of a sudden? It hadn't seemed that way when he was declaring his love.

Goddess! Had he actually done that? Why would he say something so substantial, so...irrevocable, if he didn't mean it? Like her, had he been affected by the bond in combination with the heat of the moment? Shoving that to the back of her mind for later examination, she retrieved a white button-down shirt from off a hanger and put it on, dropping the covers as she did so. Then she faced the room again. Mace still had his back to her.

Her frown deepened. "Did I do something wrong?"

He whirled around and threw his hands in the air, once more mirroring her words. "What do you mean did *you* do something wrong?" Then every inch of him froze, all but his eyes which ran the length of her body, pausing on her legs. For a second, that hunger she'd seen earlier returned, gone a moment later. He cleared his throat, shook his head, and then, as if at a loss, he gestured wildly. "You should be railing at me! Spitting curses! Throwing things at my head, or something. Why isn't that happening right now? Are you still confused, still altered by the excess blood?"

She considered that question seriously for a moment. She supposed if this had happened on day one, she would have felt the way he was suggesting. Not now, after everything they had been through. Had they really only been together a few days?

"I'm not upset by what happened between us," she assured, hoping that was enough to appease him.

It wasn't.

"I don't believe you. You can't possibly be okay with what I...with what happened." His eyes darted to the necklace that rested in the V of her shirt. She hadn't bothered removing it. "Are you bespelled?"

"What? No," she replied defensively, then thought better of it. "I...At least I don't think so." She toyed with the chain.

"Don't take it off," he cautioned.

She paused at the clasp. "Why not?"

"Just trust me. We don't know what will happen." Then he swore, muttering something about how he should have known better. When he looked at her again, his features became speculative. "You're not outraged at all? Not even a little?"

After allowing for a moment of introspection, she shook her head. Unfortunately, she wasn't exactly able to describe what she was feeling. A mass of confusion bubbled in her head. Worse, she wasn't sure how to act around Mace now. Before, she had been careful, submissive, so as not to provoke his vampire nature in any way, just as she had learned to do with Edgar. Now? Well, things were different now, weren't they? She'd already determined she could trust Mace. He'd admitted to caring about her, although, she didn't believe what he felt was love; he craved her blood because of the bond, and possibly her body too. And right now, he didn't seem happy about it at all.

"We're going to visit that witch," he announced.

Her head jerked up in surprise. "What witch?"

He gestured to the cluster of items he'd given her. "The one who sold me all that stuff. She'll free us of these hexes, and then she can explain why I should let her live."

Cora shivered at his dark tone.

* * *

The dense forest of trees passed by as Cora absently gazed at the scenery, her arm resting on the ledge of the passenger seat window. Thankfully, the evening was warm. She had kept the white button-down on, adding to it her loose sweats, but the material of both were thin. She'd tied her hair up to keep the rushing wind through the busted window from played havoc with it.

She shifted in the seat and noticed a tiny lump pressing against her thigh. She scooped out the piece of glass and tossed it out the window. Mace maneuvered around a natural pot hole in the dirt road, only to hit a smaller one, rocking the car. More glass from the back window cascaded along the trunk with the clatter of a hundred high pitched *tinks*. Some of it tumbled into the back seat.

Cora couldn't help but laugh at the destruction. Mace lifted a brow at her as though she'd gone crazy. He wasn't used to hearing her laugh, she supposed. She wasn't used to it much either.

"What's funny?" he asked.

"I can only imagine what Cortez will think of his car."

One corner of his mouth curled up. "I don't give two shits about Cortez right now."

"Me either." She laughed again.

Maybe she was going nuts. She felt more relaxed now than she had in months, and she couldn't ferret out why. Mace was clearly worried by her suddenly buoyant demeanor. She didn't want him to be, but there wasn't much she could do, besides force a somber mood. She frowned, but her ploy backfired and she laughed harder than before.

Mace pressed the gas, picking up speed. "Your emotions seem erratic. At the cottage you seemed nervous or anxious. Now you're...I want to say happy? Tell me what's going on inside that head of yours."

She leaned her head back against the seat. "I don't know. I've been trying to figure it out myself." She paused, saddened that she was actually growing serious. "I've been so worried for so long, constantly on edge, even before this mess with the blood, before you." She glanced his way, then back out the window. "And now I've nearly died, what, twice? Three times? Four? I'm losing count."

That brought her laughter back, making Mace even more concerned...she could *feel* it from him.

She sobered, for his sake. "There's got to be a breaking point, don't you think?"

"Oh, god. I broke you?"

"No, not you. It's not your fault. I'm just...I wish I could explain this better," she muttered, then added more loudly, "My life is totally out of my control. It has been for longer than I can remember. So earlier I got to thinking, and it hit me: I'm going to have to stop fighting myself and letting my fear and preconceptions get the better of me and just go with the flow already." She shrugged. "Once I decided that, it felt like a mountain of tension lifted off of me."

"Preconceptions?"

"Yeah. About you, mostly. Vampires in general, I guess."

"And when did you come to this epiphany?"

"This morning."

"By chance is that when you put that necklace on?"

She took the stone pendent between her fingers. "Actually, a little afterward."

Mace grumbled out a sound as if that confirmed his suspicions.

Cora went back to watching the scenery. She didn't feel like she was under a spell. But then, maybe that was the point.

Chapter 19

"What do you mean, she's gone away?" Mace was livid to have found an arrogantly snotty teen in place of that wretched ancient hag.

"Are you deaf?" The dark-haired girl behind the counter cocked her head, narrowing her blue eyes into slits. With thick black makeup smudged around the edges, they all but disappeared against her pale skin. "She's—gone—away."

He perched his knuckles on the counter. "Well, where'd she go?"

The girl pointed a whimsical finger at the side of her head. "Do you see information booth stamped on my forehead?"

He leaned forward with contempt, his patience gone in an instant. Cora seemed to notice the dangerous shift and placed a hand on his bicep. Her touch was like a balm.

Wisely, she took over addressing the child. "When will Ms., uh, what did you say her name was?"

"Windshaw," the girl replied, crossing her fishnet covered arms over a shirt decorated by black and red skulls.

"Right, when is Ms. Windshaw expected to return?"

The girl popped her gum. "Didn't say. Said she needed to go on business, is all, and she'd call."

Mace grumbled, "She knew I'd be coming for her ass is more like it."

The girl curled her lip at him. "Hey, what's your damage, bruiser?"

As his muscles flexed to teach this brat a lesson in humility, Cora gave a tender squeeze of her hand and then placed herself between him and the little witch.

"Okay," she said calmly. "Then is there anyone else here who knows about...magic?"

"Why are you whispering it like that? We're in a *magic* shop. And yeah, I do."

"You?" Mace scoffed.

The girl rolled her eyes. "What do you want to know?"

Cora answered, "Right, okay then. We'd like to know if there's a spell on this necklace." She lifted the pendant a few inches off her neck.

The girl reached out just as rudely as the old lady had the night before and pulled the necklace closer for examination, making Cora bend over the counter. A line of stainless steel skull rings decorated the girl's delicate hand, each with sparkling eyes of various colors.

What was with youth and their obsession with death? Especially when they all turn into a bunch of ninnies in the face of it.

"There's no spell on this," the girl announced, letting go of the necklace, and Cora along with it.

Mace snorted. "'Scuse me if I don't trust the proficiency of an inept baby witch."

The girl pinned him with a hard stare. "There's no spell on that thing, and any witch who tells you otherwise is looking to con you with an—" She made air quotes. "—anti-spell that'll do more damage than good."

"And I suppose there's been no spell placed on me, either," Mace challenged.

The girl scanned the space around him.

"No, there's a spell on you," she replied blithely, surprising both him and Cora. "Both of you actually. But it's not from that necklace."

"Wait, both of us?" Cora's voice had gone up an octave. "What kind of spell?"

"I'm not sure about him, but you're bound tighter than a nut-job in a straitjacket."

"Huh?"

She rolled her eyes. "Duh, your magic's been bound."

Cora and Mace shared a look.

"No way!" The girl said. "How could you not know? I would kill myself if that happened to me."

Cora placed her pointer and thumb over the bridge of her nose and mumbled to herself, "This is getting ridiculous." To the girl, she asked. "How do I...*un*bind it?"

"That's tricksy. Not all binding spells are created equal, and yours is a whopper. Do you know who cast it?"

Cora shook her head.

"That'll make it harder to figure out, but I can see now why you're wearing that necklace."

"Why's that?" Mace demanded, not liking any of this.

"Did you hear something?" the girl said obstinately, staring at Cora with faux curiosity. "Sounds like someone's talking, but I can't quite..." She cupped her palm around her ear.

Mace was contemplating the satisfaction of having his hand around the girl's neck, but Cora's amused smirk gave him pause. "You're actually enjoying this, aren't you?"

"Just a little," she replied, then muttered to him through the side of her mouth, "I think she's looking for an apology."

"Apology? For what? I'm the one who's been hexed by that old witch. And now I'm forced to endure this immature—"

The girl interrupted, sneering, "Whatever Ms. Windshaw did to you, your punk ass probably deserved it."

"You little wench!"

"Mason!" Cora scolded. She stepped away from him and crossed her arms tightly over her chest.

He glanced at the set of her stubborn jaw. "Oh, come on. Seriously? *That's* the line? That's what spurs you to be angry with me?"

She looked at him now as if he were the worst sort. The younger girl mimicked Cora's stance, except her expression was smug.

Mace gritted his teeth, wishing only to be out of here as quickly as possible. "I'm sorry." It wasn't as if they were getting anywhere, anyway.

"Sorry for what?" The girl asked sweetly.

"Don't push it."

She shrugged. "Fine. The crystal in that necklace is used for wisdom and clarity. It helps to see what is true while stifling thoughts that muddle the mind, like fear." The girl grew animated as she continued. "Which in turn can translate into anger, hate, self-loathing, or even prejudice. Aside from clearing the mind, this stone helps to let go of the old and anything that keeps you attached to old notions or ideals that no longer serve you." She started ticking off her fingers. "Helps with intuition, healing, balancing energy. It's a very powerful stone."

Cora's eyes darted to Mace. "Huh."

Mace wasn't sure what to think about all that. Could the stone be responsible for Cora's changed behavior? And if so... "How is that any different than a spell?"

The girl laughed. "It doesn't force anything upon the wearer that isn't natural. It only brings positive energy that encourages change."

The implication was too tempting for Mace to believe. For a brief moment in time, had Cora actually conquered her fear to see him as a man rather than a vampire? Is that why she hadn't fought the lust that drove her into his all-too-willing arms?

He chastised himself for his hopeful thoughts. Even if she had, his errant actions would no doubt reinforce the idea that he was not to be trusted, once she was free of this stone's influence. Then she'd be back to flinching from him and averting her gaze like a caged animal.

A part of him would rather she wear that stone forever. But that would be selfish, and he'd already demonstrated enough of that. "Can she remove the necklace without any adverse effects?"

"'Course. Why couldn't she?"

He pulled at his collar, revealing a line of the barest discoloration along his skin. Both the girl and Cora leaned in for a better look.

"What's that?" Cora asked as the girl shrugged, looking clueless.

"That old witch tricked me," he sneered. "This is the evidence of her deceitfulness."

Cora reached out and ran her fingers over the mark. He tensed at her casual touch, so unexpected.

She misunderstood and pulled her hand away. "Does it hurt?"

"No," he replied, letting his collar fall back into place.

Her attitude toward him had done a complete one-eighty. Was it truly the influence of magic or some silly stone? Or was it more? Once again, he rebuked the flourishing hope in favor of logic. It had to be witchcraft at work.

"That doesn't look like any spell I've ever seen."

"Well, then, if a ten year old has never seen it—"

"I'm seventeen, prick."

"So much better."

"Enough," Cora chided, wondering why Mace was being overtly aggressive. "You're both behaving childishly." She turned to the girl, her tone subdued. "Sorry, what is your name?"

The girl hesitated, her expression turning suspicious. "Saraphine."

"I'm Coraline, and this is Mason. I've just discovered I might be a..." Her lips morphed into a nervous grin and she flushed with embarrassment. "A witch, and I really have no idea what that means."

"So what do you want from me?"

"You might be young, but I'm sure you have more knowledge about all this than I ever will."

The flattery worked as intended. Saraphine's defensive

shoulders relaxed a touch. Youthful conceit carved its way into her features. "Probably."

Mace snorted behind Cora, but she ignored him, keeping her focus on Saraphine. "To be honest, I'm not sure I even believe in all this witch stuff."

"You really don't know anything, do you?" Saraphine replied. "Negativity like that harshes your magic. Not that it matters. You're bound so tightly I'm surprised your eyeballs aren't popping out."

"Can you help me to unbind it?"

Suspicion returned. "How do I know you haven't been bound for a reason? I get the sense that spell on you is seriously hard-core. Maybe your coven punished you for something heinous. You could be evil." She eyed Mace with a sneer. "You consort with vamps, after all."

Mace bared his fangs at her. Cora censured him with another look. After a stubborn hesitation, he concealed his fangs with a frown. Then his expression turned repentant. It was mystifying that she was able to corral him at all.

Cora faced Saraphine. "I don't belong to a coven. I've been on my own since I was ten. That's when I lost my family. I've never done anything more evil than steal some food when I was hungry."

"I've heard that sob story before," Saraphine replied, though her voice wavered with shaky conviction.

"So then you won't help me?"

"I didn't say that. But I *will* need to make sure you're not some psycho dark witch before I do."

Unease followed Saraphine's statement. "How?"

Saraphine smiled widely.

Chapter 20

"You can't seriously be considering drinking this." Mace glowered at the inky-liquid-filled chalice on the table, surrounded by five white candles.

Cora offered him an uncertain glance from where she sat on the medieval-looking bench, wringing her fingers.

Standing sentinel next to her, Mace had been working to bury a deep sense of foreboding ever since Saraphine had closed the store and escorted them to this eclectic back room where she'd begun brewing a mysterious concoction.

The room was rather spacious, the ceiling vaulted. The back wall housed a nook with a large wood fire pit. Over that, flames licked the underside of a bulbous black cauldron hanging by a metal bar that had been stabbed into either side of the grey brick alcove.

For the last two hours, he had watched Saraphine toss random ingredients into the boiling water. At first, all had seemed innocent: tea leaves, mandrake, honey. Then came the bones, dried tongue—hopefully from some kind of animal—and a white powdery substance before she had transferring a small amount to the metal chalice.

The final ingredient was a drop of Cora's own blood.

Mace gritted his teeth as she blithely pricked her own finger and offered her essence to the chalice. He was nearly fed up with this absurd indulgence, but at his every protest, Cora insisted she see this through.

"If I'm truly a witch, I should know for sure, shouldn't I?" she reasoned, licking clean the small wound on her finger.

Mace cleared his suddenly dry throat, struggling to erase from his expression all traces of desire to take that task from her. Hunger had been fiercely gnawing at him since this morning, as if he hadn't eaten in a week rather than a day.

"And I should have use of whatever *powers* comes with it," she continued, eyeing the chalice warily.

Saraphine took a seat on a tattered green armchair across from Cora. "This spell isn't to unbind your magic, mind you."

"Then what the hell is it for?" Mace bit out.

"It's so I can get at the truth of the situation, so I can determine whether I should help her or not."

For the umpteenth time, and without checking his tone, Mace argued the judgment of placing their trust in this baby witch, only to receive the same impatient, scathing glare from both of them.

"If she's a baby witch, then I'm a fetus, Mace," Cora said, rolling her eyes.

Allowing a small amount of his insecurity to seep into his voice, Mace admitted, "My instincts are screaming to protect you from this."

She exhaled on a lengthy sigh, focusing a blank stare on the chalice. "I know. Sensing things like that from you seems to be coming easier."

He claimed the seat next to her and slipped his hand into hers. "Then don't do this. You don't need magic. I'll protect you always."

Her features twisted as if pained, and his heart churned to retract whichever of his words had caused it.

Her shoulders hunched. "I know you mean that, Mason, and I don't want you to take this the wrong way, but in my experience, I can't rely on others. And magic, if it truly exists at all, could have saved me from some very painful situations."

At that, Mace relented. Cora was the definition of a survivor. She would use whatever means was at her disposal in the pursuit of self-preservation. He couldn't blame her for that. It was the nature of all things to try and better the odds of survival, genetically imprinted into every living molecule on Earth.

He couldn't ask her to handicap herself if there was even a small chance magic might benefit her in some way. And yet, he couldn't shake his apprehension.

Without a second glance, Cora clasped the chalice between both palms and brought it to her lips. A breath of hesitation sent a shiver over the surface of the dark liquid before she gulped it down.

Cora held back a disgusted heave, her esophagus fighting to keep the liquid down. Bile mixed with the rising fluid, burning. Scorching! She grabbed her throat, sucking fire-laced oxygen into her lungs. Her eyes watered, tears spilling in quick succession as she gasped, the inferno increasing.

"What have you done, witch?" Mace shot to his feet, lunging for Saraphine.

A ghost of his writhing fury burst through her, mingling with the agonizing heat that rose another degree, making it impossible for her to do anything but draw sharp, arduous breaths. With each one, the temperature notched higher till she thought acid was eating away her insides.

Looking monstrous, Mace had Saraphine around the neck, her feet off the ground. With a rasp, she whimpered as her legs thrashed wildly. Mace would kill her, Cora realized, as the fire in her spiked to an unbearable degree. It began to migrate from her throat to her chest, bombarding her heart and making each pulse pound acid into her veins. She fell from the couch, clutching her torso, her lungs failing.

There was a distant thud, then Mace hovered over her. Oh goddess, had he killed Saraphine? Should she care? Her mind rebelled against all thought, pain slicing through her brain to the forefront.

"Cora! Breathe!" Mace ordered, as if she hadn't been trying. She'd never seen him look so helpless.

Saraphine came into view behind Mace, her eyes wide. "You must relax," she said earnestly. "Stop fighting and let the spell take you. The pain will ease when you do."

Cora bared her teeth on a suffocated growl, her stomach revolting. Pain was all there could be, all the world was made of, and all it had to offer. Pain was life, and life was overrated. Perhaps it was time to die already, and allow that circling grain of sand to make its final descent.

A torrent of desperate worry rode the edges of her mind. It belonged to Mace and was possibly the purest emotion she had ever experienced. His concern broke her heart and managed to unravel a small piece of the barbed wire that had grown like a weed around it. When that spiky cage had come into existence, she wasn't sure, but she did know it was tightly rusted into place, and small cracks from Mason's love couldn't fully dismantle the structure now.

Still, as she gazed into his tormented eyes, her muscles relaxed and precious air invaded her lungs. With another thick breath, and another, the fire began to diminish till finally it was little more than smoldering embers.

Sitting up, she shot an accusatory glance at Saraphine.

"Don't be mad. It was a cleansing pyre spell, part of the truth ceremony. You'd never have done it if I'd have warned you."

"I might have surprised you," she wheezed, trying to pull herself off the ground.

Mace hurriedly helped her onto the couch, then turned on Saraphine with a scowl. "You did that to her on purpose?"

"It was necessary."

"The only thing necessary is death and taxes. Everything else is negotiable."

"I'm fine now, Mace." Cora resisted clutching her chest where the inferno still simmered. "Let's just get this over with so we can go home." Through gritted teeth, she added, "What's next, Saraphine?"

Sheepishly, Saraphine rubbed her neck. On closer inspection, Cora noticed a slight bruise forming. Before, she would have berated Mace for that. Now any semblance of empathy was gone, and she just raised an impatient brow at the girl.

Saraphine took her place across from Cora and hesitantly held out her hands. "Place your palms face down on mine."

Cora warily did as asked.

"The potion you ingested opened your aura to mine. Now I'll chant a spell that will allow the truth to be known."

Mason's impatience crawled through Cora's mind, mingling with her own. It didn't help that she was beginning to feel idiotic about this whole thing.

Saraphine closed her eyes and started her chant in a low timbre. "Show me the truth, by the power of three. By the power of three, I conjure truth unto me." She repeated the chant several times, till the words started to run together.

After about the twelfth repetition with nothing happening, Cora rolled her eyes and shot an apologetic glance at Mace. Mace replied with a frustrated frown.

She supposed her desperation to understand her odd predicament, and maybe even her past, had tempted her to take this fantasy further than she should have.

She was about to withdraw her hands when Saraphine's eyes flashed opened and an explosion of color crashed through Cora's mind. Her muscles tensed, her spine arching as though from an electric jolt. Vision failed her before piercing light blinded her. Images flashed in quick succession, too fast for her to get a lock on any one.

She strained to focus.

Blurred figures stood out. Two of them, no three. The third was smaller than the others. A child.

Me.

Her parents crouched next to a crying seven-year-old Cora...covered by blood. The dimly lit room came into view. Blood stained the walls in violent patterns. The expressions on her parent's faces caused Cora's adult heart to sink into the darkest pit of her stomach.

They were terrified...of their own child.

"She killed him," her mother whispered, breathless and a little hysterical. "She killed him."

Cora's tiny lungs worked harder on a sob.

"I can't believe it." Her father darted disbelieving gazes around the room. "She's too young to be this powerful."

"But she is. And they won't care that she can't control it. They'll take her."

"What happened, exactly? Her Father demanded. "Whose blood is this?"

"Adam was watching over her."

"You left her with Adam?"

"You act as though I had a choice!"

Her father's shoulders hunched. "You're right. I'm sorry."

"Last I knew they were playing blocks on the floor. I came running when I heard Coraline screaming. Adam's guts were still dripping from the walls when I came in." She pulled Cora on to her lap, bouncing her. "Hush, hush now."

Cora clutched her mother and buried her face in her chest.

"Look here." Her father retrieved a pair of shredded jeans from the middle of the room and snatched a key from the belt loop.

Her mother paled. "We're to run then?"

"What else can we do?"

The scene flashed forward in time. Cora lay asleep on the floor in a bundle of blankets. Next to her, her mother's stomach swelled with the first signs of pregnancy.

Her father leaned against the far wall. Worry lines creased his forehead. "They'll find us if we don't do something," he said.

"But bind her? She'll be defenseless. You do remember the fang marks on her shoulder just after we found her that night, don't you?"

"I remember," her father sighed. "That rat deserved what he got, no doubt about it. But she still can't control her power. She casts spells in her sleep. They'll find us if we don't. Besides, we'll be able to protect her long enough to find a coven that'll take us."

"But, her memories too? It's so extreme."

"She's traumatized. That's why she hasn't spoken since it happened. When she's older, ready to train, we'll unbind her, but I want to bury that memory forever. I want our daughter back."

Her mother turned thoughtful. "Very well."

The scene shifted again, and panic flared.

Darkness slammed around her as the building collapsed, separating her from her family and trapping her under a load of debris. Cora didn't need to be reminded of this painful memory. She knew what was to come. Days of being trapped, nearly starving, crying for her mother and father. Eventually, she managed to clamber free of the rubble and stumbled through the ruins, searching. She didn't want to relive this.

She was shown no pity, and the memory played through.

She climbed over mountains of torn chunks of sheetrock, broken glass, fallen beams, all the while kicking up dust. It entered her lungs, making it hard to breathe. Eventually, her hacking turned painful.

A shaft of light in the distance gave her strength to move her wobbly legs forward. It could be a way out. Maybe her parents had already found it and were waiting for her there.

Over the next hill of rubble, she discovered her father pinned to the hard cement floor by a barrage of heavy beams. His skin was a sickly gray, his mouth limp, his eyes ever staring through a cloud of haze.

Not far, thick strands of her mother's blond hair was visible from pinched under a heap of broken concrete chunks, dripping red.

Cora could only thank the goddess her expression was hidden under the wreckage, not like her father's.

No sign of her new baby brother.

She sat atop the heap, clutching her knees to her chest, and stared at her parents for a long while. She stared until her heaving sobs were exhausted and her eyes ran dry of tears. Till her silly child's hope that they might actually be alive and she just didn't realize it died along with them. Till she comprehended she'd never again see their smiles. Hear them laugh or fight with each other as they sometimes did. She'd never smell her mother's sweet scent, or feel the warmth of her father's bear-hugs.

Finally, as a heavy numbness flowed over her, killing the pain and dulling her senses, she stood and hobbled toward the fissure that allowed in the hated light for her gruesome goodbye.

The vision shifted again, to exactly where she feared it would.

The coming months after her parent's demise had been trying. She was tired, hungry, cold...alone. Her hair was knotted and matted to her head. Dust and dirt made a home on her skin and clothing, cracking uncomfortably with every gesture.

She found her way into a back alley that she hadn't checked in a couple of days and picked through trash, seeking something edible. Tears threatened when she found nothing.

"Are you hungry?" a cooing male voice eased up behind her.

"I'll show you where there's food."

Cora turned to face the predatory gaze of her worst nightmare, only, at the time, she hadn't known to be afraid.

"Enough," Cora cried, vaulting to her feet.

Saraphine jerked back as if stunned, her eyes stark. "Goddess, you've had it rough."

"What happened?" Mace pushed to stand as well, scrutinizing both of their strained expressions.

Cora shook her head, her eyes burning.

As if he sensed her despair, he pulled her into a tender embrace.

She forced a steady voice. "We discovered who bound my magic."

Chapter 21

Mason paced outside the changing room of the small clothing shop, drowning in Cora's melancholy. They'd stopped to buy her some new clothes before returning to the cottage. In the car, she'd explained a little about what had transpired. Her parents bound her, suppressed her memories, then up and died, leaving behind a small helpless child. No wonder she learned not to rely on others.

He stopped pacing to ask, "Do you need help in there?"

Cora sighed, the sound a bit muted by the door. "This isn't necessary. I'm fine wearing the baggy clothes back at the cottage."

"Didn't anyone ever tell you? Shopping is supposed to cheer women up."

"Then you'd better pack up this entire store because that's what it might take."

"You want it?" he replied jauntily. "I'll compel the owner to give it to you."

Cora opened the door and stepped out. One corner of her

mouth was curled in a crooked half-grin. It was better than the frown that threatened even now to take over.

"Very funny," she grumbled. The outfit she donned was the colorful dress he'd selected to contrast her mood.

"No joke. Just say the word."

"Oh, goddess, you're serious!" She slapped his chest with the back of her hand, smiling fully now. "Don't you dare." She glanced down at the flowery dress. "I feel ridiculous in this."

"You look beautiful."

She stilled and studied him for a moment.

"What?"

"You surprise me, is all. I never imagined there was such a thing as a kind vampire."

"Don't tell anyone. You'll destroy centuries of hard-earned reputation."

She gave a tiny snort. "I doubt a single word from me would send your rep crashing around you."

"Not just me, the whole vampire nation. When you're done, you'll have everyone believing we're a pack of ninnies, prancing around a field of pansies."

Impishly, she replied, "Well, aren't you?" Then she darted back into the changing room.

He laughed. "Why, you little witch." He bit his tongue on the last word as a pang blasted at him from the direction of the changing room.

Damn. For a moment, he was actually starting to take her mind off things.

"Cora—"

"Could you grab me a smaller size in this?" She flipped a pair of black jeans over the door.

"Uh, 'course." He perused the storefront for the correct rack. On his way back, he collected a few extra items, then handed them over the door.

"What's this?" she asked.

"Just something else for you to model for me."

She snorted. "Dream on. I'm not modeling this for you."

The door swung open. Cora had redressed in her original sweats and white button down. She snapped the red-laced thong at his face like a rubber band.

He caught it. "Oh, come one. Just a quick peek?"

"You sleezy old vamp." Her lips curled upward as she tried to conceal her smile.

He flashed his canines. "Later then."

"Ha! You wish."

"Like you wouldn't believe," he replied shamelessly, then gathered the pile of clothing she had set aside for purchase and placed the thong on top.

She rolled her eyes, flushing a lovely shade of pink.

For most of the ride back, a tense silence settled over her and it seemed as though she wanted to say something, but couldn't verbalize her thoughts. He attempted to ferret out her emotions through the bond, but he wasn't getting a clear read. About the seventh time she opened her mouth, only to close it and turn away, he gave up on trying to figure her out.

"What's up, love?"

She cocked her head. "You were flirting with me earlier."

"Caught that, did you?"

"But you were feeling so guilty this morning after we..."

"Yes."

"Are your emotions so easily discarded?" She didn't sound

angry, merely curious.

"I compartmentalize. With all that's happened, I figure now's not the time to deal with what happened between us. I'm just glad you're not under a spell." Pause. "Well, the spell I thought you were under."

"And what sort of spell did you think I was under?"

"Not sure exactly. Something that stripped you of your will, your inhibitions. You were very...agreeable." He smiled.

Another deep blush colored her cheeks.

"Vampire blood might make you more aggressive, spur a body's need, but it wouldn't force anyone to do something if they really didn't want to." He grin grew devilish.

"I can't tell if your ego's been inflated or if you're just naturally arrogant."

As he pulled up to the cottage, he replied, "You know, I believe there is something that's inflated, but it's not my ego. Care to assist me with it?"

She pursed her lips to fight a smile and exited the car. "You need a helping hand, huh?"

He followed her eagerly as she sauntered toward the cottage. "Indeed."

"Shall I'll check if Knox is available for you?"

"Oh, that's cold."

She laughed, opening the cottage door. Her laugh turned into a gurgled scream as a large hand gripped her by the throat and pulled her inside.

With alarming abruptness, Cora's air supply was obstructed by a strong vice-like grip. Her feet left the ground, and her back slammed against the inner wall of the cottage.

Through her panic, she assessed her situation, quickly realizing she'd taken her last breath. And though it was futile to fight, her body reacted on instinct. Her nails dug into Trent's tightening hold, drawing blood. Her legs flailed desperately.

Trent growled at her, his face filled with the purest form of hate.

Mace burst through the door, boiling over with fury. It flooded her like a crashing wave.

He lunged for Trent.

Without releasing her, Trent side-kicked Mace in the stomach. Mace flew backwards and crashed into the wall. Then Trent's hostile gaze swung back to her, his fangs bared in a snarl.

She stared back at the face of her death. Pinpricks of light began dotting her eyes as her brain was deprived of oxygen. It wouldn't be long now. Her body relaxed, giving in.

That damn grain of sand dropped, landing gracefully among the pile.

Her time was up.

Chapter 22

Click.

Mace held his aim true, cocking the gun next to Trent's head. "Let her go," he ordered in a dangerously low voice.

"Don't be a fool, Mace," Trent hissed back.

Mace's horror turned into terror as Cora ceased her struggles, her body going limp.

"Drop her now!" He tightened his finger on the trigger. "I'm not bluffing."

"That's the problem," Trent said, not budging.

"Now!" Mace screamed.

Trent snatched his hands away from Cora's throat. She crumbled to the floor, coughing and wheezing horribly. Her body curled into a protective ball.

Trent turned to Mace, ignoring the barrel trained on his forehead. "She's controlling you, Mace. She's been a part of this whole thing from the start."

Mace shook his head. "That's not true."

"She could be the ringleader."

"No."

"Don't you think it's funny that not only is she the only suspect to survive, she's turned out to be a witch? She was probably on her way to the hotel that day to take Winston out personally."

Mace shook his head.

"And lo and behold, she's bonded you to her. Can't you see how she's playing you? For the love of god, she's turned you against your own maker."

"No, that was all *your* doing," Mace accused, watching Cora from the corner of his eye. She'd dragged herself to the corner of the room, shaking and struggling to hold back her sobs. He ached to go to her. To take her from this place, this life that insisted on torturing her.

"Listen to him, Mace." Knox appeared from within the kitchen.

"Stay out of this," Mace snapped. "You know nothing about it."

"I have a say in this, and I say she's guilty."

"What the fuck are you talking about?" Mace growled, his gun still on Trent.

"She's bonded me, too."

The room went silent. Even Cora's muffled cries were subdued for a moment.

"What?"

"You deaf? I said I've been blood bonded to her," Knox hissed through clenched teeth.

Vicious jealousy raged through Mason's brain. "Impossible."

Trent turned and took a threatening step toward Cora. "Tell

the truth, witch!"

She let out a frightened cry and hid her head behind shaking arms, her knees tucked into her chest.

"Get the fuck away from her!" Mace sounded off a warning shot that missed Trent's skull by mere inches.

Trent rose to his full height. "It would be within my right to kill you for that."

Cora's eyes turned stark, almost void, as if she were escaping to a refuge inside her mind. Seconds later, Mace sensed her closing up as a mental door shut him out.

"Fuck!" Mace cursed. "Do you have any idea the damage you've done? I'd been making so much progress with her!"

"I need to get you away from her. She's warped you brain," Trent insisted.

Mace raised his gun again. "I should shoot you where you stand."

"She's bonded you in order to control you. It's what her kind does. I knew it the moment you accused me of trying to kill her."

"The man you sent *did* try to kill her!"

"I sent a woman, Mace, not a man."

"Bullshit. Cora was shot in the chest. Nearly died. She didn't *pretend* that."

"That's true," Knox confirmed. "There was a man here who claimed to have been sent by you. She would have died if I hadn't healed her with my blood the second after she was shot."

Trent traded speculative glances between Mace and Knox. "The woman I sent hasn't checked in yet."

Silence reigned again as they all took that in.

"Million to one she's dead," Mace said, easing up on the

trigger.

Trent turned to Knox "How did you come to be bonded?"

"I had a taste of her last night, just before she knocked me in the bollocks."

Mace growled. "No wonder why she was out-of-her-mind frightened of you."

Knox shrugged, uncaring. "It was miniscule. A measly couple of drops. Hardly enough to broker a bond, or so I assumed," he grumbled the last, then continued. "This morning, the witch nearly dies. Didn't realize she was a witch till I caught her reading that book. Still, I wasn't thinking, I guess. I gave her my blood to save her 'cause Mace was practically obsessing over the girl. Figured I'd do him a bloody favor." He sliced a glare at Mace. "Found out I was bonded 'bout an hour ago, when I tried to feed. Tasted like shit. Started feeling the bitch's emotions soon after."

Trent cursed. "Don't you see, Mace? She's too close to her goal. She's too close to turning."

"What are you talking about?"

"I've sired my share of vampires. I know how it's done. She's nearly figured it out!"

Though there was no change in Cora's outward appearance—physically, she remained the embodiment of a statue—her pulse spiked rapidly.

"She's not involved," Mace said. "I can't prove it to you. So you'll just have to trust me on this."

Trent shifted his gaze to Cora, debating. "And if I don't?"

"I'll kill for her. Even you."

"That only proves my point."

"It's not her!"

Trent locked eyes with Mace, the debate still waging war behind his eyes. Finally, he said, "I won't kill her, for now, but she has some explaining to do."

"You'll leave her be. Any questions can go through me." Mace realized too late that he'd overstepped, practically issuing orders to his sire.

Trent's body seemed to grow in mass, his fangs descending to their full length. "I don't think so!" His eyes flashed with the authority of a master. "Drop the weapon, Mason."

With all his fortitude, Mace fought the compulsion, even knowing he would lose this battle. After only a few short moments, he lowered his arms.

Yet he held Trent's gaze. "Leave her be for now, please. You've no idea what she been through in such a short amount of time. I sense she's ready to break."

Trent's fierce expression wavered.

"She *is* ready to break," Knox agreed, but for the wrong reason. "I can feel it. Now's the time to get answers."

Mace crossed to place himself between Cora and the two other vampires, saying with his expression what he needn't say with words; he would fight to the death to protect her in this moment.

Trent stood back, observing, while Knox advanced aggressively. "I'll not be some witch's play thing!" he growled. "Get out of my way."

Mason's muscles tensed for battle, his fangs prominent. He displayed them with a forced smile. "Come and get her, if you can."

"Stand down, both of you," Trent ordered, taking a seat on the couch.

He now seemed as relaxed as though they were gearing up to discuss the weather. He always had a way with corralling his emotions—or concealing them, Mace wasn't sure.

"She's not going anywhere." Trent stretched out his arm along the back of the sofa. "We have time to get to the bottom of this."

Disdain raged over Knox's features, but he turned away with a ripe curse, placing himself against the farthest wall in the room.

Mace let out a slow breath, facing Cora. She still hugged her legs to her chest, her eyes seeing nothing. He knelt before her and cooed her name softly.

She didn't respond.

The yellow-green bruise forming around her neck had aggression slicing through him once more. She flinched, and he worked to tamp it down. "Cora? Look at me."

She didn't. Her gaze remained on nothing in particular, her body trembling. He pinched her chin between his thumb and forefinger, tilting her head up. When she met his gaze, tears filled her eyes, spilling over.

"Let me die," she whispered, her voice like gravel. It probably pained to push that small phrase out. "Just let me die."

He glared at Trent, then Knox. Both would have heard her plea, but their expressions remained hard.

"I won't let you give up now," he said. "Not after all this."

Her already low tone became the slightest whisper. "I can't handle this. It's too much." She gasped on a sob, and her tears flowed without restraint.

He leaned in close so that the others couldn't hear him. "I can't let you go, Coraline. You're the only thing that matters to me now. I need you."

She focused on him, her tone too loud for his liking. "It's the bond. It's all because of the bond. You wouldn't feel that way otherwise. I don't want to be someone who controls the thoughts or feelings of others. I don't want you to care for me because you have to."

"I don't. You don't control anything about me."

"How can you be sure?"

Mace hesitated. "I've wanted you for months," he confessed. "Since the moment I saw you. I thought you'd begun to realize that."

She blinked up at him, her eyes beginning to clear. Then her gaze darted to Trent and back.

"He won't hurt you now. He just wants to talk."

Cora shook her head and rubbed her neck uncomfortably. She swallowed with difficulty.

Mace turned to Knox. "Could you get her some water?"

Knox sneered and then smiled cruelly. "Fetch it for her yourself. We'll watch her."

Cora trembled harder.

Mace sighed impatiently. "Trent?"

Trent remained quiet for a few beats, then looked at Knox and nodded.

Knox hissed and shoved away from the wall, heading for the kitchen. Moments later, the sound of shattering glass reverberated from the other room.

Trent called to him, "Try not to destroy everything while you're at it."

An inaudible string of grumbles bounced back at them.

Mace looked down at Cora. "I'm going to move you to the

couch," He informed her.

She gave a miniscule shake of her head, but he lifted her in his arms anyway. She stiffened, but made no other protest. After settling her on the couch, in the spot farthest away from Trent, he placed himself between the two.

"So, what has she got to say?" Trent started.

Cora just shook her head.

Knox returned and slammed a glass down on the coffee table in front of them. Then he straightened and glowered at Cora. She kept still. Her eyes were intently focused, again at nothing in particular, but a crack in her walls allowed her fear to seep into Mace.

"She's frightened enough as it is," Mace barked at Knox.

Knox cracked his knuckles. "A little terror works wonders on tight lips."

Mace shot him a warning look. "She doesn't need you terrorizing her right now."

"Don't give a shit what she needs."

Mace bolted to his feet, getting in Knox's face.

Knox smiled. "You want to dance again, sweetheart?"

"Both of you stow it," Trent said, growing impatient.

Mace waited till Knox backed up to his place against the wall before reclaiming his seat. Cora hadn't moved a muscle. She'd mentally returned to that place he couldn't reach.

Chapter 23

It wasn't so much Cora's worst nightmare as it was the most terrible reality possible come to fruition: a curse fulfilled, for that's what she seemed to be.

Cursed.

Cursed to suffer till her dying breath.

And death was preferable to being held captive by Trent and Knox. They despised her. She could feel it in spades flowing from Knox. A confirmation that she had indeed established a dark bond with him.

With the onset of such familiar yet overwhelming fright, her body shut down, her muscles nearly unresponsive. It was the first survival technique that had been beaten into her.

They wanted to talk?

No. They wanted her to admit something that was untrue. That she'd purposely bonded Mace, and now Knox. Who in their right mind would engage in such reckless behavior?

As Mace worked to explain their situation, Trent continued to demand she speak for herself while Knox trained a hate filled gaze on her, his fangs prominent as though he'd love nothing more than to rip her throat out.

But even if her esophagus wasn't scalded from Trent's greeting, she couldn't make her vocal cords work in her favor. They were trained for this. To be silent and just accept the pain. To cry and whimper only when she was once more alone. The only response her body gave at all was the falling of tears. That always pleased Edgar, made him watch her with fascination instead of malicious intent.

She wasn't sure how long it took—time had become meaningless—but eventually they realized she'd become frozen in the recesses of her mind. It was home for her there. Her last peaceful refuge. Even Mace had stopped getting through when she snuggled in and tuned out.

He'd continued answering Trent's questions as best he could, but after a while, all she heard was a mixture of deep timbres.

"I can't learn the truth if she refuses to speak," Trent said irritably.

"I've told you the truth," Mace insisted. "She knows nothing of the black-market blood or Brayden's disappearance besides what I've relayed to her. She not involved."

"You really expect me to believe she's innocent in all this?" Trent asked, incredulous. At least he had calmed down considerably.

"Have you forgotten she's bonded me?" Knox chimed in, disgruntled.

"It's your own fault," Mace shot back at him, anger seething in the layers of his accusation. "You wouldn't be bonded now if you hadn't forced your fangs on her."

"The witch was practically begging for it, batting those pretty eyes at me."

Mace clenched his fists. "Right, and she thanked you with a knee to the groin. I guess it's like you always say, you *do* like it rough."

"So will she when I'm done with her."

"You touch her and I'll slice you open, slowly. Starting with that tiny prick of yours."

"You'd better bring a big knife because there ain't nothin' tiny about it, mate."

Trent pinched the bridge of his nose. "Enough already. Unless one of you is actually going to kill the other, then shut the fuck up." He leaned back in his chair. "So, as it appears, both the *bondings* were accidental. That I'll grant, for now. But she's still a witch, and I find it hard to believe she didn't know."

Mace proceeded to explain what they'd learned from Saraphine's spell. "Before we left, Saraphine promised to start work on an unbinding spell."

"You dimwitted git!" Knox's accent had grown thick. "She's practically helpless right now, and you want to reverse that?"

"You're a real shit, Knox," Mace spat.

"Gold plated and smellin' like roses. Why is she acting so pathetic, anyway?"

"She's been mistreated by our kind repeatedly. One that I know of was particularly cruel." Mace glanced at Cora, hating that it was him explaining this rather than her. "It sounded like she and her parents had been claimed by a clan against their will or something when she was young."

Trent cocked his head. "For what purpose?"

"I'm not sure. When her parents died, she fell prey to another vamp, most likely during the end of the last uprising. A soldier. Psychotic, from what she's revealed. I doubt I've heard the full story. She was only ten at the time."

Trent cursed. Knox appeared bored, his expression blank.

Mace continued, "I realize some witches use our kind through the blood bond, but she's not like that. In fact, when she found out about the bond, she was most interested to know how long it would last.

"Probably because she has to figure out when she'll need to reinforce the bond," Knox accused.

Mace raised his voice for Knox, though he spoke to Trent. "She can hardly wait for the bond to fade."

"What did you tell her?" Trent asked.

"I thought she was human at the time. I said it would fade swiftly. She was relieved. I could feel it." He lowered his voice. "She'll be devastated when she finds out..."

"Finds out what?" Knox demanded.

Mace glanced at Cora. She stared at nothing as if she'd completely checked out. "How fast a blood bond with a witch fades is determined by the strength of the witch.

"At least, that's the theory," Trent added. "There could be other factors involved."

Knox scrutinized her. "She looks pretty weak to me. With luck, I'll be free of her by the end of the week."

"We can only hope," Mace hissed under his breath. "Just keep your blood away from her from now on."

"Well, would you say that's accurate?" Trent interrupted before another argument could erupt. "As far as witches go, is she weak?"

Mace shook his head. "With her magic bound, who can say? But she's endured more than most could even imagine. If her character is anything to go by, there's nothing weak about her."

"Are you kidding?" Knox scoffed. "Look at her!"

He did, wanting to tuck her into his side, but he feared she'd flinch away from him. Instead, he replied, "Like I said. She's been through a lot in the last couple of days."

Trent waved a negligent hand at her. "How long is she going to be like this?"

"It took me a while just to get her to feel comfortable around me, and I hadn't even threatened her like the two of you have. Not to mention all I'd had to do to prove myself worthy of her trust. You'll both need to check your aggression around her. Try to be gentle—"

Knox interrupted. "Or what? Your wee witch will crack like glass?"

"Knox," Trent chided.

Knox threw his hands in the air. "What is this, a therapy session? Sounds like you've both gone soft."

Trent displayed no reaction to Knox's jibe.

Mace struggled to remain just as calm. "I wish you would have left when I asked you to."

"That makes two of us." Knox crossed his arms. "But the little bitch has made that impossible now."

"Call her that again, and I'll shove my gun so far up your ass you'll taste copper before you die!"

"Promise you'll buy me dinner first."

Trent pushed out of the chair. "Now I remember why I separated you two." To Mace, he ordered, "Take the girl upstairs and get her some rest."

All too ready to get her out of here, Mace stood and pulled her into his arms, then headed for their room.

"And Mace?"

He paused at the bottom of the staircase.

"Watch her closely. I'm not sure I fully believe all this, and if she tries to escape, I really will kill her."

Chapter 24

Knox's narrowed gaze followed the chit in Mason's arms. Before they disappeared to the second floor, Mason mirrored his hostile glare.

The girl was good. Her fabricated grim expression hadn't faltered once. Mace was so easily duped. The moron was bonded, yet couldn't even decipher her emotions. There had been no fear in her, but for the initial impression he'd received when Trent had threatened her life. After that, all trace of emotion in her had drained away. She'd been like a bottomless pit of emptiness.

Heartlessness.

Knox had been bonded only one other time, to a human girl. He recalled the sharing of emotions to be a constant irritant. An annoyance he'd been glad to be rid of. There had been no reprieve until the bond had been severed a few very long months later when the girl had been murdered.

He clenched his fist.

He hoped Mason's witch *did* attempt to escape. If she were to die, the bond would be broken instantly. And if Trent proved to be as gullible as Mason, Knox might need to take care of things on his own. But for now, he would hold off on that route and indulge the two do-gooders who fancied their detective work.

However, for everyone's sake, there was something that required his immediate attention.

"I'm heading out for a bite," he told Trent, beating a path to the door.

Trent ran thick fingers through his dark hair. "Good idea. I'll join you."

Knox halted. "Shouldn't you make sure that witch stays put?"

"Mace is with her."

He laughed. "Lover boy is a puppet now. If she wanted, he'd carry her out on his back with two broken legs."

Trent shared in his revelry, then shook his head as if at a loss. "Alright. I'll go out once you return. Don't be long."

Strolling out the door, he called back, "I don't plan on it." It was almost too easy to convince Trent not to follow.

Thirty minutes later, Knox hid in the shadows of an alley, waiting for his prey. Most of the town had closed down for the night. Only a few working light posts illuminated the streets in sporadic patterns, and most of those buzzed loudly and flickered. The light post that fronted his little niche was off, and had been for some time.

The alley stank of trash and decay. A stack of black bags carved out a spot near the opposite end. It wasn't the best part of town, but it wasn't exactly the worst either.

After another twenty minutes, his target finally emerged from the shop across the street, unaware of his hunter's gaze. She turned her back, locking the shop door behind her. Then she crossed the street, taking the path she always did. This was his town, and he knew nearly everyone's routine. She would cross his path in three, two, one...

He whipped his arm out and snatched her around the waist. His free hand went to her mouth to prevent her building scream as he easily pulled her into the darkness and planted her against the wall. The weight of his body caged her in.

"Hello, Saraphine," he said.

Her impossibly wide eyes went even wider. Yes, she recognized him. He frequented the shitty bars in this small town often to feed from one of the locals. He preferred them to the blood whores.

He scented the sweet fragrance of Saraphine's racing pulse, mentally cursing when he remembered that there would be no pleasure in tasting it. All other blood would be like ash in his mouth thanks to Mason's witch.

"You had a visitor earlier," he said, his voice smooth. "A witch. You remember? She commissioned a spell to unbind her magic."

Saraphine nodded, fear wafting from her pores.

His eyes glowed as he weaved compulsion into his next words. "You'll proceed to craft a spell, just as you promised, but it won't do as requested. It won't unbind her powers. You're young, still learning your craft. Perhaps you add the wrong ingredient, say the wrong words. What sort of mistake is yours to choose. Nod so I know you understand me."

Her expression blanked, and she nodded again. He contemplated taking her vein, if only for nourishment, but he knew it would not alleviate his hunger. And, at the moment, he had a mighty craving for a doe-eyed blond-haired witch.

"Now forget you saw me and run along." He released Saraphine and swatted her ass, sending her on her way.

Though he'd removed her fear along with the compulsion, her natural sense of danger must be keen. Her pace was unusually swift as she headed away from him.

* * *

Cora came to as if from out of a fog. She found herself lying on a bed. Mace hovered over her. His concern pooled around her so thickly she didn't need to look up to know it was written all over his face.

"Cora?" he said as though he'd repeated it several times already.

How long had he been chanting her name, trying to bring her back from wherever it was she'd escaped to? Her throat still burned with an inner soreness, so in response, she raised her hand to stroke her fingers along his jaw, feeling a bit of stubble. He turned his head and kissed her palm.

"Here, take some of my blood." He brought his wrist to his mouth, preparing to bite down.

She shook her head. "No." The word came out like sand paper, and she winced at the accompanying sting.

"A small amount will heal you without any side effects."

"Where's..." She trailed off when her throat closed in protest.

Mace sliced a fang into his wrist and held it out for her. Warily, she eyed the deep red drop forming there.

"Please, I can feel your discomfort."

The increased agony as she tried to swallow had her relenting after only a slight hesitation. She licked away the drop and then waited. Mace nodded for her to take more, but she shook her head. She could already feel his blood going to work, like the soothing balm of a lozenge. Yet a slight tenderness lingered. Another drop might smother it, but she didn't want to lose herself to the lust that followed overindulgence. She told him as much, her voice coming clearer, and he withdrew his arm.

"Where are they?" she asked.

"Downstairs," he said. "Where were *you*? It felt like you weren't even here, yet at the same time, you were."

She sat up and surveyed the room, verifying they were alone. The instinct to escape was intense, but she knew she wouldn't be going anywhere. Not only would the other two stop her, maybe kill her, but Mace seemed unalarmed by their current situation. He was calm now, which meant he trusted his comrades more than he feared for her. Even if she begged for him to take her somewhere else, he would only make a case to stay.

"I go to a place where pain doesn't exist," she replied. "It's sort of like blacking out. It used to happen a lot when I was younger. When...well, anyway. I haven't experienced it in a long time." Then, because she couldn't help herself, she added, "Do we need to remain here? Can we go?" Involuntarily, her hands clutched his shirt.

He sighed and took her hands in his. "They won't hurt you now, I promise." He explained Trent's misunderstanding, then added, "He's my sire. In human terms, that's like a patron. Our leader. And it's his duty to protect his clan. That's the only reason why he went after you. He thought you were controlling me."

"But Knox is going to kill me. He wants to. I can feel it."

"He won't, though. He knows I'll gut him if he tried. Trent

would too, if only for disobeying a direct order."

She shook her head, disbelieving.

"I swear to you, I won't let them harm you again."

Her teeth clenched as his resolve settled over her. "You must be strong then. You should drink." She swept her hair aside.

Mace reared back. "I...I don't want you to feel forced. I can manage without."

"I can feel your hunger."

"Yes, but I can feed from others."

"But doing so would only keep you alive. It wouldn't satisfy you, or provide the kind of strength my blood would, correct?"

Mace didn't respond, which was tantamount to an affirmation.

"So then, go ahead." She tilted her head to the side and squeezed her eyes shut.

"You're only offering because you feel obligated. That's not how I want it."

As if a trap door was released, her patience left her in a rush, replaced by anger. "I don't have a choice anymore, do I?"

Mace frowned and sat back. They both remained silent for a tense moment.

She sighed, tempering her anger. "I'm accepting this, Mace. Them. You. I'm accepting my lot—"

"I don't want you to have to *accept your lot*—"

"And if I had to be bound to any vampire in the world, I'm only grateful that it was you." She edged toward him, unabashedly straddling his lap, and settled her arms around his neck.

His body stiffened, and he placed his palms at her waist, unconsciously snaking his thumbs under the hem of her shirt. She leaned forward and allowed her lips to brush his in a gentle kiss.

It was obvious he wanted more, but he kept himself in check.

She continued. "You said you loved me. I don't know if you really meant it—"

"I did."

She couldn't keep a tiny grin from conquering her lips, but they quickly settled back into a frown. "I'm going to be frank with you. I've come to...care for you. However, love is not something I can offer right now."

His features turned inscrutable, but for a thinning of his lips. She truly hated that what she said now hurt him, but she had to make sure he knew where she stood.

"What I *can* offer is my blood. So you can be strong. So you can protect me."

He grinned, but it was a bitter sight. "My little survivalist."

She ignored that. "And my body, because I know you want it."

At that, she waited for his fury to erupt. It bubbled and churned just under the surface. She waited. And waited.

Finally, he took command of himself and drew in a deep breath. "You'd sleep with me just so I'll protect you?"

She jerked her head back sharply, appalled. "No. Not for that reason." She blushed, embarrassment now overtaking her. "It was...I mean...when we...I..."

His grin became genuine, instantly placated by the rambling, convoluted confession that only two people in the world could fully understand because they were blood bonded. "You enjoyed yourself, did you?"

She rolled her eyes, smiling too wide. "Don't tease me."

"Why not? You light up when I do."

"I do not—"

He cut her off with a sudden kiss. A demanding kiss that rendered her earlier one amateurish.

When he pulled away to speak, his voice had become guttural. "You *care* for me, huh? I guess I can live with that, for now. But one day, I'll take your heart, along with your body."

He flipped her to the mattress, hunching over her as he claimed her mouth with rough abandon. He wedged himself between her legs before he ripped the fabric of her sweats straight in half down the middle.

A little bit of unease melted through the heat of her passion. "Mace?"

His smile was wicked. "Guess you'll not be wearing these again. Good thing I thought to provide you some clothing." He eyed her white button-down shirt. "You can keep that. I like you in it."

His sudden aggression was alarming at first, till she recognized where it came from. It was more natural for vampires to behave this way. Mace had been modulating himself around her from the start. Caging his urges for her. Now she had all but set him free, offered herself up to his inhuman appetites.

And she wasn't afraid.

She tugged at his shirt, wanting it off him. He obliged, shrugging out of it and tossing it aside. She ran her hands over the planes and valleys that made up the tightly packed muscles of his torso. They contracted for her in a vision of perfect masculinity.

As she allowed her fingers to play, he methodically unbuttoned her shirt, starting at the top. He must truly like this particular piece of menswear on her to take such care with it now.

After setting it aside, he dipped his head to press his lips to hers, his tongue demanding rather than asking for access. While he delved deep into the recesses of her mouth, his right palm caressed its way over her thigh and up her side to softly tease the underside of her breast. She moaned at the sensation, her skin warming with need.

His hand cupped her chest and applied a delectable pressure. Then his mouth left hers to capture her nipple instead. Her body shook as she hissed out a whimper, arching.

She heard the sound of his belt being loosened, and another rush of heat flooded her lower regions. If she didn't know any better, she would have thought she'd taken more than a drop of his blood, but she couldn't use that as an excuse this time. This time the frenzied lust was all hers.

As Mace rid himself of his jeans, she shoved her panties down, kicking them away. He entered her with a savage thrust, exquisite in its glorious carnality. In the back of her mind, she was surprised by her own ferocity, her eagerness for his voracious taking. To submit in every way and let him dominate as she knew he craved.

His hips drove into her with rough abandon, and she was bewildered by the ecstasy rippling through her, the sweltering bliss that numbed her mind like nothing she'd ever felt.

It was rapturous but for one small detail. Not having his fangs in her was a new kind of anguish, one that had never before tormented her till this moment. She couldn't think past the need to rectify the situation. Without realizing what she was doing, she heard herself pleading with Mason, begging, presenting her neck.

From somewhere deep within him, from the part of him that was purely-forged instinct, a growl ripped free. Then his fangs penetrated her taut skin. She cried out as every nuance in her body soared to the heavens, so high she didn't think she would ever return to earth again.

* * *

Mace glanced down at Cora curled into his side. Her eyes drooped languidly, yet she smiled up at him, as though pleased. He wouldn't have believed it if he didn't feel it for himself. Or if she had taken more of his blood earlier. But she actually was content, sated, maybe even a little happy.

He allowed that thought to overrule his apprehensions, though he couldn't block them out completely. He'd believed it when she told him she cared about him. And he respected that she confessed to only that much rather than professing undying love and attempting to play him for a fool. But she still only accepted him because she felt she had no other choice.

To her, it was him or death.

Needless to say, he was of two minds about it. Well, more like mind and body. He'd lost himself in her sweet flesh and even sweeter blood, allowing himself to go mindless while reinforcing their bond by taking her blood into him. She had matched his carnal demands avidly and given him everything he'd wanted.

Almost everything.

He'd win her heart if it took him a thousand years to do so.

Her brow rose at his possessive sentiment.

"What are you thinking?" she asked.

He ran the backs of his fingers along her jaw. "How beautiful you look."

"Liar." She smiled.

When first she had offered him her body, acidic rage had nearly eroded away reason. That she would debase herself like that—when she had gone her entire life without resorting to such desperate acts—riled something in him that he couldn't describe.

But then that touching coyness, that lovely flush that spread over her cheeks as she'd tried to explain, had relieved all his animosity as swiftly as water through a drain.

She might not love him yet, but a part of her wanted him desperately. He had to remind himself that they'd only been together a few short days. She merely needed time to sort out her feelings. After all, he'd had months to decipher his.

Her gaze turned suspicious, and he changed the subject. "You must be starving. When was the last time you ate?" He glanced around for some leftover fruit. When he turned back, her expression had fallen. "What is it?"

Chapter 25

"I don't want to go down there." Cora fidgeted nervously at the top of the stairs wishing she had lied about the problem with her appetite. Anxiety crept up her spine. At Mason's look, she said, "*He's* down there."

The moment she'd left the sanctity of their room, the deplorable situation crashed down around her again, and she was instantly ill at ease.

Trent won't harm you." Mace held out his hand to her, palm up.

"I don't mean Trent."

Mace pursed his lips. "You're talking about Knox?"

She nodded.

"You can sense him, huh?" Mace sounded disgruntled.

She nodded again. "A little. Not like you."

"Just keep near me. We need to find out from Trent what might be going on with your appetite."

"*You* can do that. You don't need me there."

"I'd like to prove to you that you're safe. And anyway, Trent won't want to speak to you through me." He held out his hand.

She sighed, gathering her courage. After a few calming breaths, she set her hand in his.

Downstairs, Knox relaxed on one of the couches, the bottom of his booted foot perched on the edge of the coffee table. He watched them descend, his features hardening.

Mace lifted his chin. "Where's Trent?"

"Hunting, I suppose," Knox replied curtly, then transferred his hateful gaze to her. "Not that I care. I've got a mighty hunger occupying my mind."

She edged closer to Mace, turning her eyes down.

"Don't," Mace whispered to her. "Submission encourages dominance. Keep your head up."

She began to tremble at his suggestion. By her experience, behaving otherwise brings the pain.

He turned her to him, faking an embrace as he lifted her chin with a concealed hand and said into her ear, "Keep your eyes on his, no matter what."

She swallowed the thick lump of dread that had formed in her throat just as Mace released her. She forced her chin to remain in the air when all it wanted to do was sink down. And for the first time in her life, her eyes sought to capture the gaze of a hostile vampire. It felt wrong in every way imaginable, but she did it.

Knox cocked his head, malicious interest lighting up his ice-cold eyes.

Her mind protested, bombarding her with memories of the consequences from such defiance. It became too much, the tremors spreading like a gas infused wildfire. His mouth twisted into a dark grin.

Finding her limit, she shoved away from Mace and raced up the stairs.

A string of vile curses aimed at Knox spewed from Mace in a heap. "She requires tenderness, Knox!"

"And I require food."

Mace lumbered forward and kicked the other vampire's boot off the table. "Over my dead body!"

"Don't tempt me."

Mace struggle to stow his temper and think rationally. "Look, you don't want to be bonded to Cora. She'd prefer that as well, and it's no big mystery that I'd like you gone. So stay away from her, leave, don't take her blood, and don't give her yours again. I'm sure your bond will fade, and you'll be free before you know it."

"Be assured, Mace, I won't share my blood with her again, *especially* if her life is in danger. And I know better than you that the bond will fade. I don't need you to tell me that." Knox stood. "But I won't resign myself to indefinite weakness. I'll feed from the witch until I can feed from others again. I suggest you learn to accept that."

Mace bared his fangs. "I don't have to accept shit. I could just end you."

"Love for you to try, mate. I've been looking forward to the end for a while now. But do you think you've got what it takes?"

They were nose to nose.

"Mace! Knox! Separate, now!"

They both backed up, the power of their sire's command

overruling their macabre urges to beat the other bloody.

"Sit," Trent ordered.

They claimed spots on opposite sides of the coffee table, staring daggers at each other.

Trent glanced around the room, his eyes coming to rest on Mace. "Where's the girl?"

"She's upstairs." He hated leaving her by herself, but she was overwhelmed, and he could tell she wished to be left alone anyway.

Adjusting her ingrained perspective of his kind was going to be a task. She'd find more success if she could learn to assert herself better.

"Good. I have things to discuss with you. There's already been new leads on Brayden's case. Whoever's holding him didn't wait long to start selling his blood again through new channels. I was hoping to bring you back in to investigate."

"Cora needs me." He didn't hesitate in his response. "Clearly they still want her dead, which tells me something about her is a threat to them."

"I've considered that as well," Trent replied solemnly. "And I agree with your assessment. But mostly, now that you're bonded to her, I don't have much of a choice. Your strength depends on her blood at the moment." His eyes shifted to Knox. "Both of yours does."

"You can't be serious," Mace protested. "Knox does nothing for the clan. His strength is inconsequential. He need not feed from her at all."

"Everyone is an asset, Mace. He hasn't been working for the VEA because I've assigned him to this cottage."

Mace fell silent, taken aback. "Why?"

"An entity made its presence known several years back. I fear, whatever it is, it's growing stronger."

"A ghost," Mace replied, deadpan. He turned to Knox and mocked, "You're a ghost hunter now?"

Knox sneered. "Smirk all you like, it won't save your woman from me."

Mace frowned, turning to Trent. "You can't subject her to him. She's...delicate. More so now than ever."

Trent turned contemplative, leaning back in his chair. "Knox, you'll only feed from her. You'll not harm her in any way. Understand?"

Knox waved his hand in a show on nonchalance. "Fine, whatever."

"You can't be serious. Knox just being near harms her."

"Is that so?" Mischief coated Knox's words.

Mace gesture toward him as if proving a point.

"Enough, Mace, I've made my decision. You'll both stay here with the witch."

"Then how will I be able to help with the case?"

Trent turned roguish and then headed for the kitchen, gesturing for Mace to follow. "Knox has been working on another project here at the cottage."

"Oi," Knox complained. "You're not going to show him, are you? It's not ready yet."

Trent ignored him and continued to the secret panel.

Moments later, Mace and Trent descended into the cavern. Knox begrudgingly trailed behind.

"We only just finished carving out the space," Trent declared. "Knox has been installing the power station and backup generators."

Mace paused. "Power station? For what?"

"Our new compound." Trent turned a corner and disappeared through a fissure in the wall, covered by darkness. His voice echoed back at Mace, "Eventually I want to relocate the clan."

Through the hidden alcove, and a set of heavy metal doors, Mace found himself in a large, open room, perfectly square with smooth grey walls. Light fixtures hung from recesses in the ceiling. A door on each wall led to three other rooms, all of them bare, with doors of their own.

"Impressive," Mace said. "How far does it go?"

There's room for the whole clan and then some," Trent replied. "But like Knox said, it's not ready yet. Mostly bones at this point. However, a couple rooms are set up for communication and research. That's how you'll continue your work on the case. When I get back to St. Stamsworth, I'll send you the list of new suspects."

"When are you're leaving?"

"Within the hour. I dropped my entire investigation to come see to you. Drove like a bat out of hell to get here too. I have to get back." He retrieved his phone from his pocket and scrolled through a list of messages.

Mace recognized one of the names as belonging to the captain of the human precinct who had been all too willing to cooperate with their investigation. Captain Avery. At the time, he had been grateful for the easy capitulation.

Now he was suspicious.

"With you gone, how am I to deal with..." Mace glanced around. "Wait, where's Knox?"

* * *

"Sweet frightened Coraline," Cora heard Knox purr.

Her blood stopped cold and she shot out of the bed, backing up several steps. Knox closed the door behind him and loped toward her at a leisurely pace.

She remembered Mason's words and fought to hold Knox's gaze. "Go away."

"But I brought something for you." His fangs were already extended, his intention's clear.

She gulped down the painfully hard lump that had swollen in her esophagus.

"Hold still so I can give it to you."

Her feet ached to do just the opposite, but her legs were like two shaking sticks in stormy weather. Besides, there was nowhere to run. Knox was nearly upon her. Her pulse thumped out a rabbit's warning, her brain not knowing how to respond to the message.

Knox shoved an object into her shaky palm just as he pulled her head to the side by the nape. His fangs bore down on her. There was a quick sting when he penetrated her skin, then a rush of unwanted pleasure as he began to drink her in.

Mace barged into the room, the waves of his fury mingling oddly with her pleasure. He lunged for Knox. Cora was somehow shoved out of the way as the two began to grapple. Back to her senses, she scrambled to the opposite side of the bed, using it as a barrier. Then she realized she still held what Knox had handed her: Pride and Prejudice. She gazed at the book as if it were a three-headed sloth.

Trent appeared and forced himself between Knox and Mace,

quickly breaking up the brawl. Mace made sure to back up so that he was in front of her. Knox taunted him with a triumphant visage.

Cora took in the carnage, surprised by the amount of damage done in just a few seconds.

The reading desk had been knocked over, the drawers and items inside spread over the floor. The chair had been tossed as well, along with the bags of clothing Mace had brought up from the car. The bathroom door was smashed in. She hadn't even noticed when that had happened. Had she blacked out while Knox had his way? She brought her fingers to her neck. They came away with blood on the tips.

Mace panted like any beast would after taking on a rival. So did Knox, and though he was bleeding from his nose and lip, he appeared smug and amused, whereas Mace was concentrated rage. If Trent weren't in command, Mace would have disemboweled Knox for her.

He was magnificent.

"The two of you *will* work this out!" Trent sliced his hand through the air as if this were a final warning. "And without killing each other. Mace, I expect you to be reasonable. Knox... don't be an ass." Then he surprised her by asking, "You alright, Cora?"

Her blonde hair was sweat-dampened and tangled in her face. She haphazardly brushed it back, nodding, trying her damnedest to mean it.

"Of course she's not alright," Mace bellowed. "Get Knox out of here. Take him with you."

Impatiently, Trent replied, "My decision has been made."

"Come off it, mate." Knox extended his arms outward with

his palms to the ceiling. "I was gentle, just like you said. She melted for me."

Mace hurled himself at Knox again and managed to get his hands around his neck.

This time, instead of ordering them to stop, Trent approached and used his considerable strength to hurl them in opposite directions. They barreled into the walls on either side of Cora, causing more destruction to the room.

Then Trent sent an accusatory glance her way as if she were to blame for their behavior. She cringed, wondering if he'd changed his mind and was about to kill her.

As Mace and Knox pulled themselves to stand, Trent repeated his declaration for them to "work it out." Adding, "I can't stay here and babysit you both. In fact, I should have left an hour ago."

When he turned in to the hall and headed down the stairs, Cora scurried off the bed toward Mace. He opened his arms for her and folded her in his embrace. Then, with a parting grimace at Knox, he guided her downstairs after Trent.

She tried to block out Knox's insolent satisfaction, pouring over her like sticky glue, and to her surprise, it actually dimmed a bit.

"Hold on," Mace called to Trent.

Trent looked up as he donned his coat, and Mace swiftly informed him of Cora's total loss of appetite, seeking advice.

Once more, Trent glared at her in accusation. "She's definitely primed for the change."

Knox lumbered down the stairs, joining them. His disgruntled expression matched Trent's.

"It's a process that only few have knowledge of," Trent continued, "with even fewer aware of the catalyst. When the process is prolonged, appetite is often affected." Cold eyes rolled over her as he added, "But she won't change. Just keep an eye on her. Her appetite might return. In the meant time, make sure she eats."

Mace glanced down at her, and she knew he would stock the kitchen at the first opportunity.

Before he left, Trent pulled a small package from his coat pocket and handed it to Knox. "Almost forgot to leave this with you," he said.

Knox took the item without reply.

* * *

"Try not to destroy this one," Cora said as they transferred their things to the tidy room across the hall. Once Trent had gone, and Knox disappeared to the underground compound, she seemed to relax.

She was smiling again, at least.

But Mace could tell how hard she was trying to hide the fragility of it.

He set the bundle of her clothes he'd gathered from the other room on the bed, and she dove into folding them.

He perched on the mattress, leaning his back against the headboard with one of his legs dangled over the side. For a long while, he was content just to watch her work, intent on her task. Her delicate arms moved with swift grace, her fingers nimble as she stacked the clothing and then plucked another garment to repeat the process.

He must truly be in love if he can find her sexy during the

mundane task of tending laundry. He let that thought percolate.

However, his mind soon drifted to how drastically her behavior changed around Knox. When he was near, she became like a completely different person. Suppressed. Like a flower that closes as night creeps in.

"Does Knox remind you of Edgar?" he blurted.

She froze mid-action, the shirt in her hands half finished. Unease seeped into him.

She lowered the garment. "In a way, you all do."

He frowned. How could *he* possibly remind her of a sicko like that?

As though gathering the direction of his thoughts, she hurriedly explained, "Not so much you...entirely...anymore...It's more of the situation. My life is in constant danger. I feel like I'm treading on thin ice, and at any moment, I could find myself in another chokehold."

He grimaced.

"Along with that, I'm trapped here with—"

"Trapped?" His brow furrowed.

She gave him a withering look. "Can I leave?"

He pursed his lips and settled back against the wall, not about to answer.

"Well, then." She went back to folding.

"Do you want to leave?"

She slowed, but didn't look up. "I don't want to be afraid anymore."

"Is that a yes?" His words came out harsher than he meant.

She sighed, set the garment away, and approached him. With no hesitation at all, she slipped onto his lap and put her arms around his neck. His hooked her waist.

A sadness in her contradicted her actions.

"Put yourself in my shoes. You called me a survivor, and you're probably right. I don't want to die. I *do* care about you, but part of me thinks I might be safer away from you."

His fingers dug into her hips possessively. She winced, and he forced himself to relax.

"But maybe I'm not as much a survivalist as you think. It would be easy for me to tell you that I love you, and I never want to be separated from you, but I can't bring myself to lie to you like that." She offered an apologetic look before turning thoughtful. "Then I think about being away from you, and I get a little anxious. Sad. Then I think that's crazy, like maybe I'm coming down with Stockholm syndrome, which is possible, you have to admit. Then I think about the things we've done to each other and my heart goes all wonky—"

Mace chuckled. "You're mixed up."

"Big time," she concurred. "I know what you want from me. All I can say is when I figure it out, I'll let you know."

"How sweet." From the hallway, Knox's voice curled around the corner of the open door. In the next instant, he appeared, taking up the space of the threshold.

Mace nearly shot to his feet, but Cora now clung to his neck like a spider monkey. He squeezed her closer and flashed his former friend an expression that said, "This belongs to me."

Knox inclined his head as if to reply, "If I wanted, I could take it from you."

"Can I assist you with something?" Mace hissed.

"Found this in the other room." He didn't enter, only reached his hand in to set a book on the reading desk near the door. "Someone forgot it."

Cora looked away, and Knox smirked. Clearly, whatever he intended to communicate had been telegraphed, and received.

When Knox turned to head downstairs, Cora hopped off Mace's lap and crossed swiftly to close the door. She didn't so much as glance at the book.

"What was that about?" he asked.

She shrugged, and went back to her folding. And just like that, she was closed to him.

He glowered. "Come here."

She stilled at his tone, going tense.

"Please," he added. "I liked you where you were."

After a moment, she smiled and returned to his lap. He rewarded her with a tender kiss. She leaned in, expounding upon it by running her fingers along the back of his neck.

"Are you trying to get me going?" he rumbled.

"Can't you tell?"

He had intended to talk with her more, he'd been enjoying their conversation, but blood from his brain had transferred to a more demanding region of his anatomy. "It's too easy for you."

She bit her lip, and her eyes turned sultry.

Chapter 26

Mace eased out from under Cora's limp arm, then leaned over and placed a soft kiss on her forehead. She slept soundly as he stabbed his feet into his jeans and then slipped quietly into the hallway.

It didn't take long to find Knox. He was in the living room, lounging on the couch and watching...

Mace stopped short. "For the love of god, don't watch that down here. What if Cora were to see that?"

Without taking his eyes from the porn flick, Knox replied, "Girl might learn a thing or two. Why aren't you hissing at me like a cat in heat right now?"

"I'm here to talk," Mace replied evenly.

A sardonic gaze landed on him as a climactic scene came to an end. "You're serious?"

"And I need one of those inoculations Trent left for you. I haven't had one in a while."

Knox hit the mute button, and the salacious sounds cut off. "You want something from me? I want something from your little lady."

Mason's teeth gnashed together. "Is this how it's going to be from now on?"

Knox shrugged. "Pretty much."

"And what is it you think you should get from her?"

"What do you think? I want her available to me whenever I want."

Mace glowered. "Not going to happen."

"Then I'll just *take* her whenever I want."

"You sorry son of a bitch!"

Knox sat forward. "Talking pretty to me doesn't work, lover boy."

Gnashing his teeth, Mace said, "What *will* work? What will it take for you to leave her alone?"

Knox leaned forward with unwavering seriousness. "Blood, Mason. Blood that will keep me strong and sated. Let's see... where can we find that at?"

"What about bloodletting? We could keep pints of it in the fridge just for you."

"While you get the fresh, warm stuff?"

Mace waited, sensing the offer intrigued him.

Knox's grin grew broad. He leaned back and rested one arm along the back of the couch. With the other, he pulled out a sealed syringe cartridge from a side-pocket of his black cargo pants and balanced it between his thumb and forefinger. Turning thoughtful, he began to twirl and weave the thing between his fingers like a magician with a coin. "So if I hand over one of my doses, I get Cora's blood any time I want?"

"As long as she can supply it without harming herself. Yes."

"You think she's going to be okay with that?"

"She'll have to be, won't she?"

"Since she already has you by the balls, maybe you should ask her first."

Mace shook his head, ignoring the insult. "We settle this now, tonight. I'll inform her of our decision in the morning."

Knox smirked and slid the syringe across the table. "You've got yourself a deal, mate. But...I think she already knows." He gestured behind Mace with roguish eyes.

Anger and betrayal slammed into Mace from behind. He turned to see Cora's bare feet beating a path up the stairs.

"Cora...!" With the sound-deafening spell in place, he could just imagine the door to their room slamming shut. To Knox, he said, "You really are a son of a bitch."

Knox chuckled. "Too right."

He unmuted the television.

Cora paced furiously.

She was just a product for their consumption! How dare Mace bargain her off to Knox.

The nerve! The repugnance!

"Bastards!" she hissed.

She whirled around when a crack rang out and the door burst open. The doorjamb was now splintered where the lock had been.

Mace entered.

Not even a courtesy knock, she thought bitterly.

"How much did you hear?" he asked.

"You! Selling me like a whore!" she screamed, then hurled a pillow at him.

He batted it away, and it flopped to his feet.

Her gaze darted for something with more substance. Finding nothing nearby, she settled on the other pillow.

Same as the first, he swatted it away, then lifted his palms in the air and attempted to approach her.

"Get away from me!"

He halted, his brows rising at her tone.

"I wasn't selling you," he countered defensively. "I mean, I didn't mean to...I thought it would be better this way. Less painful for you."

"Less painful than if Knox had constant access to my blood?" she replied, not quelling the sarcasm. "He gets me any time he wants?"

"No. Just your blood. I figured you would prefer it this way. Otherwise Knox is going to put his fangs in you whenever he gets a chance. I can't watch him all the time."

His words seemed a bit convoluted. "So, what are you saying? I should just accept him the same as I have you?"

"Of course not. It wouldn't be the same at all."

"How would it be different? When he drank from me earlier I felt...something." Heat ran over her cheeks.

The sting of Mason's furious jealousy sank into her. She flinched, and a darkness overtook his features.

"Unfortunately, that's to be expected with any vampire's bite," he said. "Which is why I suggested the bloodletting instead."

She stilled, her breath heaving with vexation. "The what now?"

"Bloodletting. So that he doesn't take straight from your vein."

Her brows shot up, as her shoulders sank. "Oh."

Mason seemed to relax a touch. "You didn't hear that part, did you?"

"Um...."

Mason explained his deal with Knox, making it sound so... reasonable.

Still, she held resentment. "Will he be satisfied by that? What if he changes his mind? And what's this *dose* that made you sell my blood so freely? Without even talking to me first?"

"It's not important for you to know."

She worried her bottom lip. "Are you ill?"

Mace studied her. She got the sense that her concern satisfied him in some way, which made her eyes narrow stubbornly.

"I'm not ill," he assured, not bothering to conceal his smile.

"Don't act so smug. I haven't forgiven you just yet. You still sold my blood without my permission. *My* blood. It doesn't belong to you."

His expression fell. "You wanted my protection. I've just done what's best for you."

"Well, maybe protection isn't enough. I should have a say in what happens to me."

Mace turned his head away. "We'll speak of this later. I'd planned to take you back to Saraphine in the morning. You should get some rest."

Her chin shot higher. His statement sounded too much like an order in this moment. Although, she *was* tired.

Exhausted, really.

And she did want to see Saraphine again. Not only was the young witch spunky, and snarky to Mace, which Cora found humorous, but she'd felt an instant kinship with the girl. Also, maybe if her alleged powers were unbound, she'd finally be able to defend herself—a necessity if she were expected to contend with Knox.

Goddess, she hoped this magic thing wasn't fictitious.

And yet, she couldn't let Mace continue to think she would give into his every whim. She needed to dig her heels in before it became a habit.

"I'd like some space tonight," she informed him, amplifying her conviction through the use of her emotions and tightly crossed arms.

He didn't respond for a long while, his features going dark. Finally, he replied, "Sleep well, then. I'll fetch you in the morning."

With that, he closed her in the room.

Cora sighed and crossed to the window, glancing out over the darkened forest as she contemplated how that last look on Mace's face had spiked her pulse, and not in the way she liked.

He'd reacted strongly to something she'd said, but she couldn't decipher what.

A flash in the distance drew her attention. What had that been? A light of some kind? It came again from behind a large tree, joined by another. A dark figure, low to the ground, prowled through the forest, and she realized what the lights were.

Glossy eyes flashed once more, and it reminded her of the reflection off an animal's pupils.

While the human race had been drastically diminished by way of war, poverty, and disease, the natural predators of the land had flourished. It wasn't uncommon, even in city limits, to spot deer, or foraging bears. She couldn't see it clearly through the darkness, but by the bulky silhouette, she imagined she was probably looking at the latter.

A wild beast.

She was reminded how much more similar vampires were to animals than humans. She'd be smart to remember that when dealing with Mace. He had essentially claimed her as his mate, and she'd practically rebuked him just now. Maybe that's why she'd received such a strong mixture of feelings from him. It was part possessiveness spliced with greed. A large portion had been practically uncivilized, barbaric even. And a fraction had been something else entirely, something she couldn't even begin to describe.

She shuddered, pushed away from the window, and slipped under the covers, closing her eyes.

Morning came far too swiftly. Sleep had been restless.

Insanely, she'd felt bereft of Mason's warmth the whole night. And...guilty. Had she grown so used to the security of Mason's presence in such a short time?

And had she really yelled at him like that? Where had that bravado emerged from?

She washed and dressed in a pair of dark jeans that Mace had mentioned liking. A simple midnight-blue tank hung loose on her torso, and she put her hair up in a tight ponytail.

She'd had nearly the whole of the night to rationalize his high-handed decision, and her conclusion was simply this: Though she despised that he'd made that choice for her, it actually was an acceptable option for the time being. Knox could be mollified, leaving her free of harassment.

By the time Mace came for her, the sun was just cracking the tree line.

Cora took him in.

A black jacket hugged his torso. Under that, the butt of his gun peeked out of a holster that wrapped across his torso. Dark jeans and black utility boots finished off the ensemble.

He looked formidable. Terrifying. Sexy.

When she finally looked up at his face, she found him solemn. Yet determination was carved into the creases around his mouth.

There was a lot she wanted to say. She wanted to rid them both of this tension that had settled like a valley between them. Instead, she glided forward till only an inch separated them and lowered her forehead to his shoulder.

As if he understood what she needed, his arms came around her, his palms flat on the small of her back. She didn't know how long they stood like that, but eventually, without a word, they separated and made their way to the car.

"Going into town?" Knox shoved into the back seat, popping out of nowhere. "I'll just tag along then, won't I? Wouldn't want the two of you love birds plotting to run off without me?"

Cora shrank into the passenger seat, using it as a makeshift shield against his gaze. Mace seethed, but didn't respond as he started the ignition. The engine grumbled to life, and the car jerked into motion.

"Done a number on this beauty of a car," Knox commented blithely, brushing bits of glass over the edge of the back seat with his hand.

No one replied.

"It's a right heap. I know a guy. We could trade it for something more suitable for our...growing family." The last words were growled low, soaked in sarcasm.

Cora's shoulders tensed so badly her neck started to hurt.

"Knox, shut the fuck up," Mace fired at him.

"Pull over, and see if you can make me," Knox challenged.

She caught the look they shared in the rearview mirror, but, by far, it didn't match the sense of mutual hate she received from both of them through the bond. It went beyond her, as if it had been forged in a distant past, perhaps even long before she was born.

The original emotion that formed her perception suddenly cut off. It was as if a wall slammed down so hard, she was surprised she was the only one in the car to jump from the noise.

Taken off guard, she glanced back at Knox. He returned her puzzled gaze with one full of hostility.

She turned away.

It was then that she realized he could conceal his emotions from her.

Was that learned, or innate? Was it possible she could block her emotions from him?

She wouldn't dare inquire.

Surprisingly, after the exchange, Knox quieted. Yet the duration of the trip was steeped in thickly tense silence, bubbling with tempered aggression.

Outside Saraphine's shop, Mace pulled up to the curb and stepped out. Cora joined him on the cracked, uneven sidewalk. She was sure to keep Mace between her and Knox, but at the moment, Knox didn't seem to be interested in her.

His attention was on the two-story building with its slightly dilapidated storefront. For the first time, Cora noticed the sign over the door. The words Wicked Wares had been inscribed into a slab of wood that hung from a protruding iron rod. The letters were embellished with fanciful swirls and had been painted, but the color that could have once been vibrant red was dulled to a rusty burgundy and were cracked and peeling.

She glanced around, taking in the town that had previously eluded her interest as well. Crude buildings hinted at a once glorious past. Dirt and other natural debris stained the streets and walls fronted by a road that could have been a main street, but was empty of vehicles. She'd once seen part of an old western flick and half expected to spot a tumbleweed cross the street at any moment.

"This the hovel where your pretty witch friend lives?"

Mace turned a withering gaze on Knox. "Why don't you disappear for a while? Go do something useful?"

"And what would that be?"

"Trent said Cora should continue to eat. There's not a lot of food at the cottage right now."

"You want me to food shop for your little witch?" Knox balked, then laughed outright. "We never bargained for that." He rolled a dark gaze toward Cora. "If you want to renegotiate—"

She cringed.

"Forget it." Mace directed Cora inside.

Knox strolled in behind them.

Saraphine was sitting at the register, her feet up on the counter. The black tank top she wore was designed to look like a corset with black string laced down the front and was framed by a pattern of white and pink skulls. Her arms were covered by a sheer pantyhose material that left her pale shoulders exposed. Her jeans were tight and low on her thin waist, which inspired a bit of feminine envy in Cora. When Saraphine looked up, her feet flopped to the ground, boots landing loudly as she stood.

"Hiya, Cora!" she said. She glanced past Cora and Mace, and her expression fell. A hint of green took over the color in her face.

Knox loped farther into the room. His emotions were totally blocked from Cora. Not that she wanted to experience what he was feeling...ever. But it almost seemed as if whatever wall he'd put up between them had just been solidified.

Mace, too, had noticed a change in the atmosphere, but he was focused on Saraphine. "Everything alright?"

"'Course." She smiled at him sweetly, then quickly added, "I finished the potion this morning." She reached under the counter and produced a small teardrop vile filled with a purple liquid that seemed to glow from within.

"What do I do with it?" Cora asked as she moved closer, almost mesmerized by the container. An unexpected excitement unraveled inside her.

"You just drink it." Saraphine replied. She began to wring her hands together.

Cora picked up the vile and removed the stopper. The scent of lilac engulfed the room.

She was on the cusp of something wondrous, her mind insisted. Dangerous, maybe. Frightening, for sure. But wondrous nonetheless. Would she discover herself to be a powerful, extraordinary witch...filled with an astonishing, magical ability imparted upon her from birth? Would she finally discover the means of protecting herself, rather than cowering or relying on others?

The possibilities swirled in her head.

She paused. "Is this going to hurt like your last spell?"

One of Saraphine's shoulders lifted, the gesture miniscule yet packed with significance. "Most spells come with some physical effect. Not always painful."

She didn't miss the purposeful avoidance of the question. "Good to know. But will *this one* hurt?"

A new voice answered; an older voice Cora had never heard before. "It gonna hurt like a bitch. You may even think yer dying. But it will set you free." An ancient looking woman stepped out from the back room. She pointed a stubby, thick-knuckled finger at Knox. "Threaten my granddaughter again, vampire, and I'll string yer teeth into a necklace."

Arms crossed over his chest, Knox's features twisted into a wry grin. He shifted that same droll expression toward Saraphine and it tightened around his mouth. "*Lurela*?"

"What did you do?" Mace demanded, facing Knox.

"What you and Trent are too pussy to do. You think we'll ever be free of her when she gains her powers?"

All at once, Cora understood. A dim memory rushed to the forefront. Knox had argued with Trent and Mace about unbinding her magic. He'd wanted to keep her weak. Maybe even kill her.

She shuddered at that.

Had he hunted down Saraphine? Threatened her? Harmed her? If so, Saraphine was truly brave to have defied him and created the potion anyway.

"I don't want to be free of her," Mace replied, practically growling.

Cora's jaw went slack on a gasp. Mace sent her a fleeting glance then turned back to Knox.

"Well I do," Knox growled. "By allowing this, you're signing both our lives away."

Mace gestured to the door. "Walk away. No one's stopping you."

Knox sneered at Cora, then at the bottle in her grasp. The barest fissure cracked into his wall, and she read his intend. Before he could lunge for it—her salvation!—she tossed the contents of the vile back, gulping it down. He bellowed out a harsh cry and kept coming. Mace threw himself in the way, holding him back.

Unexpected pain lacerated her every nerve, and she doubled over. White-hot tendrils of burning agony slithered over her flesh, scorching its way inside as if to her very soul. Her skin felt as though it were being flayed and ripped back, exposing the muscle underneath. Spasms cut through her. Fevered agony ignited, seeming to boil the blood in her veins and searing off the sweat on her forehead.

The blazing inferno ate away all thought, devoured hope, leaving behind only misery and pain.

She was pure anguish. Suffering, her purpose. Agony, her friend. If she breathed, she didn't know. If she cried, she didn't know. If anyone mourned for her, she didn't know, for this was surely the end, and in the end, there was nothing but infinite torture.

Chapter 27

A glorious touch of cold patted her forehead, dripping over her scalp and into her hairline. She moaned softly as residual pain simmered under her skin. Her body was struggling to make a way for oxygen to enter her throat. Something hard was pressed into her back…the floor? Gravity was being a bitch at the moment. Its pull to the Earth seemed to have increased tenfold. Her chest felt concaved. She was spinning wildly, growing nauseous. Whatever was happening, she begged for it to stop. It begged back for her to open her eyes. She tried, but failed. Blinding light sent tiny swords through her brain.

A hand slapped down on her face, and she realized it was hers. Her limbs were finding it difficult to follow orders. Gaining a bit of control, she rubbed her aching head with clumsy fingers.

Another breath found its way into her lungs, blowing them up like a balloon that was too full, but it was necessary. She needed more. She concentrated on making that happen while a crisscrossing of voices mingled around her.

"She'll be alright now," one assured.

"She'd better be," another threatened.

"The worst is over," a third added.

For some reason she expected there should be a fourth, but the first began again. "Be wary. She'll be ill-equipped to use her powers, and mayhap they'll manifest involuntarily."

The fourth voice finally spoke. "Just fucking great." This voice sounded farther away than the others hovering directly over her.

"Bring her back here in one month's time, and I'll learn her best I can."

Pause. Breathe...

A scuffling sounded along the floor moved away from her, then returned in the same manner.

"What is that?" The second voice sounded alarmed now. "No more of your spells! She's had enough."

"This'll sooth. Bring sleep. Dull the pain."

Yes, she thought. *Dull the pain...no more pain.*

She must have verbalized the last, because those around her went quiet.

There was a deep sigh. "Okay, love. The old...uh...Ms. Windshaw is going to give you something else to drink. Do you think you can swallow?"

"No more pain," she pleaded in answer, her eyelids still too heavy to open. A tear tracked down her cheek.

"This had better work." Dark implication surrounded the phrase.

Something cool touched her lips. Liquid filled her mouth. She choked as it slid down her throat, her body instinctually rejecting it. Someone ordered her to swallow. She did. And, as the pain melted away, so did the rest of her.

Mace watched with staggering anxiety as Cora went slack. The fact that she still breathed kept his murderous tendencies in check. Knox was smart enough to stand out of the way, taking up the farthest corner of the room. The two witches appeared wary, but not as fearful of him as they should be. For a brief moment as Cora had writhed with agony on the floor, he'd suspected them all of plotting to murder her, and he'd been ready to end the lot.

"You should have warned me that would happen." Mace glared at the old woman.

"Warned the girl, weren't yer ears open? 'Sides, didn't know it would be so bad," Ms. Windshaw countered. "Put the gun away."

Mace looked at his hand. At some point he must have slipped the gun from its holster. He replaced it and then gathered Cora in his arms. "What do you mean you didn't know?"

"No spell works the same for every witch. Bindings especially. This one was particularly strong. Cast by her mother, I hear." The old woman looked at Cora thoughtfully. Under her breath, she muttered, "Tough life, this one. Powerful as she be, I don't envy her." The old witch sobered. "She'll be needin' you. Don't turn yer back on her."

"I would never turn away from her. She's mine," Mace replied. His tone brokered no debate.

The old woman appeared unconvinced. "For now. Not always."

That sent a chill crawling down Mason's spine. Violent denial squashed it. "Learn when to hold your tongue, old woman, or someone might hold it for you."

"Got plenty more in the back."

From behind, Knox released a deep chuckle.

Mace ignored him, keeping his focus on the witch. "Before I leave here, you'll remove that spell you placed on me."

Her wrinkly features became stern. "Won't be removin' nothing. Get back to your cottage and let the girl rest. And let that cat in. She'll be needing it, too."

"Cat?"

Knox took a menacing step forward. "How do you know about the cottage?"

Ignoring them both, the old woman turned and disappeared into the back room. Mace rushed after her, holding Cora steady as he went, but when he crossed into the other room, he found it empty. A sharp sulfur scent lingered in the air.

Returning to the front, Saraphine just shrugged at him, slanting wary glances toward Knox. He hadn't budged from his spot, but his narrowed gaze was fixed on her.

"Knox, go outside," Mace ordered.

Surprisingly, Knox didn't argue as he headed for the door.

"See you around, Saraphine," he muttered on his way out.

Saraphine turned pale, the color starker than ever against her black makeup.

He was going to have to keep a closer eye on Knox.

* * *

Cora soared on the fringe of consciousness and mentally slapped herself awake. When she opened her eyes, she expected to see the ceiling of Wicked Wares, not yet realizing that the padding at her back was far too soft to be the wooden floor.

Something dark hovered overhead, blocking her vision. A misty grey apparition? She blinked, and it vanished. Must have been the grit in her eyes.

A constant vibration down the length of her chest drew her attention. A small grey fluff-ball of a kitten, ears too big for its body, lifted its tiny head and peeked at her with wide green eyes. When she met its gaze, it let out a half meow, half yawn, revealing miniature teeth. At the same time, little paws stretched out, exposing sharp claws before retracting.

"Well, hello there," she cooed.

The bed shifted, and she quickly rationalized that she was back in her room at the cottage, and that Mace was lying next to her.

"Cora?" He propped up on his elbow. "How are you feeling?"

She surveyed her body. "Good. Where did this little guy come from?"

"Found it scratching at the door when we returned. I gather it belongs to you."

Cora stroked a hand down its silky spine. When she brought her hand closer to its ears, the kitten nuzzled its entire head into her palm. "What makes you think it belongs to me?"

"Nipped at my heels as I carried you up here and hasn't left its makeshift nest since."

"Since when?"

"We returned yesterday. You've been out nearly a whole day."

"Is Knox still here?"

Mace scowled. "Yes. He denies having threatened Saraphine."

Cora snorted and rolled her eyes.

"I know. I'll figure out how to deal with him later. For now, I must apologize to you."

Her brow furrowed. "For what?"

"I've been neglecting your needs too long. You must eat."

She focused on the state of her stomach. "I'm still not really hungry."

"Even so, you've been losing weight. You were much too light in my arms. Before we left town yesterday, we picked up some produce for you. It's in the kitchen."

"You and Knox went to the market together?" Cora couldn't help but smile at the image.

"Hardly. I sent Knox while I kept watch over you in the back seat of the car."

"And he was okay with that? Getting me food, I mean."

"I wouldn't say he was happy about it, but the gun in my hand was fairly persuasive."

"You sure the food isn't poisoned?"

"It's not. I tested it."

"You tested it? How?" *Don't tell me—*

"By eating some of it, of course."

"What?" She shot up, displacing the little kitten to her lap. The only protest came in the form of a surprised *murrow*? "What if it *had* been poisoned?"

He cupped his hand over her cheek. His lips pressed lightly to hers for a split second of bliss before he pulled back. "Then I would have hurt for a time, I suppose. But nothing like what I went through watching you suffering yesterday. Are you sure you're better? Do you feel...different?"

Oh, that's right! She'd nearly forgotten the point of that agonizing potion. Mentally, she registered, sorted, and categorized every nuance of her body, her mind, even glanced at her bare arms and hands, flipping them this way and that...searching for any sign that magic was now a part of her. Hers to control.

Disappointment made her shoulders hunch. "I don't feel any different at all."

He returned her disgruntled expression with a thin-lipped smile, yet he appeared...relieved? At her look, he admitted, "To be honest, I'm glad. I feared you'd be a completely different person when you woke." He playfully nudged her shoulder. "Like a witch or something."

She laughed. "But aren't I supposed to be? Maybe that blood test really was inaccurate."

Mace disagreed, explaining what Ms. Windshaw said while she'd been out. The prospect of training to master her powers did nothing to quell her disappointment. She had hoped for something a little more...instantaneous.

Mace didn't allow for much wallowing. He left her side and walked around the bed to stand before her. Then he offered his hand, with it, a wicked smile. "Let me care for you."

A thrill scored through her at his rumbling voice. Who'd have thought she'd ever be hot for a vamp. And she wasn't even hopped up on the red juice.

Cora set the kitten aside, gave one last scratch to its head, and then placed her palm in Mason's hand.

* * *

After Mace had thoroughly "cared for her" in the shower, on

the counter, against the wall, Cora shuffled through her newly purchased wardrobe with a towel around her body. She had the undeniable urge to wear something Mace would like. And she knew just the thing.

After a short hunt, she found what she was looking for. Knowing full well that Mace greedily watched her from the bed—still hadn't had enough of her by the looks of him—she hooked the red thong around one finger and nonchalantly held it up for his observation.

The kitten was perched in his lap, sleeping. Mace's big hand dwarfed the feline as he petted it. How cute was that?

At the sight of the undergarment, he let out a low growl, his eyes going dark. The kitten lifted its head.

"You mean to keep me here forever, vixen."

A shiver ran through her at the prospect. When Mason's fangs began to elongate, she bit her lip, recalling the pleasure those incisors had provided only moments ago. But then he seemed to mentally shake himself.

"No more distractions. You need food. So does your little furball."

She sighed. "Alright."

After stepping into the panties, she dressed in a tan blouse with delicate frills down the front and a pair of denim jeans that stretched over her hips like a glove. Mason's eyes had gone dark again. With sure steps, she sauntered toward him and then claimed the kitten, cradling it in her arms.

Still seated, Mace swore under his breath and then grabbed her backside hard, a hand on each ass cheek, pulling her close. The pressure sent a shock of pleasure up her spine, straight into her brain. She stifled a moan. Mace appeared nearly savage as he gazed up at her adoringly. As though he were starving, and not for her blood.

It was the first moment in her life she'd felt powerful.

It was heady, seductive, addictive.

Merrow. The kitten ran its cold nose along her forearm followed by a sand-papery tongue.

"I suppose I should eat something," she murmured on a sigh.

"Then right back up here," Mace said.

Downstairs, Cora found the kitchen filled with treats. Many that a year ago, she would have risked her life to pilfer: fruits, vegetables, pastries, whole milk...pie! Several kinds by the looks of it. She might not be hungry, but there was always room for pie.

Mace took a seat at the table as she pulled one of the delicacies out of the fridge and placed it on the opposite island counter. Then she grabbed a plate from the cabinet and transferred a slice onto it. Cherry filling seeped out of the flaky cocoon like a miniature rockslide.

Mace watched her with the same adoration as she scavenged for a fork. Next to him, the kitten lapped from a saucer of milk he'd set out.

"Would you like a piece?" she asked Mace, suddenly feeling awkward.

"Later, maybe. I've already had my dessert." He smiled suggestively.

She blushed furiously.

Just as she pulled a fork from a drawer, Knox appeared in the doorway. Mace tensed, and she froze, her eyes darting nervously.

"Well, *cher*? You going to offer me any?" As always, Knox's deep tone verged on a threat.

She didn't respond. Wasn't sure she could have even if her throat hadn't grown thick with unwanted panic. That powerful feeling had fled faster than a minnow in sea of piranha. Frustration mingled with her fear. She wanted to question Knox about Ms. Windshaw's accusation, about what he may have done to Saraphine. But like a coward, she only stood there as Knox idly slid the fork from her two-fingered grasp. Her teeth gnashed at his mocking expression as he bypassed her single serving and claimed the entire tin. Then he dug the fork straight into the middle and shoveled a heaping portion into his mouth.

"Knox," Mace chastised. "That's for Cora. You don't need it."

"You're right," he replied easily, not taking his eyes off her. "What I *need* has yet to be provided. We had a deal."

"And what she needs is to regain her strength."

His gaze languidly traveled over her. "Looks healthy enough to me."

She paled, and he smirked. He enjoyed her discomfort! A small fraction of her fear morphed into indignation. She couldn't allow him to continue his purposeful intimidation. Or, at least, she couldn't let it show. Not if she and Mace were going to corral him into behaving more reasonably.

Before they'd left the room, Cora had asked Mace, "I don't understand why we remain here with him." She'd witnessed vampires kill each other over something as insignificant as a childish argument, though she hadn't informed Mace of that.

He'd simply replied, "It's complicated. Besides, this is the safest location for you right now, even with Knox, and I'm sure he will calm down...eventually. "

Feigning bravado, Cora turned and retrieved another fork from the drawer. Then she snatched her pie and crossed to join Mace at the table. She was sure the desert was savory and sweet, but to her, the first bite was like powdered chalk. For effect, she crossed her legs and tried to appear at ease.

After a moment, Knox transferred his gaze from her to Mace. "I just spoke with Trent. He wants you to get to work on his list of suspects, or whatever. I've set up an office for you down below."

"And what will you be doing?"

He spread his arm out as if to say, "You're looking at it." At Mason's glare, he said, "VEA business is your bag, not mine. Got my own shit to do. And no, we're not going to gab about it like adolescent girls." He dug into the pie again.

Cora was on her third bite, and she thought she was actually starting to taste it. It would be a shame to down the whole thing with no enjoyment. She used to love food...when she could get it.

After her marriage, Winston had introduced her to all manner of wondrous delicacies.

Honestly she didn't care that she was no longer hungry. It was actually a relief not to feel the effects of starvation. She just wished her taste buds were in working order.

When she took another bite, flavor exploded into her mouth, and she jumped at the unexpected punch. Two sets of eyes swung toward her.

"What?" Mace asked.

Instead of answering right away, she eagerly tested the pie again.

Delicious!

"I think...I think I just did magic or something."

Whereas Mace seemed instantly curious, Knox appeared horrified. Before she could explain, he tossed the leftover pie onto the counter and stormed out of the room.

Chapter 28

With that somewhat trivial, yet profound, mystical evidence of magic existing within her, Cora became ravenous for information. Over the next few weeks, she delved back into the books Mace had provided. She read and reread the pocket book of spells, all the while attempting to access her powers again. Unfortunately with no noticeable luck. The book was mostly filled with superficial spells, such as increasing energy, helping with slumber, beauty remedies. Much of it was holistic in nature. There were a few in the back that claimed her interest. A spell called The Breath of Life, another dubbed Access to the Realm of Dreams, and another simply called Truth.

Her kitten, which she'd named Meeka, remained near and followed wherever she went. If she ventured downstairs for a light snack, Meeka would bound down after her. After a while, Meeka had taken to riding on Cora's shoulder, earning her amused looks from Mace.

She came across a bit of text that suggested Meeka might be her familiar, a witch's spiritual ally. As Cora read on, she found familiars were used to maintain a rapport with nature, a reoccurring theme, she discovered. Familiars were also considered companions and often assisted witches with their magic. The timing of Meeka's arrival was Cora's greatest affirmation that this was the case.

All in all, things settled down, as Mace had predicted. Cora had begun a regiment of bloodletting. Each morning, she would fill a thermos by carefully slicing her wrist under Mace's supervision and place it in the fridge for Knox. If she weakened or grew chilled from the loss of blood, Mace offered her his vein to replenish her energy and his body to warm her. She never took more from him than was necessary.

And though she never caught Knox drinking—he was thankfully keeping his distance—the thermos was always emptied by morning. Even if the means was distasteful to Cora, the resulting peace was priceless. She'd happily bleed as long as was necessary.

Mace began to relax as well, becoming more comfortable with leaving her from time to time. He often disappeared to a subterranean complex that reminded Cora of an elaborate bomb shelter.

He'd shown it to her once. That's when he'd discovered her unique phobia.

Quickly growing lost as he led her around the many rooms and corridors, she'd begun to shake and panic for the exit. The familiar sense of claustrophobia combined with the terror of being trapped crawled over her. It was almost as if she could feel the weight of the mountain above pressing down on her. The walls seemed to constrict, twist, and close in around her. When he'd brought her back out into the less confining cavern, he'd held her till her quaking ebbed. He hadn't suggested she venture down there again.

Most of the time, Cora remained in the sanctuary that was her and Mason's room, fumbling around with magic. Both the dream spell and the truth spell required a subject, so every night, after he finished with his work, Mace would volunteer. In their room, she would spread her things out over the floor, light the required color and number of candles, and sit just as still as she was now, chanting quietly as Mace rested nearby.

Nothing had come of it, and a few of the candles were already half burned.

It didn't help that she had no idea what to expect. Or what she was doing, for that matter. By the third week, discouragement ran rampant as she repeated the incantations over and over, feeling like an idiot.

When she was alone, like now, she focused mainly on the Breath of Life. She'd found the husk of an expired moth on the window's ledge, and for three straight days, she attempted to *breathe life* back into it. A rainbow of lit candles surrounded the moth on the floor, flickering in the darkened room. Cora sat on her knees, inhaling and exhaling with an intentionally slow tempo as the text instructed. She was meant to enter a trance of sorts before she began the incantation.

Meeka was sprawled on the edge of the bed, watching curiously. Dancing candlelight refracted off her large pupils.

Once relaxed, mind focused, Cora began to mumble out the words. "*Vi tres spiro vitam tuam. Tribus offero me in virtute. Unde profecti estis Spiritu ad corpora redituras.*"

She repeated the words till they spilled from her automatically, till they ran together and rode the edges of her breath.

Then, when she felt ready, she leaned forward, put her lips together, and blew out a light gust. Air caught under the dusty wings and the lifeless moth skittered stiffly along the carpet.

She straightened her spine. A heartbeat passed. Then another. Cora realized she was holding her breath, and her pulse was oddly speeding up with anticipation. She couldn't be sure, but she thought she'd felt...something that time. A burst of energy?

When the moth remained motionless, her shoulders slumped. She was almost ready to give up entirely.

Then...a single wing moved!

She waited. Could have been a draft.

The other wing fluttered...then both jointly. When the tiny antenna shimmied back and forth, Cora slapped a hand over her mouth, unsuccessfully muffling an exuberant cry.

Just as the moth leapt into magnificent flight, Mace entered and took in her expression. "What's up?"

Rendered completely speechless, she could only point to the moth, flapping its way towards him. As it approached, he bowed backwards, and before she could explain, he swatted his palms together.

She gasped, "You killed it!"

He glanced up idly as he wiped his hands on his jeans. "What? That bug?"

She shot to her feet. "I brought it back from the dead!" Her pitch was high, her tone accusatory, and her outrage increased while he attempted to stifle a humorous grin.

"Let me get this straight. The first bit of magic you do is to zombify a moth and have it attack me?"

"It wasn't zombified."

"Didn't you see it salivating as it lunged at me? It was terrifying."

"It's not funny." She gritted her teeth against the traitorous smile playing along her lips. Determined not to be amused, she crossed her arms.

He made his expression contrite. "I'm sorry I killed your undead pet. Next time put a collar on it...with a bell maybe."

Battle lost, Cora dropped her arms and allowed a giggle to roll out of her.

He came forward and pressed an apologetic kiss to her lips.

She pulled back. "Oh, goddess! What if it had been a zombie moth? What if it had bitten you?"

"Then you'd have one sexy zombie-vamp to look after." He trapped her with strong arms around her waist and dipped his head to nibble along her neck, tickling her flesh with fleeting nips until she squealed with laughter.

When their humor died down, he said, "Come on, let's go scrounge up some more insect carcasses for your minion army."

Knox glared at the disgustingly happy couple as they practically frolicked out the door. Over the last few weeks, the witch's emotions were growing more acute, invasive, burrowing into his brain. He was finding it increasingly difficult to block her. Although it was curious that whenever she noticed him in a room, her caustic emotions would cut off, like a door slamming shut on a chaotic mental cyclone.

Not that he was complaining, but it almost made him wonder what the chit was up to. What was she hiding from him? Furthermore, was she just as easily masking herself from Mace? Served him right if he was tangled in her snare. The idiot fancied himself half in love already. Typically, Knox wouldn't give a damn about it if he hadn't been caught up in this shit as well.

He made his way up to the love-bird's room and paused in the doorway, sneering at the display of witchcraft along the floor. The recently extinguished candles still simmered with smoke. On the bed, the witch's pet rolled over and looked at him with too-keen eyes.

"Keep your mouth shut about this, cat, and I won't kill you just yet."

The cat meowed. Then it stretched in an impossible arch before settling back down and closing its eyes.

The tattered copy of Pride and Prejudice was still sitting where Knox had placed it weeks ago. Apparently, she hadn't touched it. He laughed at that. Didn't care for the memory with which it was now linked, huh?

His search began with her dresser drawers. He was hoping to find something. But what? He wasn't sure. A twinge of evidence that she planned to bond more than just him and Mace. Perhaps she had Trent in her sights. If so, the girl was a moron. There wasn't a witch alive who could control that vampire.

Perhaps, despite her protests when Mace had informed her of Trent's intentions with the underground compound, she was eager for their entire clan to relocate here.

Joke's on her. Trent had put off the move till this thing with her and the black-market blood had been solved and ordered Mace to keep her here till then. She wouldn't be crossing the path of another vampire any time soon.

Finding nothing of interest, besides the female's undergarments—Mace always did like frills—Knox moved on to search Mace's things, not really expecting to discover much. Neither of the two had much in the way of belongings. He noticed Mace's phone on top of the dresser and began flipping through the texts.

He read one from Trent that had him grinding his teeth. "Son of a bitch."

Cora was a descendant of the Conwell bloodline? Had they hid this from him on purpose? The phone groaned in protest against his hold.

Just then, the cat hissed at something in the corner of the room, her back arching. He followed her line of sight to a space that was unnaturally darkened by a writhing, sandy mist.

He'd been wondering why the spirit had finally ventured out of its impervious haven. Now he knew.

He lifted one corner of his mouth in a cruel smile. "It appears a relative has come for you at last. Don't get your ghostly hopes up. I'll kill her before she sets you free. The best you can hope for is that she'll join you in hell."

He couldn't tell if the apparition understood him or not. It remained tucked in the corner.

Disregarding it, he turned back to the phone and swiped through the photographs. Cora was the subject of dozens—no hundreds—of shots. Cora at a coffee shop, smiling at the barista as she claimed a cup. Cora seated on a leaf-strewn deck, shaded by an umbrella. Cora in a park, walking, seemingly aimlessly, her expression far-away as if deep in thought. Cora kneeling in an alleyway, handing a small box to an elderly homeless man. And countless more images. In all of them, she seemed unaware of her photographer.

Looked like Mace was getting his PhD in stalker-ology. Pathetic.

Knox came to the last photo and stared at it for a long moment.

It was a snapshot of Cora perched on a motorcycle in a porn star pose, except her expression was naively clueless. Tendrils of long damp hair clung to her neck, disappearing under the collar of a binding tan coat. The fuck-me boots hinted at a scandalous concealment. He turned the phone this way and that, enthralled.

Ugh. The witch was getting to him!

Furious, he tossed the phone aside and beat feet out of the room, noticing the apparition had vanished. The cat had once more calmed.

As he came to the bottom of the stairs, the front door opened. An exuberant Cora was laughing at something Mace had said as she entered. The sound cut off when her eyes landed on Knox. Anxiety spiked.

Your fear is wise.

As expected, the door to her emotions slammed shut. Yet then she raised a confused brow at him before averting her gaze entirely.

Out of the loop, Mace acknowledged Knox with the tip of his head and guided Cora up the stairs to do god knows what with her magic.

Idiot! You court your own destruction.

And he was blindly dragging Knox into the path of the wrecking ball. He could sense nefarious intentions in every move she made. An expert seductress if he'd ever seen one. She wouldn't be satisfied till both he and Mace were drooling after her like lost puppies begging for scraps.

Hell, he was already ravenous for the chilled thermos of

blood each morning, felt deprived when it was emptied. And that paled in comparison to the succulent memory of the warm stuff straight off the tap. He wasn't one to beg, far from it, but he feared she'd have him on his knees in no time.

Clearly, Trent had resigned them to their fate, and it was time Knox took control of this situation.

Chapter 29

Drab grey walls boxed Mace in. The illumination coming from the computer screen bounced off his skin, bathing it lightly in a harsh blue tone. After so many days down here, he could almost understand Cora's aversion to the place, even as his kind tended to prefer underground domiciles.

Going down the list Trent had provided, Mace typed in the name of the next suspect: Randall Pike. It was one of Cora's old neighbors whose wife had recently and miraculously recovered from terminal brain cancer. Mace had already gathered intel on the man when first assigned to the case.

On the surface, Randall was an entrepreneur, investor, and wealthy restaurant owner with several five-star establishments to his name. His net worth was twice what Winston's had been.

Behind closed doors, the stout, balding Randall was...boring.

He cared for his wife, was a devoted father, donated to various charities, appeared to be law abiding. And for a man of his stature, he was oddly polite to the help. Nothing like how Winston and some of his cohorts had been.

In fact, the only indication of Randall's possible involvement with the black-market blood rested solely on his wife's newly acquired good health.

Like the others, Mace checked Randall's phone records, hacked his personal computers, scanned his emails, made backup copies of his entire hard drive, and then audited his finances, noting any large or unusual purchases. He also embedded a spy program before moving on to the next name on the list and repeated the process.

Heavy footfalls at his back indicated Knox's approach. Mace glanced behind him to see the other vampire leaning against the door frame, clutching a mug. The sweet tang of Cora's cooled blood tingled in his nostrils.

Jealousy flared as acutely as his hunger.

He hated that he had to share even a drop of Cora with Knox. And not only that, Mace hadn't been taking as much from her so that she could provide for Knox, thus keeping the peace. Knox hadn't been making any such concessions. The greedy bastard downed every last drop by mid-morning.

"Can I help you?" Mace returned his attention to the computer.

"Can't a bloke come and visit his old friend?"

"Sentimental, are we? Drop the pretense. It doesn't become you."

"Not sentimental. Just curious."

After a moment of silence, interrupted by the clicking of his keyboard, Mace took the bait. "Curious about what?"

"I've been thinking—"

"Ouch, do you need something for the pain?"

"Do you honestly believe the witch—"

"Coraline."

"—to be clueless of her origins?"

Mace tensed slightly with guilt. Per their conversation with Trent, Knox was aware that, until recently, Cora had no recollection of her true nature, but Mace hadn't informed him of Cora's lineage. He was hoping to avoid that revelation as long as possible. At least until Knox's hostility died down.

"I've had a lot of time to determine the genuineness of her claim. I believe she was bespelled by her mother to forget her birthright."

"Right. And to forget her...family. For what purpose?"

"I don't know, and neither does she."

"Convenient."

"She's been alone all her life, struggling, living like a *human*."

"Such a tragedy."

Mace ignored the contempt in Knox's tone. "She might be a witch, but I guarantee she's nothing like what you've encountered. She's kind and compassionate. There's no underlying, devious plot for you to uncover here."

"Of course. Just an all-around, bona fide witch...who just happens to be a descendant of the Conwells!"

Mace's fingers halted over the keyboard. His shoulders cinched higher.

"Were you planning on ever telling me who she really is?"

He swiveled his chair to face Knox. "I'm not sure."

"And you dare bring her here of all places?"

"You weren't supposed to be here. I had no idea you'd been assigned to...whatever it is you're doing."

"And yet you stayed."

"Like I've said, this is the safest place for her right now."

Knox's features contorted into a shallow grin. "You have no idea how wrong you are."

"What do you mean?" Mace's eyes darted to Knox's hand resting on the edge of the heavy metal door, then to the blank re-enforced walls of the...cell?

As Mace came to this realization, Knox answered, "She and I are about to square things away. I think it's best you stay out of the way."

Mace lurched out of his chair as the door slammed shut, the grinding of a metal bar across the door's front barricaded him inside.

* * *

Cora lay stomach down on the bed, head propped on her elbows and Quick Spells for the Witch on the Go sprawled out in front of her. She swiped her thumb and forefinger over her tongue and then turned the page.

Yesterday, she had tried well into the night to duplicate the Breath of Life, only to be left with a pile of decomposing insect remains. It didn't help that the whole time Mace had lounged shirtless on the mattress, watching her with a smoldering gaze.

Today, she decided to find a spell that might be a little less advanced. Infusing Body Odor with Floral Scents appeared promising. All she'd need to do was hold an aromatic flower as she chanted a spell.

When Meeka sauntered across the bed and plopped her body under Cora's nose, directly on top of her book, Cora decided it was time to take a break. "Are you hungry, cutie?"

Meeka meowed and began absently licking her paw.

"I suppose I should eat something too, huh? Don't want all that pie to go to waste."

Downstairs in the kitchen, she set Meeka near the newly designated cat bowl beside the fridge and filled it with dry food from the bag she and Mace had procured in town. Meeka happily crunched away.

As Cora dug through the fridge for herself, she got the uneasy sense of being watched. She straightened her spine and glanced around, seeing no one. Yet still, she felt ill at ease. "Hello?"

She ducked into the living room. Her heart stuttered when she spotted a shadowy figure across the room. It rolled and tilted what looked to be its head like a curious animal would. Its transparent body mimicked the eerie move.

She shivered.

Then the mist sank to the ground and crawled along the carpet toward the stairs before ascending to the second floor. It paused halfway up, and she got the impression it wanted her to follow.

Though it had startled her, she didn't sense an open threat from the thing. It might not have even meant to scare her. Maybe that was why it wanted her to go to it, rather than coming to her. If it had approached, she would have headed straight down to the underground compound to find Mace. Phobia be damned.

If the apparition was sentient, it might have expected that reaction from her. Her fear could just be inherent, born of ignorance. Or perhaps not. She should have gone back and read that section on ghosts.

After several moments, curiosity won the debate in her head, and she started for the stairs.

As she skirted around the furniture, a hard wall of muscle

plowed into her from behind, pinning her legs to the back of the couch. The quick motion thrust her torso forward and she braced herself on the seatback.

"Hello Coraline." The dangerously deep voice could only belong to Knox.

Without thought, she cried out for Mace.

"He's a little trapped by his work at the moment. It's just you and me. Shall we cozy up?"

Thick fingers gripped her nape and drew her back against his chest. His warm breath whispered along her neck. She swallowed hard, feeling her pulse spike, which was probably what Knox was going for.

"What do you want?" She feigned bravado with all she had in her, but her voice still shook.

"We haven't had a load of quality time to get to know each other," he said darkly. "This is me, making time."

"What have you done with Mace?"

"Relax, *cher*. He won't be interrupting us this time." Knox ran his nose along the curve of her neck towards her earlobe. With his lips an inch away, he said, "I think you owe my aching bollocks an apology kiss."

Anxiety made her terse. "How 'bout we just shake hands and call it a day?"

A rough chuckle rumbled through him. "Saucy witch. Maybe I should give you a tongue lashing instead."

She shuddered, wondering if Knox intended the double-entendre. "Get to the point," she snapped.

His crotch pressed deeper into the crevice of her jean-clad ass, and his fist tightened in her hair before angling her head to the side. The tips of his fangs trailed along her skin, yet not penetrating. "Is that really what you want?"

Her throat grew thick, and she could only gasp at the sensation of sharp teeth grazing tender flesh. She knew she wasn't walking away from this without, at the very least, his fang in her. She had accepted that fact from the moment she'd heard his unmerciful voice. And she knew the moment he bit her she would like it no matter what—such was the nature of vampires. However, and to her utter confusion, the shiver that raked through her bordered on anticipation, rather than aversion.

What was that about?

It was only because Mace had taught her the rapture of his bite, she quickly reasoned. It was Mace she wanted breathing in her scent as Knox was now.

Knox pulled his fangs away to mutter, "Your death would solve everything. You know that, don't you?"

She froze up in his grasp.

"He thinks you're his. But you can't be his when you're mine."

"I'm not yours."

"You've made it so by bonding me," he accused vehemently.

"I didn't—"

"Claim ignorance once more. It matters not. It's done. And now I can't decide if I want to kill you or fuck you."

Adrenaline surged, and her body thrashed. He yanked her head back in warning as his thick arm snaked around her waist. As a result, her ass jutted out and her back arched awkwardly.

She let out a terrified sob, her eyes watering. "Please, Knox. I never wanted any of this."

His hand splayed along her stomach, the tips of his fingers dipping under the hem of her pants and finding the strap of her frilly underwear.

"You don't want this?" Amusement underlined his tone. His hand in inched lower.

"No."

"Then why do I scent your arousal?"

She shook her head in denial, her hair pulling taut in his grasp as she did so. She made no other response.

"It's because you're playing me," he accused. "Mace too. To be fair, he's always been a fool. And now that you have your magic, we're doomed to be enslaved by you for as long as you deem fit."

Again she shook her head.

His fist in her hair tightened to the point of pain. "I've made my decision. I'm going to eat you, fuck you, and then kill you."

Her tender flesh gave way to sharp points as his fangs sank in. Short-lived pain was slashed by near instant ecstasy, muddling her mind.

Panic ebbed, and she moaned.

Knox groaned, the sound caressing her flesh. The tips of his fingers breached her panties, brazenly descending. Her cheeks fired red-hot at what she knew he would discover.

He stilled, a barbarous sound rumbling through his chest. Then, unabashedly he began stroking her considerable dampness while greedily sucking at her neck. Her ass moved against his crotch. He rewarded her by swiping his thick finger over her clitoris.

Even as euphoria seized her, she cursed her treacherous body's response to his feral brutality. A conflict battled in her pleasure-numbed brain. This was wrong, but oh so right. He would kill her, but what a way to go. But before all that? He would take her against her will.

"Stop this," she managed through a moan.

He growled in protest, holding her tighter, sucking her harder.

Her plea vanished under a wave of rhapsody.

Then suddenly the weight of him was ripped away, cool air replacing his body heat. She shook her head hard, trying to regain her senses as she relied on the support of the sofa to keep her body from collapsing under her wobbling legs.

The fierce roar of an animal forced her attention to the right.

A massive beast held Knox to the floor by large paws and sharp talons. Their tips dug into his chest, drawing blood. The deeply golden-furred creature was nearly twice his size.

Recognition tugged at the back of her mind, but...it couldn't be the same mountain lion from before. It snarled out another roar in Knox's face. Knox growled back, but seemed unable to match the beast's strength to throw him off.

How the hell had it gotten in here?

The beast swiveled its massive head around and met her stunned gaze with intelligent green eyes.

Impossible.

"Meeka?"

The large feline chuffed and turned back to Knox, baring her teeth.

Disbelieving, she peeked into the kitchen, seeing the food she'd left out only half eaten, no cute tiny kitten in sight.

"Holy shit," she gasped.

Then her mind sharpened into focus.

She had to find Mace.

Chapter 30

"Mason!" Cora hollered into the entrance to the underground complex. "Are you in there?"

No response.

Her gaze darted nervously around the cavern. Chills crept along her shoulders. Her palms turned clammy. The thought of reentering that place terrified her, but not as much as the thought of Knox overpowering Meeka and coming after her.

As soon as she crossed the threshold into the first, perfectly constructed room, that familiar, abstract pressure closed in around her. A creaking noise made her jump. Whether real or imaginary, the ceiling bowed at the center. The scream of failing metal beams scraped her ears.

Her pulse jack-hammered, and her already overflowing adrenaline gushed out of control. A dull pain thrummed behind her ribs.

She scrunched her eyes closed painfully tight. Instead of darkness, images of her parent's demise, her own experience of being trapped for days with their rotting corpses, flashed ruthlessly. Her eyes parted wide, burning with tears.

Brushing aside the crushing terror, she forced her feet forward into the next room. Her breaths shallowed as her lungs reacted poorly to the constricting panic. Still she proceeded, determined. Knox had said Mace was *trapped by his work*, which, to her, meant he was down here, possibly locked in a room—there were so many to search!

As she maneuvered the maze, she called for Mace while chanting to herself that the roof would not come crashing down on her. The rooms seemed to be growing smaller, more confining, the farther she traveled. Mace wasn't responding to her calls. Had he been knocked out? Was he even down here?

Was he dead?

She pushed that from her mind.

What if this was a trap, orchestrated by Knox. A sick game of chase?

She quickly waved that suspicion away. Knox had already had her where he'd wanted. She'd had no hope of escaping him. He couldn't have anticipated her sweet little kitten transforming into an oversized predator with fangs larger than his.

Pride briefly overruled claustrophobia.

How long could Meeka hold him? How long had it been already? Was she going in circles? These rooms all looked the same. Oh goddess! The roof was sinking! Had that been an explosion she'd heard?

Have to get out!

Another explosion sounded, encouraging hysteria. Her boots trampled concrete as she raced back the way she'd come, or the way she thought she had come. Which door had she taken? The one on the right, or the one on the left?

Another explosion sent her to the right. Then to the left. Oh, goddess! The blasts were becoming louder, the vibration rumbling the entire building!

No. Not a building...

She forced herself to still as harsh gasps of air flooded her burning lungs, her chest heaving. She listened, managing to gulp down a bit of her fear. Her mind cleared, bringing back reality. She wasn't in the basement of a ten story building about to crash down. She was in a stable underground shelter. And those explosions weren't explosions at all, but echoes, as if something were striking metal.

Shaking, nearing exhaustion, she followed the noise.

Muffled bellows gave her pause.

"Mason!" she screamed, feeling her panic resurface.

The banging ceased.

"Cora?" Mace called, his voice filtered by several thick walls. "Cora! Are you alright?"

"I'm coming. Keep talking." The explosions were from him banging on metal, nothing more. Her heart eased its pace, though her breaths still came fast.

"Tell me you're well," Mace called. His voice was closer now.

"I'm fine," she lied. She didn't know how else to answer. "Knox attacked me, but Meeka's holding him."

"Oh, thank god. Did he hurt you? Are you..." There was a long pause. "Did you say Meeka's holding him?"

As he spoke, his voice boomed louder than ever, and she halted in the middle of the room she'd entered. He was just on the other side of a metal door to her right that looked like a came straight out of a high-security prison.

She pulled on the barricade, but it didn't budge. There didn't appear to be a lock on it. She tried again, harder this time. She thought it moved a little, but couldn't be sure. It must just require more pressure. She leaned her body into it, braced her feet on the floor, and used all her weight to slide the metal bar to the right. It screeched as it relented. Her body jerked to a stop when the bar had gone as far as it could.

Then she tugged on the door handle just as Mace pushed it open. She sighed with relieve to see him unharmed.

He swept her up in a tight hug. "I'm so sorry."

"It's not your fault," she assured.

He didn't look convinced. "Tell me what happened."

"We should hurry back first. I don't know how long Meeka can hold out."

Confusion overtook Mace's features for a moment. Then he swiftly guided her out of the complex and back into the cottage.

When they entered the living room, Mace paused. Meeka, in her beastly form, still had Knox pinned. Mace was stunned for a long while, his jaw opening as if to speak, but no words came out.

Knox interrupted his sneering at Meeka to slide his gaze Cora's way. Even though he had been disabled, he still managed to look triumphant. Some people were like that, defiant to the very end. She used to admire that trait, now it was just irritating.

As he continued to stare at her, he spoke to Mace. "We've squared a few things away, she and I. Though we didn't have a chance to finish our conversation."

"You're done." Mace sliced his flattened palm through the air with finality. "You crossed the line. I should kill you now."

Knox met Mace's hostile glare with a challenge. "I dare you."

Aggression flared between them for several long moments. Meeka kept a silent snarl trained on Knox, her head low in coiled threat. It was the strangest scene Cora had ever witnessed.

Knox's words were bold, but stupid. Mace had every advantage, and Knox had little chance of survival if Mace decided to take him up on his dare. And she really didn't think that was what Knox wanted. He was bluffing. Wasn't he?

Mace brought in a hefty breath and let it out through his nose. "Trent will be informed and will decide your fate. Till then, you'll remain in the cell you'd intended for me."

She couldn't explain Mace's easy capitulation. He should be ripping Knox's guts out with his bare hands. Not that she wanted to witness that. But vampires were ruthlessly territorial, and she was his.

Wasn't she?

Maybe that's what he would be doing if she'd told him the whole story of Knox's attack. Yet she knew she would keep a few details to herself, deciding the reason was to spare Mace.

She internally cringed at her behavior with Knox. Again, she reminded herself it was his bite that made her act so lascivious.

Meeka backed off as Mace moved to take charge. Knox rose by degrees, looking as if there were some damage to his bones. Just as he made it to his full height, Mace plowed a bone-crunching fist into Knox's jaw, sending him reeling backwards into the wall. Blood gushed from his mouth. However, Knox just straightened his spine and smiled, his teeth dripping red.

Meeka trotted over and placed herself protectively at Cora's front. On closer inspection, she wasn't exactly a mountain lion.

She was much larger, her features more menacing, if that were even possible. And with her nose still wrinkled on that silent growl in Knox's direction, she almost looked prehistoric.

Mace shoved Knox toward the cavern stairs. As Knox passed, he locked gazes with Cora. She lifted her chin, her lips pressing in a tight line. The corners of his mouth curled, as if to say, "It was worth it."

More than ever, she wished she had control of her magic so she could zap that expression off his face forever.

Chapter 31

With Knox locked away, Cora felt safe for the first time in ages. She hadn't realized how aware she'd been of his presence, and the dark stares in her direction, which she'd originally attributed to his anger over the accidental blood bond.

Now the memories of those dark stares were colored by malevolence.

And yet, a week had passed and still she contemplated his motives. Had he really endeavored to kill her? When she thought it over, she had to admit he hadn't actually hurt her. Not really. Yet that didn't mean he wouldn't have. He didn't seem the type to offer empty threats. So then why did her mind insist on analyzing the insidious exchange? She tried to recall if she'd caught a glimmer of his emotions, but even if she had, she'd been blinded by her own.

Mace had no idea she was giving Knox more than a moment's thought, but every now and then he'd slant a curious glance at her and ask what she was thinking. Her emotions must be telling, and she often swam in guilt over what had transpired.

When he inquired once more, she jauntily lied, "I'm thinking about finally training with Ms. Windshaw."

The old woman had instructed Mace to bring her back to Wicked Wares in one month. That was tomorrow.

She wiggled her fingers at Mace and grinned. "I can't wait to finally learn how to wield these suckers."

He stunned her with a wickedly flirtatious grin. "I can attest you've already neared expert status." He pulled her close and dipped his head to take her lips in a soft kiss that soon had her raring for more. He'd hardly left her side since the incident. Almost as if he were overcompensating for not having prevented Knox's attack. He'd been so concerned over an outside threat he'd discounted the danger within.

Yet she worried there might be something more to his constant attention. He seemed able to decipher her emotions better than she. What sort of distance was required before he could no longer sense her? Even stuck so far underground, would he have been, figuratively, front row and center to her encounter with Knox? If so, what did he make of it?

She didn't dare ask. The merest speculation made her feel irrationally tawdry. In fact, neither of them spoke of Knox if they could help it.

Over the last week, the shadowy entity had only appeared to her once more. She'd woken from a dead sleep one night to find it eerily floating near the end of the bed as if it were watching her and Mace sleep. She'd observed it until it skulked out of the room, presumably back to its mysterious window realm, or wherever it was that it went. At first she'd been frightened of the thing, but it hadn't harmed her, hadn't so much as brushed up against her. She got the feeling it was trapped. A spirit between planes maybe. Perhaps in need of assistance. Both she and Mace hoped Ms. Windshaw could enlighten them on how to deal with it.

Cora crawled into bed next to Mace.

He wrapped his arms around her and pulled her close, settling the crown of her head just under his jaw. "Is everything alright with you?"

"Yes. Why?"

Meeka, back in her kitten form, hopped up onto the mattress and declared herself with a strong meow. Then she pranced toward them and curled her little body into a crevice between their bodies.

As Mace scratched under Meeka's chin, he replied, "Your expression. You look melancholic."

"I do?"

"And you haven't smiled in a while."

"I have too," she argued.

"Not a real smile. Not one that reaches you inside."

She frowned at that.

"Are you happy here with me?" he asked suddenly.

She froze at the unexpected question.

Mace waited patiently for her response, his breath stunted.

"Of course I'm happy," she replied, but there was a false note.

He attempted to sift through her emotions, but lately, it was like finding one's way through a tight cluster of barbed chicken wire.

A week ago, he assumed while Knox was assaulting her, he'd

felt her calling out to him. It was like a lasso around his heart, squeezing tighter with every second he was unable to get to her. He'd never been rendered so helpless, or frightened, in his life. He'd failed her in every way. Could have lost her forever.

But then, as he had bashed his fists against the thick cell door, he'd sensed her acquiesce mingled with considerable lust, and it was a dagger to his chest. At some point, he'd fallen to his knees in anguish.

But he couldn't fault her. Knox had utilized his bite as many before him had: barbarically and without mercy.

I should have killed him.

But if he had, his own life would have been forfeited, according to clan law. Both he and Knox were bonded to Cora, and therefore, both were to be allowed full access to her. Technically, keeping Knox confined, as he was now, was considered illegal.

"You want to try that one again?" he said to Cora, distracting himself from his spiraling thoughts.

She cringed. Did she realize what he wanted from her? He had no right to push her on this. She'd been through too much in the last six weeks.

As if reading his mind, she said, "So much has happened in little more than a month. Everything I once knew has been turned on its head. I'm not sure about anything anymore. I'm no longer Coraline Gordon, I'm...I don't even know."

"You're Coraline Conwell."

"Right. Who is that person?"

"She's intelligent, beautiful, sexy as hell. I believe she's a powerful witch, though she hasn't figured it out. But she must be, because she's easily bewitched me." He took her by the wrist and placed her palm over his chest. "She has captured my heart."

She swallowed and forced a smile, then lowered her head to rest on his outstretched arm, placing her forehead down on his pectoral muscle, successfully hiding her face. He knew what that meant. He might not have her heart yet, but at least she wasn't afraid of him anymore. That was something. She only needed time to comb through her disheveled feelings.

He could only imagine how jarring it must be to have wholeheartedly believed something one month and then the opposite another. To, in fact, care for a vampire, demolishing a lifelong opinion that all vampires were evil.

Although she was not yet ready to admit how much she cared for him, her palm flattened over his heart.

Chapter 32

After stepping out of the car, Cora approached the building and read aloud the note taped over the door to Wicked Wares. "Due to a tragedy in the family, we will be closed for the next several days. Check back soon." She knocked anyway and then turned to Mace. "I hope they're okay."

"As do I." When no one answered, a shadow crossed over Mason's face.

"What's that look for?"

"Not sure. Suspicious timing, I guess."

"You don't think...Knox?"

Mace only shrugged and then guided her back to the car with his palms on her shoulders. Though she was disappointed to not have been able to begin training today, she felt a deep sense of compassion for the witches loss, whoever it may have been. She knew all too well how terrible it was to lose loved ones.

Back home, Cora bided her time by continuing her own form of training. She was still unable to replicate the Breath of Life.

She also took to exploring the grounds and was perplexed to find the vegetation nearest the cottage to be completely different from the vegetation farther out. It was almost as if the cottage was encased in a bubble. In a state of suspended animation. Flowers never wilted, that she could tell. Trees remained lush and full of leaves, yet their growth stunted when compared to the more massive surrounding forest with its thick, tightly packed trunks and towering reach.

How odd.

She immediately attributed it to whatever magic had been placed on the cottage. It only made sense. Whoever had concocted this remarkable spell must have been a powerful witch indeed.

After a heated conversation with Trent, Mace returned to his investigation of the missing vampire and black market blood. Trent was unhappy about Knox's imprisonment and had ordered his immediate release till an investigation could ensue. Mace refused, which Cora understood to be unusual. The orders of a sire didn't often go unfulfilled.

Mace frequently checked on her, clearly disliking that he had to leave her alone, but for now, she refused to venture back down into that dungeonous maze. And unfortunately for Mace, the cottage was not fitted for Internet access.

Every morning for the next three days they returned to Wicked Wares, finding the same vague note and no sign of Saraphine or her grandmother. On the fourth day, Cora hadn't expected anything different.

However, the note was removed.

Tentatively, she tried the knob, and the door creaked open.

"Hello?" She entered, setting off the retro bell chime that

hung just above the door. Was that new?

Mace followed behind her.

The storefront was empty, but after a moment, Saraphine stepped out from the back room. Cora took in the girl's gaunt appearance, unkempt hair, and dark stains under a pair of shockingly makeup-free eyes. Her outfit was still goth-girl-chic, although there were fewer embellishments than the last time Cora had seen her. Most heartbreaking, Saraphine appeared younger, yet she wore the wearied expression of someone twice her age with the weight of premature responsibility on her shoulders.

The moment Saraphine saw them, her face went impossibly pale. She dove behind the counter and retrieved a shotgun from under the counter, pointing it in their direction. The barrel appeared to have been sawed off.

Cora's hands flew up while Mace dragged her behind him.

"What's this?" he demanded.

"Is that bastard with you?"

"Who, Knox?" he replied. "No. It's just us. Lower your weapon."

Cora peeked around Mace, seeing the gun barrel shaking slightly, Saraphine's eyes watering.

"What happened?" she asked in a more subdued tone than Mace had used.

Saraphine hesitated.

"Please, Saraphine, we're friends. I promise." Cora stepped out from behind Mace. He moved to put her back in place, but she dodged the attempt.

"No. It's your fault," Saraphine accused. "She died because of you."

"What?" Stunned, Cora allowed Mace to pull her back into

the protection of his body. Her legs fumbled on the way. "Who died?"

"My grandmother."

Cora's heart dropped like a cannon blast to the pit of her stomach. "Ms. Windshaw's dead?"

"She was murdered."

Tears threatened. "Oh, goddess, I'm sorry...but why because of me?" Had Knox gotten to the old woman to prevent her from teaching Cora?

Saraphine's next words were like a kick to the solar plexus. "That other vampire you brought here. Knox? Murdered her in cold blood."

The tears that had previously remained captured escaped her lower lids, cascading down her cheeks. *Should I have foreseen this?* Could this have been prevented somehow? If she hadn't worked so hard to avoid Knox, would she have sensed his malicious intent?

"I'm so sorry," she repeated absently.

"You saw him do this?" Mace asked.

"No," Saraphine replied harshly, "but her body was found in the same alley where Knox tried to compel me to sabotage Cora's spell."

A muscle ticked in his jaw. "When was she found?"

"Six days ago."

Cora cocked her head, and began mentally counting back. Exactly how many days had Knox been under lock and key? Six? Seven?

Mace told Saraphine he'd been locked up for seven.

Could there be a chance Knox hadn't committed this crime? For some unfathomable reason, Cora truly hoped that was the case. Perhaps because if he were guilty, then in some abstract, roundabout way, Ms Windshaw's demise really was her fault. Not that his being innocent would redeem him in any way. He'd still attempted to compel Saraphine not to help her, or possibly even kill her, and then later attacked her. Plus, if it turned out he wasn't the culprit, it would mean a murderer was on the loose, whereas at least Knox was already imprisoned.

Finally, Saraphine lowered the weapon. Mace relaxed a bit.

"I don't know how long she was there. It could have been a couple of days. She had her throat ripped out." Saraphine squared her shoulders, attempting to project a hard-as-steel demeanor, but the quiver in her lip was telling.

Mace cursed to himself and then offered his condolences. "I had no idea he would take things so far. I've never seen him so out of control. Except..." Something akin to guilt flashed across Mason's face. "Never mind. If there's anything I can do—"

"Bring him to my Coven. We demand justice."

"You know I can't do that. I can have him charged with a crime, have it investigated by the VEA, but any consequences will be doled out by my clan."

"Vampire law is a joke. I *will* have justice."

"Don't confuse justice with revenge, Saraphine."

Saraphine lifted her chin defiantly. Cora received the dreaded impression that the young witch wasn't about to back down on this matter. Cora couldn't really blame her.

The drive back to the cottage was silent, with Mace seemingly lost in thought. He kept tilting his head this way and that, scrunching his lips together into a tight line. His mood seeped into her slowly, like oil dispersing over rough terrain. It was dark, yet defensive, with an underlining desperation. She was about to ask what was going on inside his mind when he finally spoke.

"I'm going to need you to do me a favor. You must come down with me to interrogate Knox."

"Why?" Anxiety colored the word.

"Through the bond you can help determine if he's being honest with me."

"I have a harder time reading him like that."

Mace swept a confused glance her way. "You do?"

"Yeah. It's like he has a way of blocking me."

"Huh. Well, I'd still like for you to try."

She hesitated. Then, with a relenting breath, she nodded. She could try for Mace and for Saraphine. "Do you think he did it?"

He didn't speak for so long, she wasn't sure if he would answer at all. "Do I think he's capable of it? Yes. But...no, I don't believe he's the culprit."

"Why?"

"When Knox kills, it's done with precision, clean. He doesn't rip out throats. Too messy, too much evidence."

"So he has killed before?"

"Of course. Most of us have."

Cora gasped at his casual tone. Although, why was she surprised to hear that Mace held human life with such little regard?

Mace frowned. "Don't look at me like that. Tell me how you fight a war without shedding blood?"

"War?"

"Yes. When the humans revolted against our kind, they were ruthless, killing without discrimination. Knox, myself, and most of our clan were called to arms. We don't kill without cause,

Cora. Not usually."

"Oh." She felt her cheeks warm. "But Knox has cause?"

Again Mace went quiet, his jaw tightening. "Admittedly, yes, he does."

"Me," Cora sighed, crestfallen.

Mace offered a remorseful nod. "But it's not just you."

They arrived at the cottage then, and before she could question him further, he was out of the car, heading inside. His precarious mood had shifted towards regret.

Chapter 33

Cora nervously glanced around Knox's small cell. The computer and desk had been replaced by an uncomfortable-looking cot shoved against the far wall, probably found in a well-stocked storage area buried somewhere within the complex.

She fought the shortening of her breath, the sensation that air was limited, the imagined bowing of the ceilings. It was all illusion, she reminded herself. All in her head. Mere residue from a tragic childhood experience. She could overcome.

She already was, to some degree.

Maybe because she was with Mace and Meeka. Or perhaps the repetition of coming down here was desensitizing her. Or had she managed to conquer a bit of her fear while stumbling through the complex hopped up on frantic adrenaline. Whatever the reason, traversing these halls hadn't been as harrowing as before.

Still, she'd had to take it slow to get this far.

Mace placed a palm on her shoulder as if sensing her discomfort. The movement parted the fabric of his coat and the butt of his holstered gun flashed into view.

She brought in a deep breath and steadied herself. Meeka's soft fur under her left hand helped a great deal as well. Upon their return from speaking with Saraphine, the clever feline had changed to her larger form as if she somehow knew they were intending to confront Knox. Now she sat sentinel by Cora's side.

On the cot, Knox was the epitome of relaxation with his back against the wall and his arm dangling over his folded knee. His expression was an unreadable mask, almost void of emotion. Except when his eyes fell on the silver thermos in Mace's hand. His nostrils flared, and she thought his jaw might have clenched. Besides that small display, he betrayed no other emotion.

When was the last time he'd eaten? The routine bloodletting had ceased the day of his attack. Yet he didn't really look worse for the wear. Was it that he didn't need to feed as often as he had been, or had Mace somehow been providing an alternative source of nutrients?

Knox's dark eyes slid from the thermos to her, and he smiled, not bothering to conceal a pair of elongated fangs. "Tell me this is a conjugal visit."

Strengthening her fortitude, she responded with an unabashed glare, setting her chin.

"Sorry, I don't swing that way," Mace replied.

Cora eyed him at the jest.

Knox smiled crookedly, the tension between them oddly broken. He lowered his foot to the ground and leaned forward to rest his elbows on his knees. "And yet you can't stand to be away from me. Watch that you don't make the female jealous."

Cora was flabbergasted. How could they behave so companionably toward each other after all that had happened?

It was then that she came to a glaring realization.

She was the anomaly in this trio. The outsider. How long had the two known each other? She hadn't bothered to contemplate it before, but their features were rather similar, both with dark hair, grey eyes. They could be blood related for all she knew, with decades of background and an unyielding loyalty she had no knowledge of. Hadn't Mace commented on the complicated nature of their relationship? Moreover, Mace was here to question Knox in the hopes that he was innocent. They acted like they hated each other, but neither, it seemed, would seriously harm the other.

Was that only because their sire had forbade it?

"Ms. Windshaw is dead," Mace blurted to Knox, losing his humor.

Knox paused for a moment. "Guess the old witch didn't see that one coming, did she?" He laughed, courting Cora's fury.

He stopped abruptly and pinned her in hard stare. She raised her jaw a fraction, staring daggers at him.

Seconds later, cold comprehension dug into the lines of his face. "You think I killed her?"

"It has been suggested," Mace replied. "She was found in an alleyway you've frequented as of late. Apparently, her throat was ripped out."

Knox rolled his eyes. "Does that sound like me?"

Through their exchange, Cora was trying to open herself fully to Knox, mentally diving into his emotions. Again she felt blocked. It was like jumping into a pool that had been iced over. Even though she broke through fairly quickly, she was already lost below the surface, floundering. And what she did glean was confusing, complicated, and difficult to decipher. Not to mention there was a good chance regular emotions, like, say, guilt, didn't plague him in the same manner it might a sane man. Hell, he might not even understand the concept.

She did manage to pin down a couple of things, however. Indignation. Resentment. Deeply bottled rage. But nothing that spoke of his authenticity, or lack thereof. Finally, she admitted to herself she was getting nowhere, so instead, she tried to scrutinize every change in his expression, as if she would discover the truth there.

Mace listed off Knox's many indiscretions, adding, "You have to admit, it doesn't look good for you. The witches will demand justice."

"Then they'd better look elsewhere. Honestly, Mace. If I were going to kill the old witch, there'd only be two ways I'd go about it. The first would be with every intention of making a spectacle, without repentance, brokering no doubt that it was me. Luckily, I'm not so stupid as that." He tilted his head up, resting it against the wall.

"And the second?" Cora brazenly demanded.

Knox looked at her. She thought she might have surprised him a little, but his features remained stony.

In a dark, hollow tone, he replied, "No one would have ever found the body."

A shiver battled its way up her spine. "You clearly don't care that she's dead," she accused, unable to stop herself.

He shrugged. "True enough. Doesn't mean I killed her."

"But you're happy about it. You didn't want her teaching me."

"Ah, but, *cher*, are you so easily disabled that a single witch's demise could prohibit you from learning your inherent craft? If so, I commend whoever took out your only chance."

She raised a brow at that. "You could have done the deed just before you trapped Mace here and then tried to kill me next. You can't deny you made the attempt."

"Is that what it appeared I was doing? That's not the way I recall it." His eyes glistened with remembered lust, and she blinked away.

"Aside from attacking me, you verbally threatened my life."

Knox laughed again. "I verbally threaten everybody. Par for the course."

"I suppose now you'll tell me you had no intentions of killing me, even though you said as much without batting an eyelash."

"I haven't decided yet," he replied flippantly, as though discussing something as inconsequential as which hairstyle looked best on howler monkeys.

And if that was the most honest thing he'd said thus far, Cora couldn't tell. She turned to Mace. "I'm getting nothing. This is a waste of time."

Mace glanced between them both. "How is he keeping you out?" Hope lit his features. "Maybe you're not fully bonded...if at all."

"Don't I wish," Knox grumbled.

Cora shrugged. "I couldn't say. But I have sensed his emotions on occasion."

"That could be your magic manifesting," Mace continued. "Ms. Windshaw mentioned something of that nature."

Knox shook his head. "Grasping at straws, mate. Her blood's all that sustains me. I'll be weak as a babe without it. Look at me." He lifted limp arms. "Already I'm wasting away."

Though he played at humor, his gaze darted toward the thermos. In an unguarded moment, she sensed his gnawing hunger.

Stupidly, she softened.

As if he could tell, he slashed her with a glare. He greatly disliked it when she read him. If nothing else, that was obvious.

Finished with his questioning for now, Mace set the thermos inside the door and then locked Knox in once more.

On their way out, Cora mused, "I'm surprised he didn't try to escape."

"I don't think he's sure what to make of Meeka. And besides, he knows I'd have shot him if he tried."

"Yeah, but that doesn't really stop your kind."

"Hurts like hell though. Especially when the bullets get stuck and we have to work them out on our own. And a straight shot to the brainpan would have dropped him for a decent amount of time."

When they made their way through the kitchen passage and the hidden panel slid closed behind them, disappearing seamlessly into the wall, Mace said, "Thank you for trying."

Before them, Meeka slipped into her kitten form. Strangely, it was like watching a balloon deflate. Then she trotted to her empty food bowl and planted her little butt expectantly.

"Do you believe him?" Cora asked Mace as she retrieved a small tin of cat food from the cabinet, pulled the tab to open it, and filled Meeka's bowl.

He paused thoughtfully. "I'd like to say I believe him, but... I'm not sure."

She hesitated. "Why do you want to so badly? What's up with the two of you?"

"What do you mean?"

"I feel like there's a history here I should know about."

His eyes tightened and something inscrutable slid behind them. Again, that guilt trickled out of him and into her.

"Let's just say I owe him," he said simply, and then turned away.

Chapter 34

Over the next week, Mace refused to expound on his comment about owing Knox, and eventually Cora grew tired of inquiring. Instead, she returned to her studies while he resumed his investigation.

Seated alone in the living room, sunlight streaming through the front windows, she opened A Witch's Guide to Demons, Vampires, and Other Supernatural Entities and began reading the chapter Ghosts, Ghouls, and Corporeal Entities. The shadowy figure had revealed itself once more. Again while she'd slept, it had hovered at the end of the bed. When she informed Mace the next morning, he wasn't sure what to think, stating, "It's not my area."

Knox's "assignment" apparently had something to do with the ghost, but he refused to enlighten them. Even when Mace threatened to stop his feedings by way of Cora's blood, which, to her relief, had been reduced to weekly rather than daily. Bloodletting wasn't one of her favorite activities.

In any case, it was time she determined what the specter was, and what she could do about it, if anything.

She ruled out ghoul instantly. They were said to wander

graveyards and feast on the dead. Yuck. Poltergeist was a possibility. They were spirits who haunt a particular place, or in some cases, a particular human. However, poltergeists were usually unruly, malicious, and troublesome, throwing objects and frightening the living with various tricks. Demon was out as well. Spectral demons were decidedly evil and often tried to possess the living for the purpose of doing evil. Interestingly enough, non-spectral demons could not possess the living as they are already connected to a living form.

It looked like her shadowy figure was an ordinary run-of-the-mill ghost. A benevolent spirit stuck between realms, unable to pass over for one reason or another.

Making contact with a ghost was another matter. Often, communicating with one could prove difficult, according to the book. Some people were born with the talent, such as mediums, lower cast witches who, by popular opinion, were considered little more than gifted humans. For others, a séance or ritual might work in forcing the spirit to move on. More powerful witches could conduct a spell to bring out a ghost's corporeal form. However, in extreme cases, exorcism is required.

Cora didn't think this was an extreme case, but then, she wasn't much of an expert.

Her mind drifted to Saraphine, the only other witch she knew. She wished she could go to her for help in this matter, but decided against it. Saraphine wouldn't want to see her. Not after the baleful look Cora had been subject to upon exiting Wicked Wares. There was no doubt Saraphine blamed her for her grandmother's death.

In part, Cora blamed herself.

She set the book down and exchanged it for Quick Spells for

the Witch on the Go, flipping through the pages. When she'd scanned it the first time, she'd thought she'd come across...ah, there it was. A spell to briefly merge realms and speak with the deceased. And it looked simple enough. Aside from the incantation, all she required was a dark space, a white candle, and a mirror.

When she informed Mace of her plan, he insisted on being present "Just in case," although he couldn't put voice to his reservations. Just said, "It sounds creepy."

She had to concur, but the creep factor didn't overpower her interest in the prospective results. Might she actually speak with a ghost? Provide assistance to a restless soul who needlessly clung to life? Acquire definitive proof that life did not end with death?

Excitement welled.

She wanted to start the spell now, but they waited till nightfall as the book recommended. Apparently, ghosts became more active after sunset. She found herself checking the time constantly. She'd already memorized the incantation, had her items at the ready, had picked the mirror in which to gaze—the eclectic, almost antique-looking round hanging mirror that decorated the upstairs hallway.

Finally, the day relented and darkness conquered the sky. Mace joined her in the hall. He offered an encouraging kiss before he stood back against the opposite wall and crossed his arms. She sparked the wick of her white candle, clasped it in her hands away from her torso, and fixed her eyes on her reflection. The incantation came on a whisper at first. After a few repetitions, her tone grew stronger, emboldened.

She didn't know how long she stood there, chanting away,

but at some point, her vision grew unfocused, darkening around the edges, while the words began to run together, their meaning melting away. A shiver eased up her spine and snaked along her neck, finding its way through the back of her head. She thought the surface of the mirror rippled then.

Was it her imagination?

There! It rippled again, this time with more kick. Then again. She almost expected to hear a splash. Inky blackness expanded from the center till her reflection was painted the color of volcanic rock.

And again, another ripple shivered over the surface...

But this time the watery substance broke. Something appeared as if from the other side. A set of black charred fingers emerged, nails the color of blood so accurate in shade she imagined they could drip at any moment. The hand was followed by a thin, bony wrist.

Cora was enthralled. The incantation still flowed effortlessly from her lips. The candle suddenly burned hotter, the flame higher. The mysterious hand reached for her. She stretched her arm toward it.

A pressure came around her waist. Her body was ripped backwards, the candle slapped away. The flame extinguished as it tumbled to the ground.

Her vision cleared, and she found herself clutched tightly in Mace's arms as he whisked her downstairs.

"What are you doing?" she demanded as he lowered her to her feet next to the sofa.

"You reached for it." His voice sounded strangled.

"I what? No I didn't."

"You did. The mirror was writhing, churning like a violent

ocean, and you reached *into* it." He put her at arm's length to examine her. His expression spurred her heart rate into a hard beat. He was utterly freaked.

"I didn't reach in. Something reached out."

His head shook vigorously. "I don't want you doing that again. Do you hear me?"

She frowned. "But—"

"At least not until you've been trained properly."

Her shoulders slumped. "And who's going to train me? Do you have any witchy friends who will look past this mess with Knox?"

"No, but Trent might know someone. People tend to owe him favors."

Cora sighed, dejected. "Alright."

In gratitude, Mace ran the backs of his fingers along her jawline and then dipped his head to claim her lips with his. She wasted no time deepening the kiss, inviting his tongue to find hers. With a few quick flicks, he had her panting for something more substantial.

As if reading her perfectly, which was probably the case, he reached for the hem of her shirt and guided the material over her head. Her delicate lace bra fell to the floor next. With a groan, he covered one breast with his big hand as he held her close to him by the waist and his mouth descended once more to hers, this time with more force.

As his kiss made her mindless with the ease of an expert, her hands moved to undo his jeans and free his shaft. Hot flesh as hard as steel met her palm. She pumped her fist to the hilt and back. He shuddered at her touch. She thought he growled something in another language but didn't have the brainpower to ask what it meant.

He shoved her jeans and panties down her thighs, settled her back onto the couch, knelt, and then lifted her knees over his shoulders. When his hot tongue delved into her tender flesh, she tossed her head back as a guttural sound of pleasure was forced from somewhere deep inside her. Another followed as he sucked her clitoris between his lips, all the while his hands traveled the length of her body, over her hips, her thighs, her belly, teasing the undersides of her breasts.

Her release came hard and fast, blanking her mind with agonizingly sweet ecstasy. Relentlessly, Mace's tongue caressed her core till she was on the verge again. Her head thrashed from the building pressure, her breaths coming in short pants interrupted by long moans. Just as she readied for the onslaught, Mace pulled away with a wicked gleam in his eyes, his fangs peeking out from under his upper lips.

Cora squirmed, taken over by demanding need as her orgasm was thwarted. Mace laughed at her dour expression, even as a jittery feeling still fluttered over the back of his neck.

That scene in the hallway had been more than he'd expected. Her entire hand had literally disappeared into a black abyss kept at bay by the mirror's frame.

He feared Cora was taking her magic too far, too fast.

"You find that funny, do you?" she purred, turning impish. She licked her lips. His cock grew impossibly hard at the sight.

She pulled her right leg back, placed the ball of her food on his chest, and pushed against him. He raised a brow, but followed her direction, rising to stand. She slid off the couch to her knees and then ruthlessly sucked his girth into her mouth. His head fell back on a rough groan, and his hips jutted forward.

Not wanting to miss a second of her attentions, he forced his eyes back to watch as her plump lips took him to the root and then slowly pulled to the tip, sucking as she went.

"Fuck, Cora! You'll make me come in no time if you keep that up."

She smiled up at him devilishly. With no sign of mercy, she drew him in again, deeper than he imagined she could go. His body shook with the threat of a burgeoning explosion, but he held back.

Her tongue lashed him as she began pumping steadily. Lightning rods of pleasure spiked through his brain, making him delirious. When he felt his release creeping up his length, he stepped back.

She glanced up at him with confusion, which turned to apprehension at his fierce expression. "What is it?" she asked nervously.

He couldn't imagine what she saw in his features, but he knew what he was feeling. The desperate need to pin her down, drive into her, and pierce her flesh with his fangs as he released into her soft body.

So not to frighten her by his vampiric nature, he fiercely tamed the intensity. Still, with one arm, he shoved the sofa away to make room for them on the floor. It slid back with a bit too much force and collided with the bookcase against the wall. A few books tumbled down.

Cora jumped and let out a small squeak, her eyes going wide. He was almost too consumed by his need to care, but he made a herculean effort. As he lowered his body to cover hers, nestling himself between her legs, he warned. "I want you now, love. I want to take you hard, here on the floor. I can't be gentle right now. I need you to understand that."

Her throat worked on a gulp, but, thankfully, after a couple tight breaths, she nodded.

He gripped her hips, his fingers digging in. He thought she might have winced at the pressure but couldn't be sure if it was because of that or because, in the next instant, he shoved deep into her warm flesh.

Her gasp mingled with his groan. Only a heartbeat passed before he pulled back and invaded her again, harder, deeper. And then again. A frenzied rhythm soon took over, his mind no longer stunted by rational thought. All sense of civility had been ripped away, overtaken by savaged desperation.

At this moment, he was pure instinct, carnal need, unrelenting desire, unquenchable thirst, and undying hunger. He slammed into her, riveted by the way her breasts bounced by the force of his actions. As her cries grew into rapturous screams, and an underline worry that he'd hurt her eased in his gut. Her nails scored his back, drawing blood. Drops of it trickle down his sides.

His fangs throbbed painfully.

As if she'd read his mind, she brushed aside her hair.

He plunged his fangs through the soft flesh at the crook of her neck. Flawless, untainted, concentrated bliss assailed him, stunning him with its overwhelming power. There wasn't a single part of him that didn't bow to its authority, give in to its rule. As his seed burst forth and he lost himself in her flesh, a simple truth branded into his mind. He was no longer the proprietor of his own life.

He now belonged to Cora.

* * *

Cora lay under Mason's quivering body gasping for air and trying to regain a sense of equilibrium. She was dizzy from the overdose of pleasure that had accompanied his carnal taking.

"Did I harm you?" he asked next to her ear. He was hunched over, clutching her to him, his breaths as harsh as her own.

She ran her fingernails through the dark hair at his nape. "No, but I'm sure I'll have trouble walking for a while after that."

He exhaled as his form relaxed. His lips come down over the spot where he'd bitten her. The action was so tender she almost couldn't stand it. She'd never before felt emotions like the ones rolling off him now. They were so raw, so piercing; she didn't know what to make of it. The sheer magnitude of them was frightening.

As if she'd known how to do it all along, she slammed a mental barrier down between them. It wasn't that she didn't want to experience his feelings. It's just that it was almost more than she could bear. Crushingly so. The excessive intensity threatened to tear her apart from the inside.

Mace didn't appear to notice her blockade. Good. She wasn't ready to discuss the extremeness of what was happening between them. It was all too much too soon. She'd met him not even two full months ago.

Exhaustion crept over her, and she yawned.

As if she'd issued an order, Mace rose and then lifted her in his arms to carry her to their room. She sighed and rested her head on his shoulder, taking in his scent and daring to admit one thing to herself: judging by the budding strength of her feelings for Mace, one thing was certain....

She had never really loved Winston.

After Mace tucked her into bed, he collapsed beside her and soon began a slow rhythmic breathing. How was it men could always fall asleep so quickly?

She watched him for a long while, running her gaze along the perfectly sculpted planes of his face, his hard, yet tender-to-the-touch lips. He really was a stunning specimen of masculinity. *My stunning specimen of masculinity.*

She didn't bother to fight the small grin that slipped over her mouth. Her eyelids drooped.

Before she closed them completely, a dark movement brought her attention to the foot of the bed.

The shadowy figure was back.

Only this time, it was slightly more visible, more solidified. The edges were no longer a misty tempest, but a vaguely blurred outline in the shape of a human.

Stabbing fear had her freezing into place, her body stiffening. Her mind flailed frantically when she realized it wasn't fear that rendered her motionless, but something else. Flat on her back, she couldn't move. She couldn't even use her lungs to scream, only to breathe.

The darkness crawled over her, creeping like an intelligent creature, hovering inches from her impossibly wide eyes. Though she surveyed nothing but a dark vortex of tightly packed mist, she got the horrific impression that it was looking back at her...and smiling.

If Mace sensed her terror, it wasn't enough to wake him.

Was her wall still up?

The apparition closed in. Icy air surrounded her, coating her lungs with a layer of frost. When she exhaled, condensation wafted out in a tiny cloud, dissipating swiftly. The dark creature sank lower, till it lightly brushed her skin, and then sank farther still, past her flesh, into her heart, her mind. The pressure wasn't painful, but it was distressing as hell. Like being compressed to death with no ability to stop it, and yet not feeling a thing. The specter breached her very essence, invading, shoving her consciousness into a dark corner somewhere deep inside and effortlessly locking her there.

Her surge of unmitigated hysteria was the very antithesis of her body's calming reaction. Her heart slowed to its normal speed, her tense limbs eased against her will.

Then, without her approval, she sat up. Her feet slipped over the edge of the mattress, landing softly on carpet. Next, her body eased out from under the covers, taking care not to disturb Mace, before skulking into the hallway and down the stairs.

Cora squirmed in protest when she realized where her hijacker was taking her. *No, no, no. Are you crazy?*

If whoever was now in control heard her, they didn't respond.

The panel opened. She entered the darkened cavern moments before the torches burst to life. Her hijacker didn't slow, heading straight for the fissure that marked the entrance.

When she stepped through, into the vast complex, with its confining square rooms and oppressive low ceilings, there was no rush of adrenaline, no choking anxiety...because she no longer ruled her body. There was, however, a sense of giddiness that didn't belong to her.

Although she wanted to deny the horrid suspicion, she couldn't quite manage in the face of the familiar path being taken. *You can't go there. He'll kill me!*

Her feet continued with swift, sure steps, and her plea went ignored. She struggled to regain authority over her actions, to push the overpowering consciousness out of her mind. It worked only to exhaust her, causing her to lose even more control.

When her hand reached for the metal door barricade, she screamed *No!*

She thought her body flinched, but it did nothing to keep her hand from sliding that heavy bar to the right and tugging the door open with much more ease than she'd been able to before.

Knox sat up on the cot in nearly the same position as before, only this time it was as if he'd been caught off guard by the visit. It appeared to take him a moment to realize she was alone. When he did, his expression became a mixture of roguish interest and leery suspicion.

Cora expected him to do something: make another conjugal visit comment, move to attack, or merely shove right past her to freedom. The opportunity had to be too good to pass up. But he did none of those things. He only tilted his head and studied her with an ever narrowing gaze. Could he somehow tell she was different?

In a throaty seductive voice Cora had never before utilized, she heard herself speak. "Hello, Knoxy." Then, to her horror, she leaned against the door frame flirtatiously.

Knox grinned, the expression triumphant. "Hello, Sadira."

Don't worry readers, Cora's journey is just beginning. There's a lot more in store for her. I have a lot of twists planned for the series and all the characters in it. Stick with me because it's only going to get better.

For news about the next book in the Creatures of Darkness series, sign up to Kiersten Fay's newsletter at
www.kierstenfay.com

Other books by Kiersten Fay:

A Wicked Night

Demon Possession

Demon Slave

Demon Retribution

Demon Untamed

Next in the series:
A WICKED NIGHT

About the author

Kiersten Fay is the author of the steamy romance series, Shadow Quest, in which she combines paranormal and sci-fi with loose concepts from lore and mythology. In 2013, her short story, Racing Hearts, was published in The Mammoth Book of Futuristic Romance. In 2012, via gravetells.com, she won Favorite Story of August 2012 for Demon Retribution, the third book in her Shadow Quest series, and received a nomination for favorite author in that same year. Before becoming an author, Kiersten worked as graphic designer, and now loves creating her own book covers.

While fully intending to continue her popular Shadow Quest series, she is currently working on a new dark fantasy series called Creatures of Darkness, set in a war-torn world featuring magic, witches, vampires, and whatever else she decides to throw in.

To learn more about Kiersten Fay, or to get info about upcoming release dates, go to www.kierstenfay.com

Or follow her on Twitter @KierstenFay, and on Facebook. www.facebook.com/KierstenFay